Dedicated to
my wonderful aunts and uncles:

Madeline Sowles,
Sydney Brucker Sowles and Jim Sowles,
Beatrice Bickford Hicock and Burt Hicock

DREAD
OF
WINTER

SUSAN ALICE BICKFORD

KENSINGTON BOOKS
www.kensingtonbooks.com

KENSINGTON BOOKS are published by

Kensington Publishing Corp.
119 West 40th Street
New York, NY 10018

All Kensington titles, imprints, and distributed lines are available at special quantity discounts for bulk purchases for sales promotion, premiums, fund-raising, educational, or institutional use.

Special book excerpts or customized printings can also be created to fit specific needs. For details, write or phone the office of the Kensington Sales Manager: Kensington Publishing Corp., 119 West 40th Street, New York, NY 10018. Attn. Sales Department. Phone: 1-800-221-2647.

Kensington and the K logo Reg. U.S. Pat. & TM Off.

ISBN-13: 978-1-4967-0597-6 (ebook)
ISBN-10: 1-4967-0597-1 (ebook)
Kensington Electronic Edition: November 2019

ISBN-13: 978-1-4967-0596-9
ISBN-10: 1-4967-0596-3
First Kensington Trade Paperback Edition: November 2019

10 9 8 7 6 5 4 3 2 1

Printed in the United States of America

Praise for Susan
masterful sus

A SHORT TIME TO DIE

"*A Short Time to Die* held me captive from the first page to
the last. Vivid settings, cold and alive, and strength of character,
both evil and good, kept me reading late, late into the night,
all the way through to an ending I never expected."
—Taylor Stevens, *New York Times* bestselling
author of *Liars' Paradox*

"By the end of the first chapter I was totally hooked
on *A Short Time to Die*. I couldn't have closed the
cover on Marly's story if my life depended on it."
—Lisa Black, *New York Times* bestselling
author of *Suffer the Children*

"Gripping."
—*Publishers Weekly*

"Bickford's debut is an intriguing tale of murder and corruption
that spans more than thirteen years. Riddled with twists and
turns, *A Short Time to Die* features a family that is so evil the
reader will likely be looking over their own shoulder. The
resolution is highly satisfying, more so because of Bickford's
phenomenal writing talent. An A-plus for this great book!"
—*RT Book Reviews,* 4 Stars

"Bickford's tale of revenge, the dark reach and power of generational
crime and violence, and of two brave and bright girls who become
capable, fearless women is gripping, chilling, and original. Add in a
keen, exacting eye for character and place that transcends 'genre' and
A Short Time to Die is sure to stay with you for a long, long time."
—Eric Rickstad, *New York Times* bestselling
author of *The Silent Girls* and *Lie in Wait*

"Susan Alice Bickford's first novel, *A Short Time to Die,* is disturbing,
tough. It's close to the bone, with a good dose of class consciousness
and moral ambiguity. It's fun to read. You care about Marly, and
you keep turning the pages. That is a very good thing."
—*Utica Phoenix*

Also by Susan Alice Bickford

A Short Time to Die

1

Welcome Home

As the car rounded the last bend, Sydney tried to lean forward to catch a glimpse of her mother's house. She moved too fast. The seatbelt froze, retracted, and moved up to cut off the circulation in her neck. Resistance was futile. She would have to stay firmly pinned to her seat for a couple hundred more yards.

Midway through the turn, the back end of the car fishtailed on an icy patch hidden under the gray slush covering the road. Sydney pressed her right foot on the phantom brake on the passenger side.

Francine Buckley deftly straightened the vehicle. "Damn town. That curve isn't banked properly and they know it. Bad enough in the summer, but ice builds up there all winter, no matter how much sand and salt they throw on it. Every time I drive through town . . ." Her voice trailed off in a string of grumbled obscenities.

Sydney lifted her foot. She didn't exactly disagree, but driving a bit slower might have solved Francine's problem without any investment required by the town road crew.

"Too bad about your mom, kiddo. Man, that was fast. Glad you were able to get back in time from Colorado." Francine thumped her hands twice on the steering wheel.

"California," Sydney said. After driving in silence for over an hour, her companion now seemed to be in a mood to talk. She vaguely remembered Francine as one of the lunch ladies at the high school and wondered how well she had known Sydney's mother. Perhaps that was a silly question. Everyone knew everybody in a tiny town like Oriska, New York.

"Oh yeah. Well, a long way. I guess it goes to show. You never know when your time's going to come up. I bet you never thought you'd be coming home like this."

"I never thought I'd be coming home, period," Sydney said. She slipped the fingers of her left hand between the seatbelt and her neck.

"They don't got weather like this in California, do they?" Francine pointed her chin toward the steep drifts left by the snowplow on either side of the road.

"There's snow up high in the mountains, but it never snows where I live."

"No kidding. Sounds boring."

"I'm not complaining."

"I hear Randy didn't come to the hospital."

Sydney felt a bubble of pain move down her chest. "I kept calling his cell number and left messages. Maybe he's out of town."

"Out of something, that's for sure. Up to no good, as usual." Francine continued with a barely audible string of epithets and made a jerking-off gesture in her lap with her right hand.

Sydney had to clear her throat before she could speak. "Are you saying he's been cheating on my mother?"

"I'm saying he is a sweet-talking, good-looking guy, way younger than your mother, who has always done exactly what he wants. Just like the rest of his family. Those Jaquiths have no impulse control. What could possibly go wrong? What? Don't look at me like that. Am I right?"

"I'm not arguing with you, Francine. At least he can't cheat on her anymore. That's the upside of being dead."

Francine snorted and sped up for the last fifty feet. "Okay, here we are, then." She stomped on the brake and jammed the gearshift into park. "Looks like you got some visitors."

Sydney freed herself from the seatbelt as she studied the large black SUV with a Quebec license plate in her mother's driveway. *"Je me souviens,"* she said, reading the bottom of the rear plate. *I remember.* "I would definitely like to remember that license plate number. Just in case." Her phone was buried in a bag. She grabbed a pen from Francine's pile of possessions scattered along the dashboard, and scribbled the number on the palm of her hand.

"Whatever. Let me know about your mother's service. And put the pen back."

Sydney climbed out and gasped at the cold. She had forgotten how subzero wind could suck the breath from her lungs. *Welcome back to Central New York. Let me give you a hug.*

She wrestled her luggage from the back of Francine's car: a backpack, a wheeled suitcase, her travel purse, and a brown paper bag with her mother's effects from the hospital. She reopened the passenger door and held out two twenty-dollar bills. "Thanks, Francine. I really appreciate the ride. It would have cost a fortune to take a car service all the way from Syracuse. It was nice of you to stop by to see how she was doing."

Francine snatched the bills and stuffed them down the front of her shirt. "Sure thing. I had to take Gladys up for her chemo today. I like it when I can get a round-trip. I thought I might be taking your mom home." She paused to cough up something disgusting into a dirty hankie. "I don't suppose you could pay me for taking your mother to the hospital, too?"

Sydney straightened up to give this some thought before she leaned into the car again. "I thought she called an ambulance."

"Ha! She'd still be lying in there today if she'd done that. She said to put it on her tab. Want to settle up? I'm never going to collect from *her,* that's for sure. Eighty-five bucks."

Sydney fished into her handbag for more bills. It appeared that settling her mother's estate would be full of surprises. Expensive ones.

She handed the bills to Francine, who put them in the same warm spot.

"Now shut the door," Francine said, checking her side-view mirror. "It's fucking freezing out there. And slam it hard. It don't like to catch in cold weather."

Sydney slammed the door as directed. She turned to study the Canadian vehicle. All she wanted to do was get inside out of the snow and cold, and find some solitude so she could cry her eyes out.

She didn't feel like entertaining visitors, and she didn't *souvenir* anyone from Quebec. Something wasn't right.

"I don't suppose you'd be willing to come in with me," she said, looking over her shoulder. But Francine had already slammed the car into drive. The backend fishtailed as her car leaped forward, showering Sydney in a spray of semi-frozen salt and sand.

"Never mind." Sydney waved at the receding rust bucket.

The house didn't appear changed from the outside. It had always been a lovely façade—a charming village farmhouse with a large, two-story living section and a single-story kitchen wing—facing the road as if it had nothing to hide.

Inside would be different this time. No screaming, no slamming doors, no tears except for her own.

She slipped on the backpack and tucked the paper bag under her left arm along with her travel purse. About eight inches of snow covered the driveway, and Sydney quickly realized the snow was too deep for the wheelies on the suitcase. Dragging the case like a dead body, she made a mental note to figure out who did the plowing around here. Maybe her mother kept a snowblower in the barn.

The barn was a town barn—a modest structure created for the non-farming family who built the house. It was directly attached to the house, connected via a large mudroom and laundry area. Back in the day, it must have held a couple of cows and horses and a carriage, but in recent memory it functioned as a garage and storage facility for tools and out-of-season items.

Sydney paused to glance inside the SUV. Fast-food containers littered the floor and backseat. There were no fast-food joints within twenty miles if memory served. These guys weren't local.

Two sets of footprints—boot prints, size large and extra large—led from either side of the car to the barn. The sliding door into the barn was open about two feet.

If this were California, she would have turned around. She would have called the police on her cell phone. She would have walked—no, run—to a neighbor's house.

But this was Oriska. Central New York. Somewhere between Syracuse, Binghamton, and Nowheresburg. It was January. There was no cell phone coverage. The closest neighbors had undoubtedly gone to Florida or Arizona for the winter. The police were still not her friends.

What the hell. She pushed through the last few feet into the unlit barn.

The change stopped her in her tracks. Her mother's car—a Subaru—sat waiting as expected. The rest of the interior was packed top to bottom with furniture, books, crockery, newspapers, file cabinets, old shutters, old food containers. Dirty food containers.

When had her mother turned from a collector to a hoarder? In their phone conversations, her mother raved about her thriving antique business. One more lie Sydney would never be able to put to rest.

The door to the mudroom hung wide open, spilling heated air out of the house. The boots of the two men had left clumps of ice and snow in lacy patterns. Sydney closed the mudroom door and dropped her bags before she followed the prints through a second door and into the house.

Her first impression was that black bears had come out of hibernation and invaded the kitchen and family room. Two large bodies in heavy coats and boots lounged across the couch, their feet resting on the marble coffee table—one of her mother's genuine antiques. Cigarette smoke filled the air overhead.

"Well, hey, Leslie. We've been waiting for you." The man closest to the mudroom slammed his feet to the floor and stood up.

"I'm not . . ." Sydney started to explain she wasn't Leslie and stopped. Maybe she should keep her mouth shut.

"Yeah," said the other man. He waved a tumbler filled to the brim with a golden liquid—apparently poured from the bottle of expensive scotch on the coffee table. "We were about to leave and tell Randy to take care of his own business."

"Have we met before?" Sydney asked. She decided not to ask their names but mentally labeled them René and Pierre. Their lightly accented English was excellent and colloquial, delivered in a slightly stilted, clipped manner.

"Nah," said René, the first man. "Randy said to give this package to his girlfriend at this address. He didn't want to carry it over the border." He picked up a bag with a Wegmans logo on the side and set it on the coffee table with a thump.

"Perfect. We'll take off now," Pierre said. "Thanks for the scotch."

"You're very welcome," Sydney said, eyeballing the Wegmans bag. *This could not be good. No one needs to smuggle vegetables or maple syrup from Canada.*

The two men gathered their gloves and clumped in their heavy boots toward the mudroom. Up close, Sydney could see that their eyes were bloodshot and she could smell that they hadn't bathed recently.

"Tell Randy we'll be stopping by his cabin tomorrow for the money." Pierre leaned in close, giving Sydney the opportunity to count the blackheads on his cheeks. She also noted that Pierre had never received the grooming memo that it was okay to clip nose hairs. On the bright side, his pupils were normal. He wasn't a user, even if he was too drunk to drive.

René pushed his partner aside and tapped Sydney's chest with his right forefinger. "And no sampling the merchandise. Randy says you got a taste for this stuff, so hands off. This is pure, uncut china girl. It'll kill you." He raised the finger to her face and grinned. "And that would be such a waste."

Sydney blinked and took a step back. She wasn't entirely current with drug slang, but she recalled that *china girl* meant "fentanyl."

The two Canadians disappeared into the mudroom. Sydney moved to the sitting room windows facing the driveway and watched them slog through the snow to their car. Pierre turned and waved as he climbed in.

Sydney waved back. "Yeah, yeah. *Va t'en faire foutre,* asshole." *Go fuck yourself.*

She kept watching until she was satisfied the car was out of sight before she made the rounds of locking every single door to the outside world, including the one into the barn.

Each room except the kitchen area was filled with stacks of collectibles and useless crap. Sorrow descended like a dense fog, tugging at her feet, pushing down her shoulders. By the time she returned to the kitchen sitting room area, she could feel her knees threaten to buckle.

"Did you know your mother was abusing narcotics, Ms. Graham?" the young doctor in the ICU had asked.

"Lucerno. My last name is Lucerno," Sydney answered. She forced herself to look away from her mother and the beeping machines. The doctor's nameplate read: DR. K. SINGHAL. He had introduced himself as Kamal. His brown eyes seemed warm and not judgmental. "We aren't very close. It definitely didn't come up in our phone calls. I don't see her very often."

Three times. Three times in the last thirteen years.

"I thought you said she had the flu."

"She does," Kamal replied. "The problem is that opioids suppress breathing and that led to complications."

"Pneumonia."

"Correct. She was taking a lot of codeine for the cough, in addition to her normal habit, and didn't realize she was in trouble until it was almost too late. Now she is also going through withdrawal. It's a tricky balance for us to manage."

"She's not going to make it, is she?"

Kamal put his hand on her shoulder. The nurse standing on her other side patted her back.

"We're doing all we can for her. It's good that you were able to make it here today. Why don't you go talk to her? She can't speak because of the ventilator, but she can hear you."

Sydney grasped her mother's hands and rolled them around

in her own. Why were Leslie's hands so warm if the woman was dying? Sydney memorized the freckles along her mother's knuckles and the little hairs sprouting at the base of each finger. She held up her mother's right palm and measured her own against it. Identical.

All the while, Sydney spoke of cherished childhood memories, reminded her mother of the fun they had during Leslie's infrequent visits to California, and made promises for the future Sydney knew would never come to pass.

From time to time, her mother would open her eyes and gaze at Sydney with no sign of recognition. Several times, with her eyes closed, her mother squeezed Sydney's hand.

The squeezes grew fainter. Lulled by the rhythmic beeps and clicks of the machines, Sydney fell asleep with her head resting on the blankets next to her mother's chest until the beeping gave way to a final, sustained wail when her mother's heart stopped.

Now her mother's body was on its way to Martinson Funeral Home in Hartwell, and everything she took to the hospital was jammed into a brown paper bag in the mudroom.

Sydney sank to the kitchen floor. She howled like an orphaned animal and kicked her heels. She pressed her hands to her eyes and tears finally began to flow. Between moans, she screamed and thumped her head against the tiled floor.

She should have never run away. She should have stayed to protect her mother. Or at least come home to drive away Leslie's demons.

Now Sydney and her mother would never be able to take the slow route from New York to California or drive from Vancouver to Tijuana following Route 1. Leslie would never meet Sydney's someday children.

Sydney would have to live forever with a hole in her heart where family belonged.

2

Forty Below

Forty below zero. Exactly the same temperature in both Fahrenheit and Celsius, Sydney noted as she studied the old-fashioned thermometer mounted outside her mother's kitchen window. Genuine cold, not wind chill cold.

"Wind chill is what people without real winter use for bragging rights," her grandfather used to say. According to him, no place in the world had more snow or lower temperatures than Central New York in January. Or was a better place to grow up.

After thirteen years away—a lifetime of dog years—Sydney knew better. The Sierras in California received a lot more snow—thick, dense stuff fresh off the Pacific Ocean they called Sierra Cement. Not that she had ever gone to check it out. Not even once.

Still, forty below on any scale was plenty cold, and a good three plus feet of snow covered the ground—higher counting drifts kicked up by snow plows and the winds. That was more than enough.

Sydney checked the time on her watch—just after midnight. The temperature might even drop a few more degrees before dawn. She knew there would be no room for carelessness whether it was minus twenty or minus forty, and she had serious business to conduct.

She needed to pin down Randy in his precious cabin before he had time to squirm away. Timing was of the essence. He needed to acknowledge he let her mother die on her own. He also needed to accept responsibility for the Canadian package deposited at the house. Given Sydney's own teenage legal entanglements, she could not risk being caught with a large quantity of drugs—substances largely responsible for hastening her mother's death.

She bent and hefted the small backpack at her feet, testing the weight. The package from the Canadians wasn't heavy. She added an additional bag of her own. How had her mother accumulated so many pills and powders and liquids for getting high?

Sydney had spent all afternoon checking every single hiding spot she had used during her own junkie phase and found something in each of them—and this was probably the tip of the iceberg. Why couldn't her mother have been a normal, run-of-the-mill alcoholic?

Time to go.

Sydney slid an antique Luger pistol out from its fancy leather holster. She rolled it in her hands, admiring the exquisite workmanship, and checked to make certain it was loaded. Her great-grandfather had brought this handgun back after World War I. Her mother treated it like a museum piece, but Sydney had fired it many times as a kid under her grandfather's guidance.

She suspected the Luger wasn't registered, and she knew this was a big no-no in New York State. If she was caught. She would have preferred a revolver since a revolver wouldn't kick out empty cartridges after firing. Hopefully, that wouldn't matter—as long as Randy and the Canadians minded their manners.

Sydney added a water bottle and the Luger to the backpack and made her way to the mudroom, where she had piled up every bit of cross-country and downhill ski clothing she could find. Her old thermal underwear layers were a bit snug, particularly across the chest, but the rest seemed roomy enough. She was particularly pleased that her old outer jacket and pants weren't too small. Normally they would be too heavy for cross-country, but she would need them tonight for both their warmth and camouflage. The jacket was primarily white with gray patterns, and the pants were a darker gray with the same patterns in white and black—the perfect combination to move across the winter landscape at night. She tucked her cell phone into an inside pocket next to her skin. As far as she knew, coverage was still spotty to nonexistent, but she felt naked without it.

Last came the black neck warmer that covered her head, ears, nose, mouth, and throat, followed by her padded black hat with ear flaps, a head-mounted flashlight, and clear goggles. There was no point in freezing her corneas if she could help it.

She stepped into the barn and realized she might not be as overdressed as she thought. Closing the door behind her, she shouldered her backpack and picked up the cross-country skis and poles.

Fortunately, she wouldn't need the flashlight for the first part of the trip. The full moon was directly overhead in the cloudless sky, lighting up the landscape in a brilliant pale-blue glow, reflected and amplified by pristine snow. Only the shadows remained pitch-black.

Sydney waited for a truck to roll by the house before she began her slow trot up the road, carrying her skis and poles. *Old habits die hard.* She didn't want anyone to be able to trace her tracks directly back to the house from Randy's cabin on Hangnail Pond.

She paused every few paces to listen for traffic. This was the riskiest part of the trip. If a car came along, she would have to launch herself up and over the high banks left by the town plow.

Her timing was perfect. No one was driving after midnight. She reached the plowed driveway to an old farm after about a hundred and fifty yards.

She wondered if the Blanchards still owned the place and if their big German shepherd, Spotty, was still alive. Not likely, she decided. Perhaps he'd been replaced by a younger, equally vicious guard dog.

She put her skis on by the road and slipped past the darkened barns and farmhouse, out onto the open field. All was quiet. No Son of Spotty.

3

Hangnail Pond

A few yards into Bancroft's field, the moon revealed a network of crisscrossed snowmobile tracks. Following those would be a big time and energy saver—like finding a bluebird in the middle of winter.

Sydney threaded her way along the tracks until she reached an ancient stone wall separating the dense woods that enclosed the field on the far edge. She slowed to search for the break leading to a path downhill to the Hangnail.

She felt her pulse pick up. The break wasn't where she remembered it. She turned and backtracked, hearing the snow squeak under her skis. Had trees been cut? Had new ones grown? She was forced to pick her way carefully as the cold started to penetrate more deeply.

There!

She stopped to flip on her headlamp and slipped over saplings and past tumbled boulders into the woods. The moonlight filtered through the naked branches to leave lacy patterns on the snow—lovely but disorienting. A minor fall could be fatal in this cold. Sydney considered this possibility as she dusted herself off after an unexpected tumble underneath a clump of cedars.

Was this the right path? Nothing looked familiar. She pressed on, forcing her skis to move at a walk rather than a gliding stride. If she didn't find familiar landmarks within ten minutes, she would turn around.

Over a hasty dinner of peanut butter and jelly sandwiches eaten standing at the sink, she had considered driving to the far side of the Hangnail. Even in summer, access to Randy's cabin was a challenge without a truck or SUV that could handle the deep, muddy ruts down the steep dirt track from the lake road to the cabin. In winter, the lane down the hill wasn't plowed, or at least it never used to be. Randy liked it that way.

She would have had to park on the narrow lake road and ski or snowshoe in. Plus, Randy might hear her car arrive. Noises traveled with crystalline clarity in the dead of winter.

This route was safer, but it was longer—and no longer familiar.

A new doubt crept in. She could be operating on the false assumption Randy would be at his cabin. After all, the place was lonely, isolated, and lacking in basic amenities such as insulation, central heating, phone service, and indoor plumbing.

She pushed aside her qualms. *No.* She was quite confident he would be there. Leopards do not change their spots. Even after thirteen years, she felt certain Randy would be hanging out in his beloved "hidden villa," staying up until all hours.

That wasn't to say he would be happy to talk to her, but he would let her in. On the other hand, if his father was visiting . . . That's where the Luger came in.

Sydney had mixed opinions about Randy on a personal level. As a drug supplier to lower-level junkies like herself back then, he could be tough and nasty. He required careful handling, but he wasn't psycho.

His father, Zile, operated on a different level altogether. Growing up in Oriska, she had only met one other person who scared her more than Zile—and he was dead.

The woods were growing thicker. The path disappeared into a thicket of sumac. As she started to turn around, an odd, bumpy shape on a nearby maple tree caught her attention. She grinned. It was her mask.

She moved closer and leaned in to study the crude carving. It had held up well over the years. She was surprised Randy hadn't cut down the tree.

She had been sixteen, a junior that fall. Randy found her here in his father's precious woods, hacking away with a chisel and hammer. She had completed the basic outlines and was about to start on the serious carving. She didn't hear him coming and screamed in shock when he smacked her upside the head and pushed her down.

"What the fuck is this?"

"It's a mask," she answered, scooting away on her butt. "Onondaga. I found a picture online."

"How dare you? These are sacred things, to be made as part of secret and special rites. Not by stupid white girls like you."

Sydney grabbed the hammer and chisel as she regained her footing and danced back from the tree.

"I wanted help. I needed . . ." Sydney's voice failed her, and she clamped her mouth shut.

Randy's eyes were still angry, but he stopped yelling. "Give me a break. What do you have to worry about in your life? Besides, this isn't even the right kind of tree. Maple is too hard and brittle. Didn't your online source tell you to use basswood?" They stood facing each other until Sydney started to cry.

"Do you want me to cut down the tree?" She wiped her nose on the sleeve of her sweatshirt.

"Shit. No, if my mother finds out about this, she'll skin you alive. She takes her heritage very seriously. Even I wouldn't be able to get away with something like this. I'll take care of it. Do me a favor and stay away."

Randy never did take care of it and now she knew exactly where she was.

Sydney glided through the trees at a faster pace. After a few yards, her way was blocked by a fence of blue plastic tubing, connecting two tree trunks. Puzzled for a moment, she realized she was at the edge of the Blanchards' maple sugar grove. With the branches of leafless maples arched overhead, the tubes formed a web, laced from one trunk to another, leading deeper into the forest. It was way too cold for maple sap to flow now, but she knew the lines would lead her down to the Blanchards' sugar house on the near side of the Hangnail.

Within five minutes she stood at the eastern edge of the narrow, frozen lake and stared across at the lights of Randy's cabin, looming over the opposite bank.

She eyed the snow-covered surface of the water. Cutting across would save her at least ten precious minutes—the cold was now settling deep into her bones.

In theory, the surface should be frozen solid. In practice, she remembered that snow was an excellent insulator, and this end of the lake was swampy with underground springs that flowed all winter. Better to take the long way around the northern end.

It was a crappy little body of water. On official maps, it was called Hartwell Lake, but locals called it Hangnail Pond as a joke, to contrast it with the picturesque, elegant Finger Lakes that etched into the state. The Hangnail was skinny, shallow, and murky in the summer, teeming with undersized perch and sunfish, as well as vicious pickerel that no one wanted to catch or eat. Presumably, they were slumbering in the mud under the ice, waiting for spring. Waiting for someone stupid enough to cross the lake in winter.

At least she wouldn't have to contend with the stinging nettles and poison ivy that grew along the shore in warm weather. According to Randy, *Oriska* meant "place of nettles" in Mohawk, and they were delicious if boiled three times. She had never been tempted to test that recipe.

Sydney crossed the frozen marsh at the north end and followed the shoreline to Randy's boat access. The slatted wooden dock had been pulled out for the winter and lay on its side against a clump of cedars next to a tall post topped by a large skull. This was a new one since her last visit. Black bear?

The skull rested on a horizontal board with letters carved in relief from the surface. She paused to run her encased fingers over the board, dusting away the snow.

Kanonwarohare:

She mouthed the word, trying to recall the basics of Mohawk pronunciation. *"Gah-non-wah-lo-ha-leh."* Head on a stick. It did seem to summon the spirit of this forlorn spot. And a warning.

Sydney clambered up the steep hill and forged her own path through the woods until she stood about ten yards from the side porch. The light switch was still there, protected from the elements by an old telephone box on a two-by-six post.

Randy hated to be surprised, and she doubted that had changed, given the bear skull. Every person designated as a friend was assigned a code. Visitors after dark were to stand at this box and flip the switch off and on to enter their code, which would cause the overhead light in the living room to relay the presence of the visitor.

All very Hardy Boys. Without the benefits of mobile phone coverage and no landline, there weren't many choices. Such arrogance. Here was Randy, still waiting for the mountain of technology to come to him.

She flipped the light: *up long, down quick, up long, down quick.* That was the code for *friend.* She paused. The connection to the living room light still worked, casting flashes out onto the snow. Now for her personal code. Short, short, short, long, long, long, short, short, short. SOS in Morse code.

She needed to get indoors and warmed up soon. If Randy came out shooting, she would turn and ski away, no matter how cold it was, and take her chances on making it back to her mother's house with sufficient blood flow in all her fingers and toes.

Where is he? Maybe he wasn't home after all. In which case, she should break in and warm up.

A large form moved along the windows and the door onto the porch opened. Silhouetted against the lights, Randy stepped out, looming against the narrow doorframe, holding a shotgun. The porch light flipped on, flooding the yard. Sydney edged into the circle of non-moonlight.

Randy leaned forward. "Who's there? Who are you?"

She pulled down her neck warmer and pushed up the goggles so he could see her face. "Please let me in. I'm not used to this cold." She glided forward and kicked off the skis at the edge of the porch.

She could see his body relax. He stepped back but still barred her entrance to the interior of the cabin. "Sydney! After all this time. What the hell are you doing here?"

Even at forty below, Sydney could smell the bourbon on Randy's breath. No time like the present for bad news. The warm glow called to her and pulled her in like a moth. She needed to get inside.

"Don't you ever check your voice mail, asshole? My mother died this morning."

4

Revelations

Sydney didn't wait for Randy to respond to her news. His mouth hung open and he squinted as though he was staring at some sort of phantom, giving her an opening. She shouldered her way into the cabin, pushing him back on his heels.

The warmth generated by the woodstove hit her like a tidal wave. Her eyes teared up and her nose began to run before she had taken more than a few steps into the living room.

She knew she needed to allow the heat to reach her body as soon as possible, but part of her brain wanted to stay bundled up. Fighting against her basic instincts, she peeled off her jacket, hat, and neck warmer, and flung them to the floor. The fabric of her jacket crackled as it landed.

As she bent over to undo the Velcro down each leg of her ski pants, the door closed with a slam. In a half crouch, she looked up and met Randy's eyes.

He wasn't surprised. Shocked, perhaps. His shoulders seemed to sag under his heavy sweater and his face looked pasty, but his eyes were not angry or snapping with indignation. They were sad.

He slumped against the door and stared at the glowing stove before he set the stock of the shotgun on the floor and eased the barrel to rest against the side of the threadbare couch.

"She overdosed, didn't she?" His voice was raspy and sounded clogged.

Sydney finished removing her ski pants and contemplated her response. She had braced herself for a fight, an argument, lots of yelling, and denial.

The ghosts of the place took advantage of her pause. The smells of the cabin in winter—must, mold, mothballs, bad cooking, the chemical toilet off the kitchen—filled her thawing nostrils and with them came a rush of memories. Every corner held a first—first kiss, first sex, first pills, first time using a needle.

She moved closer to the stove and held out her hands. "Technically she died of pulmonary complications from the flu. Pneumonia. That's how the polite death certificate will read, more or less. In reality, she died because she was an addict. The drugs she took—your drugs—masked her symptoms and suppressed her breathing." She took a deep breath. "You're a killer."

Randy grunted and sank onto the couch. "They weren't my drugs. I never let her have any of my shit. She preferred all the prescription stuff. No needles."

Sydney did some mental math. He was only about seven or eight years older than she was. At thirty-eight or so, he was a young man.

He still had the kind of looks that made both men and women look twice. His mother, Lilith, was Onondaga on her father's side and Mohawk on her mother's. He mirrored her heart-shaped face, soft brown complexion, and dark hair. Like Zile, his white father, Randy had grown tall and broad-shouldered. The taunting look in his green eyes and his wicked grin were entirely his own.

Most people would still consider him handsome, but all she could see was the ghost of Adonis, entombed in a layer of age and unhealthy living. His face was puffy, and jowls were creeping along his jaw. The heavy winter clothing couldn't conceal that he had thickened considerably around the middle. The tawny strands in his shoulder-length dark hair were fading to silver.

She had been ten when he entered their lives. He appeared at their house one fall day for a tutoring session with her mother, then a high school French teacher. Tutoring soon became a daily event.

Sydney didn't fully understand the unfolding drama until much later. She was profoundly interested in sex and romance, but those were still foreign lands.

She could see Randy was not like other scrawny high school boys. In those days, he wore his long hair in a ponytail or a braid, and a pendant in the shape of a turtle around his neck. He was already tall with a fully developed, rangy physique—those broad shoulders, narrow hips, six-pack abs, powerful arms and legs. He had downy hair on his shins and under his arms, and he exuded a pleasant musky smell. When he smiled at her, she felt a glow rise to her face.

Small wonder her divorced mother had fallen for him.

According to Leslie, their courtship was the most romantic adventure since Romeo and Juliet. According to everyone else—including her grandfather, the high school principal—the same events were scandalous, a violation of school ethics, possibly a criminal offense, and definitely a disgrace.

Fortunately, Randy dropped out of school when he turned eighteen that winter, sparing Leslie a host of legal complications. She lost her job. David Graham, Sydney's grandfather, was forced to resign several years ahead of his planned retirement, forfeiting a calling he loved and the prestige he craved.

Meanwhile, Sydney was stuck with being the butt of every joke and snide remark for the next seven years.

Something about her expression prompted Randy to speak. "Come on, Sydney. Leslie and I have been together almost twenty years. I loved your mother, but I couldn't help her."

"Don't give me that crap, Randy. You may not dirty your hands with direct sales, but you know you stoked the fire that killed her."

"Get down off that high horse, Sydney. For your information, half of the money for my deals usually came from your mother, and a good chunk of the profits would be headed her way, too. Do you think she could live the way she does selling knickknacks and collectibles?"

"Past tense. Lived. Now dead and soon to be buried." Sydney extracted the two bags from her backpack and tossed them onto the stained coffee table in front of the couch.

Randy leaned forward and looked in each bag. "What the hell are these?"

"The one on the right has all the drugs I could find in the house. Her stuff. I don't want it there. The other is from your Canadian friends. They were waiting for 'Leslie' and gave it to me."

Randy offered her one of his famous grins. "Aren't you afraid I'll sell her stuff?"

"I plan to pour or throw all of it down your sink. Or maybe into the chemical toilet. Your friends said they'd be coming here for their money today, by the way."

"Today? Damn." He was not grinning now. "I thought I had a few more days. That might be a problem."

"Yeah, well, not mine. Why do you need to sneak things in from Canada? You could go to Akwesasne and walk the stuff across the border, all safely within the reservation boundaries. That's what you used to do."

Randy grunted. "Let's just say I'm not as welcome there as I used to be."

Sydney headed for the kitchen. What kind of adult would prefer to stay in a stinky, half-winterized, overgrown shack in the dead of winter? No Internet, no television or radio reception, no telephone service, no cable, no cell phone coverage, no reliable electricity.

Living off the grid was one thing, but Randy was theoretically running a business and as far as she could tell, having your finger on the pulse of events around you was critical—even more critical if your career was not exactly on the up-and-up.

She grabbed a glass from a shelf over the sink and ran it under the water to scrub off some of the smudged fingerprints. She could hear the small motor under the cabin pull water up through a buried pipe from the lake. The mechanism was supposed to inject tiny amounts of chlorine. Anyone who thought lake water was pure and pristine was an idiot. She sniffed the water in the glass. *Slightly fungal.*

Back in the living room, she added a purifying dose of no-brand bourbon to her glass from the bottle sitting next to the drugs she'd delivered.

"Why didn't you call me back?" she asked. "I left messages." She examined the overstuffed chair on the opposite side of the room. It was filthy and coated with crusty bits here and there, but nothing as toxic as what she had carried. She eased gingerly into the musty cushions.

Randy pulled out two cell phones from his pockets. "I never take my personal phone when I travel on business." He placed a glossy iPhone next to the bourbon bottle and poured himself a fresh dose. "I definitely do not check messages or do anything traceable, even with *this* phone." He put down the second phone, some sort of cheap model he must have used as a burner. "I only got back this morning. If you'd sent me a text, I might have gotten it. They sometimes come through, especially if I go upstairs."

"She was already dead by this morning. Actually, yesterday morning." Sydney glanced at an ancient wall clock over Randy's head. It was now three a.m. "She was still alive twenty-four hours ago. She died at five yesterday morning."

Randy shifted in his seat. "You got there in time?"

"I got the call on Sunday evening, flew on Monday, and arrived at Hancock just before midnight. The hospital let me stay with her all day Tuesday, and I slept in her room off and on."

"Did she ask for me?" Tears started to flow. Randy poured himself more bourbon.

Sydney wanted to say yes, but she felt compelled to tell the truth. "She was on a respirator. She seemed to know who I was some of the time but mostly not. I told her I called you."

"Did your grandfather visit?"

Sydney winced and decided more bourbon would be welcome. "No, I have to go talk to him later today. He was in the infirmary at his senior living place with a cold. They didn't want him to expose others or go out in this weather." She settled back with a fresh glassful of golden liquid. "I talked to him on the phone, but I'm not sure he really understood what I was saying."

A soft silence drifted down around them like winter rime. Wood in the stove crackled.

"When she was upset, Leslie would always say that I was the reason you ran away," Randy said after he drained his glass. "Is that true?"

Seventeen-year-old Sydney screamed inside her head. *Of course it was your fault. Who ruined our lives thanks to your hormones? Who introduced me to drugs? Who talked me into selling for you? Who showed me how to use a needle? Who tried to get me into bed that fall?*

Sydney scrubbed her face with both hands to squeeze her teenage thoughts back into their bottle. "No, it wasn't you. You were part of it, but it was everything here. That brief spell in juvie was the best thing that happened to me. I got straight. I realized this environment was killing me. I knew if I stayed, I'd be dead. I had to clear out."

Randy pulled out a joint from his back pocket and lit it. "Okay. I'm not going to offer you any of this, then."

"Fine with me."

"You're not planning to stick around, I gather."

"You've got that right. I've got a job and a life to get back to. No way I'm staying." She drained her glass. "As soon as I've taken care of the funeral and the cremation, I'm out of here."

Randy scowled. "You shouldn't cremate her. You should bury her with her head to the east and her feet facing west, toward her final journey."

"Is this a Mohawk thing? West is the way to heaven, I suppose."

Randy gave a snort. "Your attitude hasn't changed much, I'll say that. It's the same for all the Iroquois as far as I know. You'll be happy to know there is no heaven or hell. We go to where our souls were created."

"Very reassuring. You know perfectly well no one is going to be buried at this time of year with the ground frozen under all this snow and I'm not waiting around for spring. Plus her ashes will be going west. Back to California with me."

"This is a bad way, Sydney. Terrible things could happen when you don't follow proper rituals."

"Oh, please. You pull out this stuff only when it suits you."

"I do when it's serious. Besides, don't my wishes count?"

"If you wanted some say in this, you should have married her. I'll leave you some of her ashes. I had no idea funerals and cremation would cost so much. I would appreciate getting back Mom's share of the money for this deal immediately."

Randy took a long toke on the joint and held his breath before expelling a cloud of smoke. "I can't do that right now. My finances aren't very liquid. Don't forget, you'll get a lot more if you wait."

Sydney tapped her glass on the side table in rhythm to her angry pulse. "I don't want more. I don't want less. I want it now."

"Here's the thing. It's not all yours. You're going to have to split it. Everything. Including the decision about cremation."

"What? Give me a break, Randy. Spit it out."

Randy stood and picked up a log for the fire. Studying his posture from the back, Sydney could see his shoulders were raised and tight.

"When you go, I want you to take Maude with you."

"Your sister?" Sydney thought back to the gangly kid she knew back when. She must have been only six or seven when Sydney had scampered out of town. Tall for her age, a miniature Randy aside from the honey-blond hair.

"No, Sydney. Not *my* sister. *Your* sister."

Sydney snapped bolt upright, wide-awake. "Repeat that."

Back on the couch, Randy clasped his hands between his knees. His gaze certainly looked sincere.

"I can't believe you didn't figure it out. After everything started blowing up with the school, your mother went away for a while. Don't you remember that?"

Sydney fought back a lump that was rising from her stomach.

Randy was about to tell her something terrible and she knew it was going to be true.

"That was an awful summer," she said. "I had to stay home alone with Grandpa. No one would play with me."

Randy raised his eyebrows. Did he really not understand how much she had suffered? No. Probably not. This was Randy.

"She went away to have the baby. *My* baby."

"And your parents did what? Adopt her?"

"Something like that."

Sydney's sight was filled with a long-forgotten vision of her mother, sobbing at the kitchen sink.

"Why would Mom let them do that?"

Randy spread his fingers wide. "It was all beyond crazy. I was so young. Your mother was a mess. The neighbors wanted to lynch us. And you know my mother would never allow one of her family to be raised by white people."

Sydney snorted. "In case you forgot, your father's white. Plus look how great you turned out. Pushing forty, pushing drugs, killing friends and family."

Randy licked his fingers and pinched out the moldering joint between his thumb and forefinger. "Yeah, well, that's easy to say in hindsight. It's true. I'm screwed. There's nothing else I know how to do. That's why I want you to take Maude with you."

"She's, like, what? Eighteen? Nineteen now? I bet she's a real bundle of joy. Something tells me you're setting me up."

Randy tilted his head back on the couch. His voice slowed and deepened. "Please, Sydney. At least get to know her. She's your sister."

Sydney tilted her head back, too. Days of minimal sleep, anger, and bitter cold took their toll, draining every bit of energy out of her body. Sleep was closing in.

"Get to know her," Randy said. "Did you hear me?"

"Yeah, yeah. We'll see."

5

Nasty Business

Sydney's snore snapped her head into an upright position. Or maybe it was Randy's snore. His jaw hung slack with his head resting back on the couch cushions. *So much for Adonis.*

The cabin was still with only a small buzz from the bare light-bulb overhead. A snap from the stove told her the fire needed stoking. The clock read 4:30. The mid-January dawn was hours away.

She leaned forward and pressed her hands to her knees, pushing herself up to a stiff and achy stand. She stumbled to the stove, looking for a pile of logs.

As she approached the clear glass of the side door, she paused to stare at blinking lights up the hill. In her semi-stupor, it took her several moments to process that what she was watching was not normal. *WTF?*

Her eyes popped wide open. Those were flashlights.

"Randy! Randy!" She rushed to the couch and shook his legs. "Randy, people are coming down the hill. I see flashlights."

Randy blinked twice and leaped to his feet. "Damn. The Canadians."

He looked around the room and started gathering up her jacket and other clothing.

"Get behind the closet. Now. Stay there until I come get you."

Sydney knew where he meant—a pocket tucked under the

staircase to the upstairs, at the back of a cramped coat closet. She had hidden there long ago during a raid by the sheriff's department. That incident had ended in her arrest, but she didn't know where else to suggest. She scooped up her gear and tossed everything to the back of the closet.

Randy picked up the two bags of drugs and hefted her backpack.

"What the hell is in here?" He fished out the Luger. "Shit."

"Don't you have a gun?"

"Only the shotgun." Randy pulled the Luger from its holster and stuffed it down the back of his pants, under his sweater. "Does it shoot?"

"It did the last time my grandfather used it thirteen years ago." Sydney's breath was coming in gasps. "Don't you want their drugs out here?"

"No, they can't know I've received them already."

"They'll want money." Sydney could barely speak. Her teeth chattered and spasms tightened her back and stomach muscles. "Don't you have it?"

"Some of it. We need to come to the right agreement. Now get into the closet and stay there. I'll put these bags someplace else." Randy grinned and returned the bags to the backpack.

Sydney didn't see the humor, but there wasn't time to argue. This cabin had been built in fits and starts—lots of orphaned spaces tucked in here and there.

She bent over and pushed aside the line of coats. She squeezed to the back and slid back a set of rough boards at the rear of the closet, revealing a ninety-degree turn into the cramped space under the stairs.

She knew she needed to settle in quickly. Noise from any movement could carry throughout the cabin.

The heat from the stove didn't penetrate much of this area. She coughed and cleared her throat as she spread her ski clothes on the frigid floor. She yanked a couple of coats off the hangers and covered herself up before sliding the boards into place. Hopefully, she wouldn't cough from all the moldy dust or freeze to death while Randy conducted business.

Coming here had been such a mistake. She should never have trekked through the cold. She should have stayed in a cramped motel up in Syracuse. She should have stayed in sunny California. Even in death, her mother had sucked her into the bottom of a deep well.

No. No blaming. She needed to own her own role in this situation. She needed to breathe slowly, evenly, not in jerks and gasps that made her cough.

She could hear Randy moving about the living room as clear as if the walls around her hiding place were made of paper. He walked into the kitchen, returned, and did something near the stove. There was a squeak of hinges from a source she couldn't identify. Was he hiding the backpack and the money?

A clinking sound told her that he had opened the woodstove door, followed by a clunk. That was more obvious—he had fed the fire.

Moments later a heavy thunk was followed by a second set of rumbling sounds. The visitors had reached the porch.

Another squeak. Randy must have opened the door.

"*Bonjour,* Randy. *Ça va?* Ready to do business?" The voice was a bit faint but familiar. She thought it sounded like the guy she called Pierre.

"What's wrong with you, coming at this hour?" Randy's voice was clear. He was probably standing in the doorway. "Creeping up like that could get you shot."

"Hey, stop waving that shotgun around. Put that on the porch for now. We just want to finish up and get the hell out of here." That voice belonged to the other one—René.

The exchange was followed by some grunts and foot stomping and the sound of the door closing. Sydney felt the pulse in her temple throb and surge faster. She cleared her throat and swallowed one last time. Now that all three men were inside she would need to stay completely still.

"You here alone?" Pierre asked. She could hear him pacing back and forth in front of the woodstove.

"Sure," Randy answered.

"Why are there two glasses on the table?"

"Because I am a terrible housekeeper. You want some of this bourbon?"

"No, I don't want any fucking rotgut liquor. I want my money."

"Where's your girlfriend, Randy?" That was René. It sounded as though he was standing at the base of the stairs, just on the other side of the layer of pine boards that hid her from view. If she rolled slightly, she would be able to see him through one of the cracks. Sydney resisted the temptation.

"I dunno. Not here."

Pierre picked up the thread. "Funny thing. We went to her house and waited. We gave our package to a woman there. A young woman. Nice looking, about so tall with dark hair." Pierre moved across the room. "But later we talked to my buddy in Syracuse. Your girlfriend is older. Older than you."

"Who the fuck did we give that package to?" René asked. His voice was soft and low, but Sydney picked up an edgy menace. She hoped Randy was paying attention.

"You must be kidding. How the hell should I know? You show up and just hand over the merchandise to someone who happened to walk in? It might have been the cleaning lady for all I know."

Uh-oh. Not good. What kind of game was Randy up to? Maybe he was telling the truth when he said all the money wasn't at the cabin.

René spoke. "Randy, I saw that house. It's a mess. That was no cleaning lady."

Pierre chimed in. "We stopped back there tonight. On our way here. Lights out. The doors were locked this time. Nobody home."

Sydney mouthed a silent curse. What would they have done if she had been in the house? The shadow of a different future passed over her heart and moved on.

"Now we want the money." That was René.

"Sorry, guys. No merchandise, no money."

"Not a good answer."

"Hey, I'm sure we can figure this out, just not at oh-dark-hundred in the morning."

Sydney squeezed her eyes shut and bit her lower lip. She tried sending telepathic messages to Randy. *What are you playing at? This is stupid. Make a deal about the money. Or give them back the drugs.*

"Listen, even if I wanted to, the money's not here. I didn't expect you guys 'til later," Randy said. "Let's have a drink. When it's light, I'll go straighten all this out."

"That's not going to work for me," René said.

The tension was more than she could stand. Sydney pressed her fingers into her ears. She could still hear the voices, but at least the words were muffled. Even so, she could tell the anger and tension were building.

She heard a shout. This was a train wreck she could not stop. Should she reveal herself? She could reassure the Canadians and let them know that their merchandise had been delivered. Would crawling out into the middle of this scene make things worse? They would want to know why she had been hiding.

The voices stopped. Sydney wanted to groan with relief. This had to be almost over. She unplugged her ears and risked slowly easing her left leg into a new, less cramped position.

The first shot sounded like a bright thunderclap. It was so close to her hiding spot that it must have come from René. Sydney yelped and clamped her hands over her mouth.

Before she could worry that she had revealed her position, there were shouts and five more shots were fired: another one from René, one from the stove area—Pierre?—and three from the far side of the living room, two in quick succession and the third after a short pause.

Sydney squealed into her hands as one round blasted through the pine plank inches over her head. *To hell with not making noise.* She rolled herself into a tight ball and tried to claw herself back into the main part of the closet.

Shouting gave way to grunts and swearing in French and English. She heard thudding footfalls moving across the floor and the door open, followed by more heavy movements.

There were three more shots, but it sounded like they must have been fired outside, followed by a thud as a large object—or body?—landed on the floor.

Sydney held her breath and assessed the sudden silence, straining to pick up any movement. All she could hear was a faint creaking noise. The air that leaked into the closet was growing colder. After several minutes, Sydney rolled to her knees. Safe or not, she knew she needed to check what was going on.

"Sydney." The voice was faint and her ears were ringing from the gunshots.

"Sydney." A mere whisper.

Sydney pushed through the hanging coats and eased the closet door open. Her leg muscles were cramped into tight knots, forcing her to crouch down on all fours and crawl out like a baby. She was crying like a baby, too. If a bullet waited for her on the other side of the closet door, hers was not going to be a dignified death.

6

Deadly Consequences

The source of the creaking sound was the door to the side porch. It stood wide open, swaying in a frigid breeze that pushed sub-zero air into the living room.

Randy was lying feetfirst toward the door. His head had landed on the threadbare braided rug close to the couch. She could see he was still alive. Blood pumped steadily from at least one source hidden by his heavy sweater, spreading a metallic smell along with a sticky red puddle. His green eyes blinked like a semaphore.

She picked up the Luger lying a few feet away. Ignoring the thick coating of blood on the stock, she checked the number of rounds. Five were gone. She staggered to her feet and looked out the open door into the winter night.

Illuminated by the porch light, she could see the man she called René had fallen backward from the porch stairs onto the snowbank, his legs twisted underneath him. Blood stained the snow around his body, and his eyes gazed up at her, unseeing.

Pierre made it a bit farther. He sprawled, spread-eagle, about twenty feet away. The footprints leading to his body were tinged with blood, and he lay facedown in the snow. His legs were twitching in a way that reminded her of a dying rabbit.

Sydney considered where to turn first. René was dead. Randy was definitely still alive. Pierre probably was not, or not for long. If he was still alive after she had checked on Randy, she would see what she could do for him.

She picked up two revolvers from the porch floor and returned inside, closing the door behind her.

Kneeling on the floor, she picked up Randy's left hand. It was cold to her touch, but she could still feel a pulse in his wrist. There were three bloodstained holes in his sweater. One was low on his right side, another was closer to his collarbone area. Both looked small. More worrisome was a larger wound, dead center in his chest.

She lifted up his sweater to check the damage. The scent of fresh blood wafted out, flooding her breathing. She swallowed so that she wouldn't gag, and tried to assess what she saw based on ancient Girl Scouts first-aid training.

There didn't seem to be a lot of blood on his upper torso, but judging by the amount flowing from underneath his body and seeping into the rug, she guessed there were larger exit wounds on his back. This was not good news.

She studied Randy's face. His eyes were closed now, but the lids flickered. He was very pale, and his lips were tinged with blue.

Circulation, airway, breathing. She could remember that much from Girl Scouts. She had to stop the bleeding first. As she stood to go to the kitchen, Randy's hand grabbed her arm and pulled her down. His eyes popped open.

"Randy. Let me go get some towels."

Randy grunted. His voice came out in a low rasp. "No good. Can't feel my legs. Bleeding out."

"You don't know that. Let me pack in a bunch of towels. I'll ski home and call for help."

"Too late. Stay." Randy rolled his head back and forth on the soggy carpet. "Take the ring."

Sydney wasn't sure what he meant. He wasn't wearing a ring on either hand.

Randy raised his left hand and fumbled at the top of his sweater. Sydney leaned closer and caught a glimpse of silver. She gingerly prodded the folds of his neck until she located a chain.

She needed two hands to rotate it around his neck so she could undo the clasp and pull it free along with the ring dangling from the middle.

Cradling the ring and chain in her right hand, she recognized it as the same design as the ring her mother wore—a ring now sitting at the bottom of the brown paper bag from the hospital. A promise ring, her mother had called it. Like her mother's, this was also modeled after a puzzle ring with strands of gold and silver that nested together. Her mother's ring had separated into four separate, interconnected rings when the nurses removed it. Randy's ring was held together by small gold bands.

She looked away from the ring and into Randy's eyes. "Don't call cops. Call my father," he said in a wheezing whisper.

Sydney recoiled. No way she wanted contact with Zile.

"No cops. Let him handle it." Randy took a labored breath. "Promise."

"Okay, okay." She wasn't looking forward to this.

"And Maude. You take Maude away from here. Swear it."

"I swear," she said, dabbing at the tears that flowed down his cheeks with a glove.

He blinked once and stared back at her. He did not blink again.

Although she was quite certain it would do no good, Sydney moved closer to his head and covered his mouth with hers and tried to revive him. The taste of bourbon, cigarettes, and marijuana made her stomach revolt, but she kept up her task for a good fifteen minutes, interspersed with chest compressions.

By then his face was pasty white and his lips were purple. The pupils of his eyes were fully dilated and had taken on a slightly cloudy appearance. Blood no longer pumped from his body, and there was no pulse in his neck or wrist.

Death had come for Randy.

Only twenty-four hours earlier, she sat beside her mother, waiting for the final breath. Now, for worse and not for better, her mother's longtime soul mate was dead as well.

She dropped her head to Randy's chest and sobbed. She closed his eyelids and kissed the palm of his left hand before she sat back with her knees tucked under her chin, her arms wrapped around her shins.

She didn't have to use what was in that package of drugs to feel its poison. She should have handed it back to the Canadians that morning.

Speaking of which—where did Randy put all that crap? And was there a bag of money or not? She pushed to her feet and scanned the room. There was no sign of her backpack or any of the contents. She made a quick tour of the kitchen, the shed, and the dining room. No luck there, either. She recalled hearing Randy move around after she'd crawled into the closet. He hadn't gone upstairs to the bedroom area, so he had hidden those little treasures somewhere close by.

Sydney glanced out the window in the porch door and groaned. Time to check on René and Pierre. She wondered if they carried identification. Under the circumstances, she wanted to know their real names.

She pulled on her jacket and gloves. As an extra precaution, she pulled on a pair of Randy's large rubber boots, standing beside the stove. She had been mildly paranoid earlier. Now she wanted to leave as few traces of her presence as possible. Stepping into her own tracks, she ventured outside.

René's eyes were still open. She could not find a pulse, and no blood pumped from the gunshot wounds to his chest and back. Blood and some sort of nasty gook covered his mouth and nose. The man was dead.

She patted the pockets on his jacket and heavy canvas pants. In the back pocket, she found a wallet. The name on the driver's license was Bernard Peillion. She tucked the wallet back into the pants pocket.

She climbed onto the porch and scanned the yard. A faint gray hinting at dawn cast a dim pall over the area. The moon had retreated below the horizon.

Looking down, she noticed two cartridges where the hot metal had melted holes through the ice and snow on the porch.

Those must have been from the Luger since the other handguns were revolvers. She picked up the casings and put them in a small pocket in her insulated thermals and reminded herself to pick up any others she could find in the living room.

Sydney made her way to Pierre. He was no longer twitching. No pumping blood, no pulse. His face made a perfect mask into the snow.

When she rolled him to check his jacket, she found another revolver buried in the snow beneath his hips. *Sneaky bastard.*

She fished into his pockets and came up with a cell phone, which she put back. It had the look of a burner phone, but that didn't mean it wasn't traceable. His driver's license revealed that his name really was Pierre. Pierre Bedard.

Sydney made her way back to the living room and stoked the fire. Her thoughts were running in circles. She needed to slow down and plan her next steps.

She paced the room, picked up her bourbon glass, and carried it to the kitchen for a thorough washing. What else had she touched?

Back in the living room, she pulled all her ski clothes from the closet and started to put them on, but stopped when she allowed herself a glance at Randy.

She could not leave him like this, rotting by himself as the weather warmed. Not Pierre or Bernard, either. At least Randy would be inside the cabin. Outside, feral cats, crows, coyo dogs, and other creatures would come to feast despite the cold. No one deserved that.

Calling the cops was the right thing to do. What could be clearer? She should ski out and go to her mother's house and make the call.

Sydney jammed the poker into the fire and stared at the coals, looking for answers. First of all, any dealings with Randy's family would immediately draw suspicion from the police. She knew she'd need to justify her presence at this scene.

Second, her past interactions with the local law as a teenager had been problematic—with good reason.

What about outstanding warrants?

She could ask Steve, her mother's lawyer, but that would be later when they met about the will.

Third, she had promised Randy she wouldn't call the cops, and promises to the dying weighed heavily in her world.

Still, contacting Zile seemed even more perilous.

A sharp buzz caught her attention. Randy's personal cell phone gave a little bounce on the coffee table. She walked in a wide arc around Randy's body and picked up the phone.

Happily, Randy was a trusting soul. The phone was not password protected. The buzz had been a calendar reminder. Randy had a dentist appointment later in the day that he would have to miss.

The screen showed zero bars, but Sydney recalled Randy's statement that sometimes he could get text messages. She scrolled through his contacts until she found the one she wanted—*Zile*.

Zile—Ozias Pitts Jaquith—Randy's father, would be the last person on earth she should contact, but he was also the first person on earth who would come to the aid of his son.

She dressed for the trip home. After a quick search, she gave up looking for the packages of drugs and money. The money was tempting, but it was easy to abandon.

She did pick up all shell casings from the Luger. She stuffed the museum piece firearm into its holster and tucked it into the back of her ski pants.

Ready to leave, she scanned the cabin. She had probably left a few fingerprints, but Zile didn't have a laboratory and he would make sure the police stayed away from this place. She hoped he would stay away from her mother's home, too.

She went upstairs and walked from bedroom to bedroom until the phone registered one bar. She entered Zile's cell number into the texting application on Randy's burner phone and typed with trembling fingers: *shot @ cabin bad news*

Sydney pressed send and waited. Once she was convinced the message had been sent, she walked back downstairs and set the phone down next to Randy's body.

Minutes later she glided on her skis down the steep embankment. She covered the ground around the frozen marsh and started the uphill slog through the woods on the opposite side of the Hangnail. She didn't need her flashlight or the moonlight. This time she knew the route by heart.

The temperature was slightly warmer, and the smell of a coming snowstorm spread through the woods. Full dawn would be upon her soon. She needed to cross the Blanchards' field and make it back to her mother's house before road traffic picked up.

Close to collapse from mental exertion and physical exhaustion, Sydney paused at the break in the stone wall leading to the Blanchards' field to wipe away her tears. Zile was nobody's fool, but unless he had changed in recent years, he wasn't exactly smart. With any luck, he wouldn't think to tie her to the death of his only son.

Yeah, right. Good luck with that.

7

Assisted Memories

Sydney pulled into the parking lot of the Valley View Senior Living Center and located a spot in the far corner. The illuminated clock in her mother's rusty Subaru Forester read 12:15. She leaned her head back and tilted the seat back as far as it would go.

Her mother's smell permeated the car, piercing the stench of oil, old food wrappers, and road salt that Sydney recognized as soon as she opened the car door. Odd that she didn't notice that scent in the house. Perhaps there were too many other distractions, like the piles of items her mother treasured too much to even organize.

Her mother's hoarding habit often made Sydney—a lifelong neatnik—wonder if she weren't adopted. It was as though her mother had to be able to see and touch everything she owned while neglecting precious objects at the same time. Which was pretty much Leslie's approach to parenting, too. A little bit of maturity and a lot of therapy had gone into coming to terms with her mother's clingy, obsessive waves of attention and indifference.

Now Sydney needed to bask in her mother's imperfect scent before she talked to her grandfather. Driving had been torturous with the sun reflecting off the snow like floodlights pointed at her face. She couldn't even make out the readings on the dashboard when she looked down from the road. She had never needed sunglasses as a kid, but now her eyes were fried. What was that about?

She could have sworn she had only blinked, but the clock suddenly read 12:45. Sydney jumped out of the car and swayed, coat-less, allowing the winter air to jolt her back to full-alert status.

She should never have allowed herself to doze on the couch when she returned from Randy's cabin. Then she was tired and exhausted. Now, after several hours' sleep, she was groggy as well as tired. Punch-drunk.

The intense cold made her nose hairs stand on end and cleared her head. She pushed thoughts of Randy away. He had all the time in the world now. He could wait.

She had reassessed her options on the drive in the cold light of day. She was sticking with plan A for the time being. Zile Jaquith would notice her text message soon, find his son's body at the cabin, and handle things from there. She would stay out of it.

If there was no word about Randy within two days, she would implement plan B. She would say that she had wanted to tell him about her mother and wondered if he might be at his cabin. She would hike in from the road, find his body and the others, hike out, and call the police. All very innocent. No one could possibly suspect her of anything. Otherwise, she would have to come up with plan C.

Meanwhile, the living were more important—specifically her grandfather. She hoped he remembered her phone call from the hospital. She knew his memory was not always good and he didn't hear well. On the phone, he had been very quiet and said almost nothing. She really did not want to repeat the news to him that his only child had died.

The main building was a three-story undistinctive brick structure. Perched on a high ridge, it did have valley vistas, and views of Skaneateles Lake as well. The lobby was bright and clean, with fresh flowers and no hint of sour odors.

"I'm here to visit my grandfather, David Graham," she said to the pimply teenager in an oversized suit behind the counter.

He pushed a ledger and pen her direction. "Dr. Graham's room is 301. Third floor on the far end of the left corridor."

As she bent to sign in, a tall woman who appeared to be about fifty, with dark brown eyes and short, wavy graying hair, came out of an office door next to the reception area and held out her hand. "Ms. Graham? I'm Patricia Atwood, managing director. I am so sorry to hear about your mother. I wonder if I could talk to you before you go up to see your grandfather."

Sydney took the woman's hand and felt the firm touch of someone who dealt with grief on a regular basis.

"My last name's Lucerno," Sydney said, and felt her cheeks glow. She didn't intend to come off as prickly.

"Oh, of course. I assumed that since your mother used Graham as her last name, you would, too."

"Word travels fast. I didn't realize you already knew about my mother."

"Your grandfather told us immediately and we followed up with the hospital."

"I wasn't certain he'd remember. I hated to tell him over the phone."

Atwood leaned back as if to get a better look. Something seemed to please her because she offered Sydney a smile that appeared to be a bit more genuine and the faint wrinkles around her eyes relaxed.

She ushered Sydney into her office and took a seat behind a plain blond wooden desk. "To get straight to the point, Ms. Lucerno, I wondered if you are now going to have power of attorney for your grandfather."

Sydney blinked several times and sank into one of the chairs on the opposite side. "I hadn't even thought about that."

"Not unusual in cases like this. That's why I wanted to make sure you and your family take care of this issue right away. Your grandfather is in reasonably good health for someone ninety years old, but he could have a health crisis at any time. As you probably know, he has been diagnosed with the beginning stages of dementia."

"I thought it was mild cognitive impairment."

Atwood busied herself with pulling out pamphlets from the file drawer next to her desk. "Right. MCI. That might progress very quickly or very slowly. It might turn into Alzheimer's, or it may stay as typical 'old age' dementia. You should consult his doctor on that. My job is to make sure that we are prepared to help him over time. For example, right now he is in our Independent Living section with his own kitchen, even though he doesn't use it much."

"I'm sure that's what he wants."

"Of course. No one likes to admit they need more help. In his case, your mother was the one who paid all his bills and set up his medical appointments. Recently he has asked us to help him get going in the mornings. Getting dressed, medications. Things like that."

"I suppose that costs money," Sydney said.

"Absolutely. We aren't heartless, but we don't have limitless resources. It might be time for him to move to our Assisted Living section, where many of those types of things are covered as part of the service."

Sydney closed her eyes tight to keep back the tears. Her chest tightened. "I have a meeting with my mother's lawyer after I leave here. I have no idea how things are set up."

Atwood placed her pile of brochures into a file folder and handed it to Sydney as they both stood. "It's a bit daunting for the uninitiated. Work with your lawyer and feel free to call me or come over. You'll figure it out. You look smart." She paused. "And you aren't a junkie."

Sydney dropped the folder and stood stock-still as Atwood bent to pick up the papers. "What?"

This time Atwood wrapped her hands around Sydney's as she handed over the folder. "I can see it in your eyes. In your face. Your mother had a habit. She hid it pretty well, but I'm a nurse by training. I could tell."

"She didn't overdose, you know." Sydney's voice rose higher. "It was the flu. Pneumonia from the flu."

Atwood patted Sydney's shoulder. "Good. Be sure to put that in her obituary. These days when younger people die with no reason given, we assume it's due to heroin or some other substance. It's a real epidemic around here."

The managing director looked up and down the corridor as if to make sure they were alone. "You would think that a place like this would be the last spot on earth to find opiate problems, but you would be wrong. We must be constantly on the lookout. Older people have many medical issues that require pain management. Sometimes they sell the pills they don't need. Sometimes . . ." She stopped and fixed Sydney in a long stare. "Sometimes, younger relatives steal those pills or force our residents to turn over their meds and prescriptions."

Sydney felt the pressure of Atwood's hand on her back. She stopped in the doorway and studied the older woman the way she had studied so many women who were approximately her mother's age over the years. What if this woman had been her mother instead of Leslie? Would her life have been better? Worse?

"Do you have children, Ms. Atwood?" she asked.

Patricia Atwood tilted her head back and guffawed. "Nope."

Sydney resisted the urge to ask if Atwood would like to adopt her, and headed down the hallway. Conscious of Atwood's watchful gaze on her back, she struggled to pick up her feet and not stumble on her way to the elevator.

Despite the managing director's words, she felt like a junkie again. Her head ached and she felt a knot in her belly that she used to get when the need to get high started to rise.

Nuts to that. She had been clean for a long time and was going to stay that way. She was tired and terrified—for her grandfather, for herself, and maybe for this new sister—but she would remain clean and straight. It was the only way forward.

David Graham was swaddled in a comforter and tucked into a comfy chair Sydney recognized as one that had been his favorite for many years. He blinked several times before he rose out of the quilting, like a baby born from a fluffy womb.

A very skinny and ancient baby. Wrapping her arms around her grandfather revealed he had shrunk in both width and height. His head rested easily on her shoulder now. His halitosis swept over her and she fought back a gag, but otherwise he smelled of mild soap and some sort of garden fresh laundry detergent.

This was a pleasant place, she decided. A small galley kitchen, half bath, and storage closet led into a large, open room filled with living and dining room furniture, familiar from her childhood. To her left, she caught a glimpse of an ample bedroom, presumably with its own bath, and to the right, she could see a small office nook. Directly ahead across a snow-covered porch, a spectacular view opened up, revealing a steep-sided moraine with a faint hint of a long, skinny frozen lake at the bottom.

She squeezed her eyes closed as she hugged her grandfather to her chest. "I've missed you," she whispered in his ear before she remembered he couldn't hear much these days.

Her grandfather patted her back and sank into his chair as a young woman about the same age as Sydney emerged from the bedroom. She wore thermal underwear under her short-sleeved, purple-themed Hawaiian-style surgical top, with pants in the same purple. Her badge identified her as Lily, a nurse's aide.

"How are we doing, Dr. Graham?" Lily turned to Sydney. "We wanted to keep him in our infirmary area, but he seems to have stabilized."

"*Doctor* Graham," Sydney's grandfather said, parroting Lily's chirpy voice. "Of course, I only had a PhD, but I was a teacher, a leader, a principal. I shaped so many lives. I'm so useless these days. What does all that matter now?"

Lily didn't seem offended. She handed David two pills and a large bottle of water. "This is your antibiotic and the cold medicine. I expect you to drink that entire bottle of water this afternoon. I'll stop back in a few hours." She folded the quilt around his legs and patted his shoulder in a way that made a lump form in Sydney's throat. Her grandfather was well looked after.

"How cold is it outside?" Sydney's grandfather asked.

"It was minus forty last night. During the day it's been about minus ten." Sydney tossed her jacket on the couch and pulled a dining room chair close to her grandfather. "I'm not used to this anymore. They say the weather should break tonight."

"That will mean snow." Her grandfather turned to look out the window. "It never snows when it's this cold. But it's hardly ever this cold these days like when I was growing up. I miss it."

"I can't say that I miss it." Sydney wiggled her backside into the chair, trying to figure how to move the conversation onto critical topics.

Her grandfather lowered his head and looked at her from under his craggy brows. "You shouldn't be here, Sydney. You need to leave."

"I don't intend to stay any longer than I have to, Grandpa."

"No, I mean go to the airport and fly out today. You are still in danger."

Sydney leaned back in her chair and gathered the threads running through her brain. "I think the statute of limitations has passed on all that crap I did."

Her grandfather wagged his head, keeping his eyes fixed on hers. "The statute of limitations doesn't apply to some crimes."

Like murder.

Sydney felt her jaw clench. She swiveled her head to check for Lily. Thankfully they were alone.

She leaned forward and clasped her grandfather's hands. "Yes, but we don't talk about those topics, right, Grandpa? That's what you always said."

David Graham pulled his hands into the depths of the quilt. "Did I? I suppose things weigh on me now that my time is short."

Sydney cleared her throat and studied her empty palms. "Remember, this is our private thing. We don't share that. We don't even mention it."

Her grandfather looked as though he might cry. She knelt beside him for a hug. "Okay. Don't worry. I will leave as soon as possible."

She felt his body relax. The crisis had passed.

She eased herself back into her chair and wiped away a tear. Her lifelong confidant was gone. All these years, she and her grandfather had shared secrets, but now he was disappearing behind a veil of imperfect memory. *Forget telling him about Randy.*

Sydney changed topics. "Meanwhile, there are some complications."

"Such as?"

"I hear I have a sister, for one."

Her grandfather wiped his face. "Oh, Sydney. I'm so sorry. I tried to get your mother to assert custody and take her back when she was born, years ago. I tried to be a grandfather, or at least a friendly presence in that girl's life."

"Is she really so awful? I don't remember much about her. Tall for her age. A smartass."

"No, not awful. Prickly. Temperamental. Stubborn. Typical of those Jaquiths. It's like she's been raised by wolves. At times I find it hard to believe we're related. Smart but an indifferent student. I hear she tried out community college."

Sydney chuckled. "I dropped out of high school, remember? And did my share of community college."

"Yes, but that was to escape." David inhaled and tilted his head, his mouth spreading into a soft grin. "I'm so proud of you. You got your GED and fought your way through college, even though it took years. Now you have that wonderful little place in Silicon Valley and a great job in high tech."

"I'm not a Silicon Valley billionaire, Grandpa. I'm not even a millionaire. I have a good, solid job—one I need to get back to."

"I loved visiting you out there every fall. Of course I didn't go this year."

Sydney frowned. Should she mention it had been three years since his last visit? "Would you like to move there? With me?"

"Your place is too small, sweetie."

"Maybe a place like this." Sydney waved her hands to the apartment around them.

"This is my home, Sydney. Not only this facility. I belong

here in the deep cold in January and the steamy heat in July. These valleys are embedded in my heart." He coughed from a deep well in his chest. "Besides, I don't think we could afford anything close to this out your way."

Sydney suspected that was the truth. Silicon Valley was so expensive. "You do know that the staff here believes you should move to the Assisted Living wing soon, right?" She leaned forward and pushed the bottle of water into his hands.

"That part of the facility is on the first floor. No views. I want to stay here. I can still look after myself." Her grandfather set the bottle on the table next to the chair. "I'll have to pee if I drink all that."

"I think that's the idea. In fact, I'll make myself some tea if you don't mind."

"Nothing in the kitchen except some vodka under the sink. I'm going to stay here and pay for extra help. Period."

Sydney wandered to the kitchen and verified the empty cupboards and the vodka bottle.

"Can you—can we—afford that?" she asked as she closed the cupboard doors. "Your school pension and Social Security can't amount to much."

"I still have some savings. Plus, that's where your mother's money comes in." David Graham crossed his legs and wrapped the quilt tighter.

Sydney crept closer, her chest tightening with each step. Could it be that her mother really did "invest" with Randy?

"She didn't earn much from her so-called antiques business, Grandpa."

Even with her standing over him, her grandfather would not look her in the eye. "Do you have prescriptions for stuff like Norco or Oxy?" she asked.

Her grandfather shifted his body under the quilt. "Vicodin. For a while. I decided I didn't need it anymore."

Not after her mother had taken it or stolen the prescription. Sydney realized that was what Patricia Atwood was trying to tell her.

She clenched her teeth. Who was she to be so judgmental? She had stolen plenty. The ache of desperation was not so distant that she couldn't feel its tentacles reach out to her.

"You need to talk to Steve. He's the lawyer. He knows all the details about your mother's finances," her grandfather said, shooting her a furtive glance.

"I'm going to meet him right after I leave here."

Her grandfather grunted and stood up, taking a moment to steady himself before he headed for the small office nook. "I want to show you something."

Sydney followed and stood next to him as he settled into the chair at the antique mahogany desk she remembered from her childhood. The lid folded down, revealing a row of cubbyholes and a little door in the center.

"I don't want to linger, Sydney. It's important you know that."

"You have a 'do not resuscitate' order and all that, right?"

Her grandfather waved his hands impatiently. "Years ago, Dr. Wagner said I'd have a heart attack around the age of ninety. Given that it takes at least thirty to forty minutes to get to the nearest hospital—and that's after the ambulance arrives—he said I'll be dead before I get there."

"That's a good thing?"

"A very good thing as far as I'm concerned. The problem is he's not always right."

David leaned forward and pulled out the secret vertical box next to the little door on the desk. "You remember this little place, don't you? Not really a secret for those familiar with these desks, but secret enough."

He turned the secret box upside down and several cellophane packets with pills slid out. "I hid these from your mother. From the staff, too. They don't exactly approve of what I have in mind."

Sydney's voice failed her. She reached out and squeezed her grandfather's shoulder.

"If I don't die of that heart attack, if I'm miserable and want to go, I'm going to take these. But I forget so much these days. I might not be able to recall where I put them. Or I might be stuck in bed. I want you to know where these are so you can help me. Can you do that?"

Sydney forced herself to breathe as tears rolled down her cheeks. "Shit."

"Good. I'll take that for a yes. Now I need to take a nice nap." Her grandfather replaced the pills in the hidden drawer. He collected his legs underneath him and pressed with his arms to stand. He stroked her cheek and shuffled toward the bedroom.

Sydney caught up with him to offer a goodbye embrace.

"Promise me, Sydney."

"Okay. Yes, I promise," she said, even though this was one promise she didn't think she could keep.

"I'll hold you to that."

"Drink your water, Grandpa."

"It makes me pee and I don't always make it to the john in time. You go talk to Steve, Sydney. He'll explain a lot of things," her grandfather said, and closed his bedroom door.

8

Irrevocable

In the time it took Sydney to drive the twenty-odd miles from Valley View Senior Living to the town of Hartwell, the weather turned from bright, cutting sunshine to cloudy malevolence. The good news was that according to the temperature reading on the car's dashboard, it was now a balmy five degrees Fahrenheit and climbing.

The bad news was that snow was on the way. Sydney didn't need the radio to tell her this. As soon as she stepped out of the parked car, she could smell it. Odd that she had forgotten about that odor for so many years but could recognize it in an instant, like the stench of rancid, overcooked popcorn in a cheap movie theater. And just about as welcome.

On the bright side, snow could hide a multitude of sins. Covering more of Hartwell might be viewed as a positive, from what Sydney could see. The place had not improved much during her absence.

A brief burst of prosperity driven by woolen mills in the late 1800s had triggered the creation of many classic storefronts along its primary streets with two or three stories above the stores for apartments and offices. Sadly, the twentieth century had not been kind. Hartwell remained the central town for little satellite villages like Oriska with the high school, two supermarkets, a bank, a pharmacy, a liquor store, a diner, and a few bars. Sydney noticed that many of the storefronts were empty with plywood covering the windows, and several had been ravaged by fires and not rebuilt.

The town plow hadn't allowed for much on-street parking, so Sydney drove past the building housing Steve's law office and wedged her mother's car between two enormous trucks in the drugstore parking lot around the corner.

Access to Steve's office was through a door next to the Kaffe Klatch Kafe, one of the few remaining businesses she remembered from childhood. The stairs rose steeply, creaking with each step. No sneaking up on Steve these days.

When she'd needed his services years ago, he operated out of his parents' house in the upscale section of Hartwell. She remembered cooling her heels on a hard bench by their front door.

Now he had a genuine waiting room with real walnut paneling and fake antique folk art on the walls. The soft, upholstered chairs showed signs of stains and abuse from too many clients, but Steve's trim and prim receptionist had not changed—his mother. She must have been seventy if she was a day, but she sat perfectly coifed with her Queen Elizabeth hairdo behind an elegant mahogany desk, studying Sydney over her bright red reading glasses.

No introductions were necessary. "Take a seat, Ms. Lucerno," she said with a sniff. "My son will be with you shortly."

Sydney opened her mouth but decided no words would help. She took a seat. At least Mrs. Lee had not called her "Syddie"— a slight status improvement.

She had barely placed her butt on the most inviting chair when the door into the inner sanctum swung open.

"Sydney, Sydney." Stephen Lockwood Lee held out his arms, not really for a hug, but rather to usher her into his office.

"Steve, Steve," Sydney said in echo. Once he closed the door, she did a three sixty in the center of his office. "Nice upgrade. Very nineteenth-century power broker."

Steve offered a grin, like a kid who had lucked into finding the executive lunchroom. "Pretty neat, huh? There have to be some advantages to hanging tough in this burg."

Sydney wandered to one of the enormous windows overlooking the street. Individual snowflakes were already swarming, getting ready to wreck collective havoc.

Steve circled to the elegant chair behind his desk as Sydney took the long way around the room before she landed in a comfortable club chair facing him across an acre of mahogany. The journey gave her the opportunity to study Steve. She assumed he was doing the same to her, and wondered what he saw.

Of all the people she had known, she suspected Steve was the most capable of discerning what residual crap she still carried—and what she had shed.

She figured Steve was in his early forties now. Back when he represented her, he confided he grew a beard to look older and more dignified. Now he had matured into the look. He had definitely missed the memo about business casual attire. Despite the weather and isolation, he wore a gray wool suit that did not look cheap, a crisp white shirt, and a tie that she thought might be considered stylish—she saw them so rarely in California.

"It's great to see you again, Sydney," Steve said as he scooted his chair up to the desk and adjusted his gold rim glasses. "I'm sad about the circumstances, but you do look good."

"Better than our last meeting, that's for sure," Sydney said. Seeing his eyebrows meet, she continued. "County jail? Fourteen years ago, almost to the day."

Steve took off his glasses and wiped them with a pressed handkerchief. "You forgot about your court date. You cleaned up real nice. That's why I was able to get you into an excellent diversion program and your record expunged." He sat back and replaced his glasses. "Looks like that program stuck."

Sydney waved her hands. "It was a great first step. And thank you for that opportunity. The reason it stuck was that I ran off as soon as I got out. I was starting to use again. I needed to leave before I could get sucked back in."

"Point taken. I'll give you that."

Mrs. Lee opened the door without knocking and deposited a tray with two steaming mugs on Steve's desk. "Tea," she said, turned, and left the room.

"If you want milk or sugar, you're out of luck." Steve pushed one mug her direction.

"Maybe in a bit." Sydney took a deep breath. "Before we get into the details of my mother's estate, I want to know if you knew she was a junkie."

She should have remembered that Steve never, ever overreacted to any surprises. Based on his lawyerly composure, she might have been asking about the weather. He took a cautious sip from his mug and set it down. "Let's back up. First and foremost, I'm very sorry about your mother. Second, I did not know about her habit. However, I didn't see her very often. So, third, if what you say is true, I'm not entirely shocked. It's a pervasive problem these days and not always obvious. And then there is the issue of the company she kept."

"Meaning Randy."

Steve wrapped his long fingers around the hot mug. "How he has managed to escape being picked up for so long is beyond me. I always figured I'd have guaranteed employment thanks to him someday. But not so far."

Make that not ever.

Sydney fought back a surge of tears. She wanted to tell someone Randy was dead, and who better than a lawyer? She reached for the mug of tea and swallowed a scalding sip to keep the words inside while she regained her composure.

"Did you know she was dealing?"

This question hit its target more squarely. Steve squirmed in his chair, and he studied the interior of his mug before he answered.

"I will say this. Your mother had me set up an irrevocable trust. Within that trust, there is a fund for your grandfather and another set of accounts that transfer on death to her heirs, along with a few bequests. There is also the house, the furnishings, and the assets of her business."

"Most of which are junk."

"Precisely. I don't have much visibility into her transactions, but every year she provided an update on the value of various assets and the amounts in her bank and investment accounts.

I'd say that there is a reasonable amount of money in those, considering."

"Like how much? Ballpark."

Steve opened a drawer on his side of the desk and pulled out a thick hanging folder. He extracted a sheet of paper from the top of the pile.

"Maybe a hundred thousand for the house, if you're lucky. She listed all the so-called antiques as worth over two hundred thousand, but I suspect that's grossly inflated. However, she had close to one hundred thousand in her brokerage account and about that in her IRA. Your grandfather's trust has about fifty thousand. She also listed her savings account as having twenty thousand or so and about ten in her checking account."

"For real?" Sydney slumped back in her chair. By Silicon Valley standards, these were very modest amounts, but her own personal wealth was less than six figures, not counting a lot of underwater stock options.

"Straight up."

"That's more than I expected. Still, I thought drug dealing paid better."

Sydney let the ticking of a grandfather clock in the corner fill the space for a minute.

"Let's suppose that she came by that money by funding Randy's drug deals or other monkey business," she said at last.

"If you like."

"Could the cops or feds or whoever come after that money?"

Steve tapped his fingers together. "Possibly. The good news for you is that your mother filed estimated taxes and yearly taxes like clockwork. They would need to have some reason to come looking. As your lawyer, I would advise you not to give them any excuses."

"Such as?"

"Bragging about it. Talking about it." Steve paused. "Taking any money at all from Randy Jaquith. Or giving him any."

Sydney looked Steve straight in the eye. "That is not going to be an issue."

Steve laid his arms down on the desk and leaned forward. "Good, because this is about to get complicated."

Stevie boy, you have no idea how right you are.

Sydney leaned forward as well until their noses were inches apart. "I assume you are talking about my sister, Maude."

Steve sat back and removed his glasses. "I didn't think you knew."

Sydney pushed back her chair and moved to the window. Winter twilight was setting in, but she picked out a familiar form stalking across the street below—Lilith Jaquith, Randy's mother. Her lanky stride was unmistakable even under a long, heavy coat. Her long hair had changed from jet black to iron gray, but it still flowed like a proud flag in the building storm.

Several steps behind, a tall form sauntered, seemingly untroubled by oncoming traffic and the decreased visibility, lugging what looked like a very heavy duffel bag. The figure was too bundled up to betray any details.

"My grandfather spilled the beans," she said. She figured this white lie was safe enough. "Please tell me I don't have any other surprise siblings."

A bell rang on Steve's desk—an apparent signal from his mother in the lobby that company had arrived.

Steve replaced his glasses and stood, straightening his tie and rebuttoning his suit jacket.

"I think you'll find that Maude will add up to more than a whole roomful of brothers and sisters. And then some."

Sydney turned from the window to face the office door. "I'll start counting my blessings."

9

Divide and Conquer

Mrs. Lee opened the door from the reception room. Before she could open her mouth to announce the visitors, Lilith Jaquith hip-checked Steve's mother to one side and pushed her way into the office. Once she had reached the middle of the room, she stood with feet planted and scanned the entire space with an icy gaze.

She shrugged out of her long, padded coat and half tossed it to Mrs. Lee in a lateral pass. Steve's mother raised one eyebrow as she drilled her son with a flat-eyed stare and left the office, coat in hand.

Aside from many more gray hairs, Lilith had not changed one bit.

As a kid, Sydney was fascinated by this tall, elegant Native woman. Back then, Sydney took Lilith's stony contempt to be a reflection of some personal failing on Sydney's part, and she had tried desperately to eke out a kind word from Randy's mother, always failing to grasp it was a lost cause.

Now Sydney was an adult, and she knew a lost cause when she saw one. Case in point, Lilith glaring across Steve's office. Lilith was as formidable as ever and did not seem pleased to find Sydney back in town.

Sydney felt a familiar tightening in her throat. She opened

her mouth to offer some sort of mealy-mouthed greeting but stopped as the second visitor shuffled into the room.

Maude. It had to be.

The visitor threw behind a chair the large duffel bag she was carrying and swept off her woolen hat to shake out a long mane of dark hair with honey streaks. She looked first at Steve and turned her gaze to Sydney, fixing her half sister with a pale-green fire from her hazel eyes.

As Maude shed her gloves, heavy coat, scarf, and fleece vest, she emerged like a butterfly from a cocoon. Sydney had no words. Maude was gorgeous.

There was no mistaking Randy's look, transformed into this tall female creature, still blessed with the skinny limbs of youth, radiating her contempt for everyone in the room.

Sydney raised her hands to her mouth, searching to pull out the right words, when Maude snuffed out her suspicious glower, tilted her head, and tucked her chin in a gesture straight from their mother's playbook.

Who was this creature barging her way into Sydney's family? Seeing her mother's smile combined with Randy's features made the hair on the back of Sydney's neck prickle.

She was being played. She was sure of it. How many times had she been sucked into one of Randy's schemes or agreed to some harebrained idea of her mother's based on a simple smile or gesture? *Too many.*

Sydney forced what she hoped was a warm smile and pulled Maude into her arms. The last time she'd seen Maude, she was a scrawny, chest-high kid. Now, Sydney's chin barely reached Maude's shoulder. A total stranger.

Sydney felt Maude stiffen and arch her back. At least the awkward feeling was mutual.

Maude grabbed Sydney's arms and pushed away. "Nice to meet you," she muttered, and shifted her eyes toward Steve.

Sydney tilted her head, trying to hold Maude's gaze. Her artificial smile froze. Maude had pinpoint pupils in a room with bad lighting.

Was her baby sister a junkie? She stepped back and turned away, hoping she had hidden her shock, only to come face-to-face with Lilith a few short paces away. Lilith's pupils were normal sized, and the set of her jaw indicated she was pissed off.

"Mrs. Jaquith . . ." was all Sydney could manage before Lilith injected words of her own.

"They say a bad penny always turns up. That's you. So like your mother."

Lilith's words hit like a whip, wrapping around Sydney's head, yanking the words from her mouth. Sydney felt her insides revolt in protest. She stepped forward, mesmerized, to take a closer look into the eyes of someone so devoid of empathy.

Perhaps it was Sydney's look of fascination that hit Lilith, but she blinked and averted her eyes and stepped back. Sydney moved smoothly into the gap, tilting her head to study Lilith's darting eyes, her fury mounting by the second.

I know something that will yank your heart straight out of your chest.

She opened her mouth to tell Lilith that Randy, her no-good misbegotten son, was dead. But the words caught in her throat. She swallowed and began to speak. "I know . . ."

In that brief pause, with her back against the door, Lilith's eyes filled with tears. Fear. Sydney could smell it. What did Lilith fear?

Sydney leaned back and coughed. Lilith sagged against the wall.

"Let's get this meeting started," Sydney said. She clapped her hands together to hide the trembling that rattled her limbs. She needed to sit down and collect her wits.

She grabbed the older woman's arm to guide her back into the middle of the room. "Here's a chair, Mrs. Jaquith. If you want to stay and listen, that's fine, but this is a meeting for my sister and me." With that, Sydney sat down in one of the two chairs opposite Steve and motioned for Maude to grab the other spot.

For two ticks, she could feel the room hold its breath, waiting for Lilith's response. Meanwhile, Sydney sank into her chair.

One demon confronted. A single battle won. Perhaps she had grown up a bit after all.

Death and dying turned out to be complicated stuff.

For the next hour, Sydney took notes at a frantic pace, covering pages of yellow paper, including notations up and down the margins. Steve refused to let her record the meeting on her cell phone, but he did pull out a whiteboard and allowed her to snap photos with her camera.

At the thirty-minute mark, she turned her focus to Maude to see what her sister was making of all this. To Sydney's surprise, Maude slouched in her seat, her head nodding forward with eyes closed and snapping back, trying to stay awake. Lilith, on the other hand, was leaning forward from the middle of the room, eyes glittering with apparent keen interest.

"Stop snoring," Sydney said, and gave Maude's elbow a whack with her pen.

Maude snorted and sat up, eyes blazing. "Jeez. I got it already." She slumped again and spoke to the ceiling. "All the money and the house are in an irrevocable trust with lots of little pieces. There's a trust for her father, some investment accounts, and some money in the bank to be split between you and me. It adds up to a lot of money, but you control everything because she appointed you to handle it. Leslie wanted some of her money to go to Middlebury College and some to people in Oriska. God knows why. And ten thousand for my father." She leaned forward and rubbed her face. "By 'father,' I mean Randy. Is that about right?"

Sydney wagged her head sideways. "It's not a lot of money in the grand scheme of things, and there's a lot of extra work to get access to it. Original wills, death certificates, papers to fill out. And we have to arrange to sell the house and all that furniture."

"*We* don't have to do anything. *You* do. You're the dominatrix."

"Executrix," Sydney said as she studied her notes. "An unpaid position, by the way. All the work and none of the glory."

"Half the glory." Maude tilted her head to one side and

cracked her neck. "I want the house and I want the car. You can have all the furniture."

Sydney felt her neck stiffen. "I was planning to torch that place, furniture and all, but if you want to spend your life in Oriska, I'm sure we can work something out."

After opening and closing his mouth several times, Steve caught up with the conversation. He pressed both palms up and down toward his desk as if to calm overexcited toddlers.

"You two can do anything you want once all is safely transitioned. Maude, you are going to have to sign a number of papers, but your mother worked with me to set things up to be straightforward."

Lilith chose that moment to speak up. "Meanwhile, that girl gets to live in the house and drive the car."

Sydney swiveled in her seat to face Lilith. "*Totek Hatwus.*"

Lilith stiffened, her eyes wide. Sydney had picked up the Mohawk phrase for "shut up, go away" from Randy. He used it so often when she was thirteen she thought it was a Mohawk nickname—until Lilith set her straight.

"Lilith, at the age of thirty, I get to be a woman. If you insist, I will stay in a motel over by Ithaca, rent a car, and charge it to the estate."

"That's why I'm coming to stay with you at the house," Maude said. "And you can drive me around."

Steve and Lilith shifted their focus to Maude.

"Don't you have a car of your own?" Sydney asked.

"She has a truck. And a DUI. Suspended license," Lilith said with a bark and a huff. "Go ahead, kiddo. I'm tired of driving you all over and sick of you living in my house, mooching my food."

"I'll be able to drive again in a couple of days," Maude said.

"A month if it's a day. Don't think you can fool me."

Sydney raised her voice to a low yell. "Fine. Fine, fine, fine. Maude can stay at the house. We'll work out the transportation details."

Lilith offered a parting remark. "You deserve each other," she said, and stalked from the room.

"Let's go." Maude motioned to the duffel bag she had dumped in the corner. "I'm all packed."

"Hold on," Sydney said, and sat down in the chair. "I need to review next steps with Steve."

Steve wiped his mouth. He looked eager to bring the meeting to a close. "Uh. I think you've got it. Why don't you go home and get some rest? Call me if you have any questions in the morning."

Maude stuffed herself back into her vest and coat, swept up her duffel, and left the office. "Hurry up," she called over her shoulder. "I'm hungry."

Sydney took her time gathering her papers and regaining her composure. Maude could wait. Ready at last, she shook Steve's hand with a mutter of thanks.

Steve returned the shake and offered his final words. "Don't let her drive, Sydney. Just don't."

10

ABS

"You should give me the keys," Maude said.

Fortunately, thanks to her big duffel, Maude was lagging several paces behind Sydney in the slippery snow that coated the sidewalk, and the keys were not within reach.

"No."

"You aren't used to driving in slop like this. I should drive."

"No."

"Don't worry about the DUI. No one will see us in this snow."

"No."

"I need to pick up my truck at my father's."

"What?" Sydney stopped dead in her tracks and turned. "You mean Randy's nasty double-wide on Dugway?"

"Not so nasty these days. He sort of fixed it up."

"The answer is no. You'd still have to drive. We're going to the house. Our mother's house. Make dinner, make lists. Tomorrow I'll ask whatshername, the real-estate person, to drop me down there and I'll bring the truck back for you."

"Lists? What sort of lists?"

"Lists of what it is going to take to get out of Oriska. For good." Sydney started walking again but turned back. "Why do you need your truck if you can't drive?"

"I can drive. I just can't get caught." Maude grinned, looking for all the world like Leslie. "I have a job to do for my father."

Sydney squinted and blinked away the sticky snow clinging to her eyelashes. "Meaning Randy or Zile?"

"Zile was Dad, now Granddad. My father is Randy."

"Glad we have our terminology straight. I gather you've known for a while. You were one ahead of me."

Maude spat onto the sidewalk and rubbed the mark with the bottom of her boot. "Randy is counting on me."

As she swiped at the swarm of snowflakes that threatened to cover her face, Sydney's brain connected the dots. "Delivering for Randy. Shit. You are going to pick up his packages and make deliveries, right?"

"None of your business." Maude hefted her heavy duffel and took the lead. "But if you don't let me get the truck, you'll have to drive me. If you don't, you'll have to answer to my father."

Sydney inhaled. All day she had been mourning Randy for all his good points. Wasted sentimentality. "I would be happy to have that conversation with Randy."

She trailed after Maude, her feet sliding in the thin layer of accumulating slush. "I used to do that for Randy and Zile, you know. I didn't have a car because I was only fifteen at first. That's when I teamed up with Caleb," Sydney said after they crossed the next intersection. "That's how I got picked up by the cops."

Maude dropped the duffel with a grunt. "Man, that's heavy. Do you mean Caleb Elway? The one who killed Sheriff Carver? Was he really your boyfriend?"

"Yeah, the first love of my life, even if he did work for Randy. He didn't kill anyone, not even *that* asshole."

Maude stared at Sydney as if seeing her for the first time. "That's not what most people think. That's not what the cops think. They think he was hiding out and ambushed the sheriff. They think he ran off with you."

Sydney felt her feet root in place, right through the snow, straight through the sidewalk. Words came and went before she could speak. "With me? Really? Caleb disappeared in September. I left in November."

"Yeah, well, that's still what most people think and that he's living with you in California."

Sydney felt all the life drain from her heart as a deep, aching numbness spread to her limbs. "I wish with all my heart that were so."

"What's that? What did you say?" Maude leaned in to stare into Sydney's eyes.

"Nothing. Let's get going."

"Okay." Maude didn't seem convinced. "We'll move faster if you help me carry this."

The duffel was heavier than it looked. Sydney was glad when they reached the car. She clicked the key fob to unlock the doors.

Maude opened the back door and slid the duffel across the backseat. "You should let me drive."

Sydney shed her heavy coat before climbing behind the wheel. "No."

There was something to be said for muscle memory, Sydney thought. She had been nervous as all get out about driving in the slippery snow, but after a few miles, it came back to her like pulling on a familiar pair of gloves.

"You don't have to pump the brakes, you know," Maude said. "Cars like this have ABS. Automatic Braking System."

Sydney waited until she had finished the turn and reached the flat stretch heading to Oriska, about seven miles away. The snow was flying straight into the windshield, but she could make out the reflective markers for the snowplows on each side of the road. As long as she could see at least one side, they'd be okay.

"I'm sorry no one called you and told you Mom was in the hospital," she said. "I didn't know about you until yesterday or I would have figured out how to get in touch."

Sydney risked a sideways glance at the passenger seat. Maude's face looked rumpled in the blue-green lights of the dashboard.

"The story of my life," Maude said, her voice soft. "Too little too late. But at least she told you at the end."

Sydney focused on keeping the vehicle between the reflective markers. How much faith should she place in ABS in this upcoming curve? How honest should she be with her newfound sister?

Their mother hadn't been able to speak thanks to the ventilator, and it was Randy who had broken the news about Maude. But perhaps these details were best kept to herself for the moment. A minor sin considering some of the other secrets she carried.

"When'd you figure out that Randy and Leslie were your parents?" she asked instead.

"I knew something was off by the time I was ten. For one thing, I was old enough to realize I wasn't enrolled as a Mohawk member. That made no sense because my 'mother'—Lilith—is enrolled and she takes this stuff very seriously. Only children of enrolled women can be enrolled. Strictly matrilineal. A lot of tribes don't follow that rule, but it's a big deal here. So why wasn't I enrolled?"

"I never realized that. I assume you asked."

"You betcha. That led nowhere. Plus, Randy would bring me over to the house all the time, especially after you'd gone. It was too odd, the way that Leslie would hang all over me. And her father, our grandfather as it turns out, was so attentive that it was spooky. Helping me with homework, taking me on little excursions."

"What about Randy?"

"Oh, I don't think he gave a shit. Not about raising me, anyway. He loved me, but I think he kind of liked the situation. Even after I figured things out, nothing changed with him."

"So how did you work it out?" Sydney asked, braking into the next curve.

"A silly thing. I had the trick that no one in my family could do. I could roll my tongue over. One hundred eighty degrees."

"Oh yeah," Sydney said. "I can do that. A lot of men can't do it."

"Well, my grandmother can't do it, either. Randy took me over to Leslie's house one day, and I showed her. She laughed and did it right back. I knew, right then and there."

"That seems kind of thin on the evidence side."

"True," Maude said. "But I told Francine when I saw her at Brochu's. I was so proud I'd figured it out. She said, 'That shit about the truth shall set you free is crap.'"

Sydney let several glowing markers go by before she spoke. "Do you think she knew all along, or was that one of her wisecracks?"

"Both?"

As if on a signal, the sisters turned their heads and stuck out their tongues at each other—rotated one hundred eighty degrees. Sydney cackled and turned her attention back to the road.

Perhaps some conversations are best had in the dark with the snow threatening to push you into a ditch, Sydney acknowledged, as the car passed under the first streetlight over the welcome sign to Oriska: POPULATION 208. FOUNDED 1792. Make that population 206, because she was not sticking around to replace her mother, that was for sure, and Randy was not coming back, either.

She navigated the zigzag route through town. Left, right, left, until she passed Brochu's General Store. What kind of twisted main street was that? No wonder Oriska was such a backwater.

"I want to stay in Mom's room," Maude said, her voice testy again.

"Suit yourself. You'd better change the sheets and scrub down the surfaces."

"You mean she really did die of the flu? I thought she OD'd."

"Welcome home. She did not overdose."

Sydney pulled into the driveway at top speed and slammed on the brakes. Sure enough, the ABS worked like a charm. The car stuttered and heaved but did not swerve, and stopped mere inches from the garage door.

11

Good Elves, Bad Elves

Sydney studied the cracks in the plaster ceiling above the bed in her childhood bedroom. There were fingerprints embedded deep in the edges of the plaster that probably dated back to the 1800s, pressed in by the men who built this place. How had she forgotten them—only visible when the gray predawn light filtered through?

The house was still. Her head was clear. Finally a pause. A chance to sleep in a real bed for close to eight hours worked wonders. She now could consider the merely important tasks she needed to take care of that had been overtaken by all critical ones—like people dying.

She rolled over and checked for a spare place on the floor to place her feet. How had her mother squeezed so much crap into this room? Sydney had tossed piles of books and old newspapers onto older piles to clear the bed. Her suitcase was still in the hallway, her dirty clothes draped over a carved wooden bear in the corner.

Who the hell is going to buy that?

It was tempting to use her time to clear space for her own stuff—a bit of closet, a few drawers, some floor space for walking—but that was a slippery slope. A tiny crack of accommodation might convince her that she could actually stay here, and that would be a dangerous delusion. She needed to get out as soon as possible, and she needed to make sure she had a life to get back to.

Heading to the hall bathroom, she started on her mental list. Her company in California was reasonably progressive and offered a modest bereavement policy. She needed to call HR bright and early Pacific Time to buy herself a couple of weeks of paid leave. After that, she would need to use her accumulated vacation. *A month?* By then it might not matter. She'd probably be out of a job. Maybe she could fake working remotely for a while, but she knew she had better be long gone from here by then.

All the more reason to reach out on social media now. LinkedIn. Facebook. Start making her case for why she might need to look for her next position without alarming her current company. She could also enjoy some warmth from her friends— using the Internet portals to the different life she had forged.

After a shower, she would make coffee and start her lists. Then . . . then . . . then . . . She could visualize the tasks spread out ahead of her like infinite strings of pearls into the future. She would not clear out her bedroom.

The kitchen and family room appeared to have been invaded by elves. Bad elves.

Good elves were like her roommates in California—Lakshmi and Angelica. They brought in the mail and stacked it in clear piles. They cleaned up the dishes even when it wasn't entirely their mess. They wrote down messages and took out the recycling. They wiped down the countertops and vacuumed.

They had good jobs in high tech and paid the rent on time. They owned small, energy-efficient cars—not big trucks—and did not use them to deliver drugs. They never left their dirty laundry scattered on the kitchen floor.

Maude did not appear to be a good elf.

Sydney picked up a pair of jeans and a shirt from the floor next to the refrigerator and tossed them on top of Maude's duffel bag, still sitting in the middle of the foyer next to the kitchen. Every cupboard door hung open and piles of plates, glassware, frying pans, and plastic containers now crowded the counters.

"Somebody" did find what they were looking for because an empty bottle of rotgut bourbon sat next to the sink snuggled next to a motley collection of half-drained gin and vodka containers.

Sydney grabbed the edge of the sink with both hands and bent at the waist to study her feet. She had done her best to clear out her mother's drug stashes before visiting Randy the night before. What were the chances she had missed a few? Probably good.

Given the evidence, her guess—her hope—was that Maude unsuccessfully searched for drugs and settled for liquor. If so, a small but significant blessing.

In order to make coffee, she needed to excavate the coffee-maker from under the piles of dishes and heavy pans. Putting things away created a cathartic clang and clatter, and also revealed the little mystery packet of powder taped to the underside of the top for an ancient Dutch oven. She stared at it as if she had found a black widow spider, waiting to pounce.

Back in her day, she would have cut it open and dumped it down the sink. Or used it. These days, she knew some opiates were so potent that fatal amounts could be absorbed through the skin, or accidentally inhaled. She pulled out a white trash bag from under the sink, lowered the top and the bottom of the pan into the bag, and twisted the top into a tight knot.

Now what? Maybe one of the local police departments or the sheriff had a drop-off for such things. An anonymous drop-off.

As she set the bag down by the mudroom door, a groan followed by a thud rose from the couch in the open-plan family room adjoining the kitchen. Peeking over the back of the sofa, she could see Maude sprawled on the floor.

"Shit. What's all that noise? Why'd you push me off the couch?" Maude rolled to her hands and knees and rotated to sit on the coffee table—fortunately a sturdy piece.

Sydney decided not to argue and scrubbed her hands and lower arms in the sink instead. "It's time to get up. The realtor lady and her estate disposal pal are going to arrive soon. Why didn't you sleep upstairs?"

"Ugh. Too germy. You freaked me out with that stuff about the flu. What's for breakfast?"

Sydney dried her hands and opened the refrigerator. "We ate almost everything last night. We'll have to go to Brochu's later. I guess I could make French toast. It looks like there's some ancient maple syrup way back in there."

"I hate maple syrup."

"Okay, plain butter for you, then. Pick up your stuff and take it upstairs. I'll help you clean Mom's bedroom later. Take a shower and come down presentable for company. I'll have breakfast ready."

"You aren't the boss of me," Maude said, but she picked up her duffel and grumbled her way toward the stairs.

"Not to worry," Sydney said under her breath. "I'm under no illusions."

The storm from the previous night had left almost a foot of new snow, and more continued to drift down. After gulping her French toast, Sydney suited up and attended to snowblowing the driveway and shoveling off the steps.

Happily, the old machine was in fine shape and ready to go. After a few turns up and down the driveway, Sydney had adjusted to the noise and pacing.

Close friends and family came through the barn and the mudroom, but other visitors usually climbed up onto the porch off the kitchen and family room wing of the house since it was closest to the driveway. The accumulated ice on the porch flooring was so thick, she needed to hack it away with an ice chopper—a long-handled metal rod with a flat blade on the bottom. Another old, familiar task.

Sweating under too many protective layers, her mind was full of Randy, which pissed her off. She should have been thinking about her mother—remembering the good times, planning a memorial service—not Leslie's boyfriend. The guilt and strain of waiting for him to turn up dead were wearing her down.

Finished for the time being, Sydney left the shovel and ice chopper on the porch. They'd be needed again soon.

She was stripping off her outside layers in the mudroom when she heard the doorbell ring and Maude's voice greeting Cindy Rose, the realtor, and her friend, Noleen.

"Perfect timing," Maude said. "We've been clearing the driveway for you."

Sydney emerged and there were handshakes all around before the four women crammed into the small family room area. Maude, all smiles and charm, poured coffee.

"We're so sorry to hear about your mother," Cindy said, accepting a steaming mug. "We were classmates of hers, you know."

"Hartwell Central School, class of 1982," Noleen said.

"My sister and I are very pleased you can help us with this part of our mother's estate," Sydney said. She watched them closely for a reaction.

Cindy and Noleen looked at each other. Cindy smiled ever so slightly. Noleen raised an eyebrow one notch. Definitely an I-told-you-so communication, Sydney thought, exchanging a similar look with Maude.

"Our goal is to sell this house and the contents as soon as possible," Sydney said, pulling the attention of the two visitors back to her. "We realize that means setting the right prices."

Cindy pursed her lips. "Even during warm months, this is a tough market. But sometimes there are bright spots. Just last week I sold a similar place to a college professor at Colgate and her husband. It's a long commute, but some will pay for charm and a bargain."

"Of course there is the issue of all the furnishings," Noleen said, casting a timid glance toward Maude.

Sydney set down her mug. "As you know, my mother was in the collectibles and antiques business. Maude and I might pick out a few family items, but we're counting on you to help us. Everything must go." In the back of her mind, a little warning bell went off. How many other deadly packets might be hiding in all this trash? "We cannot afford to be sentimental."

Cindy picked up her yellow pad and pen. "Let's get started," she said. "You can fill us in as we go."

* * *

Cindy's portion of the assessment was over rather quickly: size and age of house, features, lot size . . . Noleen had a much harder task. Sydney noticed that she stopped taking notes and filled the silence with grunts and sighs.

Maude drifted away before they had even finished with the first floor. *Up to no good, no doubt.* Sydney attempted to keep her focus on Cindy and Noleen, but she was mentally trying to trace her sister's movements. Hopefully, Maude was cleaning their mother's bedroom.

After an exhausting and exhaustive examination of all the rooms and piles of Leslie's precious accumulated estate, Sydney escorted Cindy and Noleen back to the kitchen.

"It will be tough to sell this place until spring, and probably impossible before it is emptied. Still, I'll start a listing right away. I'll drop off the paperwork tomorrow," Cindy said.

Noleen pulled on her winter parka and shoved her hands into her gloves. "You and Maude put stickers on anything you plan to retain. I'll start making plans for an estate sale. We'll probably have more than one, but most of the good furniture and antiques will go in the first round. How long will you be here?"

"Do I have to be here for any of this?" Sydney asked. "I do have a job in California."

Cindy and Noleen exchanged another I-told-you-so glance, perhaps combined with a touch of envy.

Noleen put the top back on her pen and gathered her papers. "You're so lucky to live in California. No weather like this. We'll take care of the paperwork right away. In a lot of ways, it's easier if you and Maude aren't here."

Cindy reached for her coat. "You might have to come back for the signing, but we can figure that out."

Sydney resisted the urge to kiss the two women, as the weight of the entire property seemed to slide off her shoulders. Now all she needed to do was figure out how to fulfill her promise to Randy and get Maude away from here, too, and develop a plan for her grandfather.

She followed Cindy and Noleen out onto the porch. A light dusting of snow covered the planks again. She was waving fare-

well to their car when a loud siren blasted across the village—
the signal from the Oriska Volunteer Fire Department.

Sydney stepped out onto the driveway to scan the hills and village, looking for smoke. She didn't have to look far. Across the
road, a large, open field tilted downward toward dense woods.
From the look of the smoke pouring into the gray sky, the fire
was on Dugway, the road on the opposite side of those woods.
She tried to recall what houses or barns were in that area.

The kitchen door banged open. Maude ran out, pulling on
her jacket and carrying the keys to Leslie's car. She jumped into
the car.

"Wait. Where are you going? You can't drive." Sydney
pounded on the driver's side door.

Maude cracked the window as she turned the key in the ignition. "That's Randy's place. I'm sure of it."

"I'll drive you. Hold on while I . . ." Sydney jumped back to
avoid having her toes crushed as Maude put the car in reverse
and hit the accelerator.

". . . get ready. Shit. Okay. Please don't crack up the car."

When the tires hit the roadbed, Maude slammed the car into
drive and headed down the hill toward the center of Oriska, going well over the speed limit.

"And don't get caught!" Sydney yelled.

She went back inside and started dressing for a short cross-
country ski trip over the field and through the woods to Randy's
house. There were several houses along that section of Dugway,
but in her gut she knew Maude was right—it had to be Randy's
double-wide trailer—his official residence when he wasn't living
here with her mother, or hanging out in his cabin, and probably
where his body was waiting to be found.

The chickens had come home to roost. The other shoe had
dropped. Shit was going to hit the fan. As she set her boots into
the ski bindings, her brain kicked out one trite saying after another. It was an earworm she couldn't shake, but they were all
true. All hell was about to break loose.

12

Fire Retardant

It was all downhill on skis to the fire scene—deceptively easy to arrive, hard to escape—once she committed.

Sydney balanced against her ski poles on the edge of the woods overlooking the organized chaos below. The space between her viewpoint and the road gave way to a steep slope filled in with treacherous snow covering hidden hazards. It looked deceptively easy to cross. Next, there was a six-foot barrier on either side of Dugway, consisting of packed ice and salt, formed by daily passes of the town sander and snowplow.

Parts of the ice wall were already breaking down thanks to water from the fire truck tankers, the heat of the fire itself, and the intrusion of the massive firefighting vehicles, which were not going to be intimidated by mere man-made heaps of snow. Portions were refreezing, other spots were melting, and everything was being dusted by a steady influx of snowflakes, swirling in packs like hyenas on the hunt.

Man, I hate winter. At least her perch on the hill gave her a chance to assess her options.

From her high vantage, it appeared Maude had parked up the road, well away from police vehicles. Good move, but probably a happy accident.

Not so happy was the sight of Maude fighting her way through the line of firefighters and law enforcement to gain access to

Randy's double-wide and the two EMT ambulances idling next to it. They did not seem happy to see her, as evidenced by a flock of uniformed personnel surrounding her at the end of Randy's driveway. Sydney felt a flicker of sympathy for their plight.

Sydney sidestepped down from the tree line. She removed her skis at the plow drift and stuck them upright into the snow before she slid down onto the roadbed on her backside. No one appeared to notice her, which was a blessing.

She made her way to Leslie's car, tossed the skis and poles into the back, and dusted off her gloves. Glancing inside the driver's side window, she saw the keys were still in the ignition. She opened the door and transferred them to her pocket. *One problem tackled.*

Sydney shut the door and leaned back against the car as she considered her options. The wind was pushing the smoke away from her, but the stench of melting man-made materials filled the air, and she had no desire to get any closer to the source.

Maude seemed to need help trying to reach Randy's house, but Sydney had to agree with the cops that this would not be a good option. Maude might be more tractable if she wore herself out a bit. Sydney decided to wait and figure out her new plan.

"Well, as I live and breathe. Sydney Lucerno." A deep, raspy voice made Sydney jump.

For a second, she could have sworn Sheriff Homer Carver had come back to life. His eyes glared at her, his voice rattled her bones. Her legs coiled, ready to bolt.

Her initial panic subsided. This man wore a Hartwell police uniform. His eyes were gray, not blue.

"You startled me, Officer Carver." Sydney's nerves continued to tingle. The resemblance was uncanny. In thirteen years, Michael Carver had metamorphosed into a scrawny version of his father. Although not exceptionally tall, he had long, rangy arms that dangled out of the official uniform, exposing raw wrist bones and reddened hands. Even though he was dressed in puffy winter clothing, she could see the man was lean to the point of being gaunt. *Eaten alive?*

"That's Chief Carver now, Sydney. I'm running the Hartwell police force. You remember Detective Payne?"

"Sure, sure." Sydney nodded toward Oliver Payne, who stood nearby. If Michael Carver had grown more gaunt, the weight seemed to have transferred to Ollie Payne. His uniform strained across the middle, and his neck had thickened. "Glad to see the *cream* rises to the top. Congratulations."

Payne's face turned red and Michael Carver stiffened. His eyes appeared to darken. "What ill wind brings you back to town?"

Sydney wiped her nose to hide her inner cringe. When would she learn to keep her mouth shut? She tried a new tone. "Sorry. My mother died very suddenly yesterday. No, I guess it was two days ago. The obituary will be in next week's *Hartwell Gazette*."

Payne caught Carver's gaze and raised an eyebrow. "Very suddenly?" Payne asked. A knowing smile spread across his plump lips.

Sydney felt her cheeks glow as she remembered what Patricia Atwood at Valley View Senior Living Center had said—these days *sudden death* were code words for drug overdoses. "Pneumonia. Complications from a bad case of the flu." She tried to bite her tongue. "I'm glad I had my flu shot. I was able to hold her hand when I said goodbye. I hope you guys got your flu shots. You come in touch with so many people. It was an awful way to die."

Both men shuffled their feet and took a step back. A loud, cracking sound pulled their attention toward the fire, where a section of the double-wide collapsed.

"What's the story here?" Sydney asked. "That's Randy's place, right?"

Carver pursed his lips and turned to face her. "Three bodies inside. The fire department guys pulled them out right away. Unofficially, one of them was Randy. The EMTs are ready to take them away."

Sydney clapped her hands to her mouth as genuine relief and grief bubbled to the surface. At last, she could mourn Randy.

"Oh, my God. I can't believe that. I just . . . I couldn't reach him from the hospital," she said, lying through her teeth with every syllable. "Was it smoke inhalation?"

Carver and Payne seemed to be watching her intently. Sydney hoped her face displayed shock. Carver snorted before he spoke. "Since you're not actual family, we can't say."

"But Maude is my family." Sydney pointed with her chin toward the tall figure screaming at the firefighters. "And she is his daughter. And my mother's."

Payne cleared his throat. "Your sister. That's official now?"

"Please don't tell me I was the only one who didn't know."

Carver waved his hand at Payne, who seemed to understand the signal. Payne strolled down the hill to the now-hysterical Maude and began guiding her back toward Sydney and the car.

"Yes, I guess most of us had known for a long time." Carver kicked at a block of ice that had tumbled down onto the road. "Where did you say you were living these days?"

"In denial, apparently."

"Isn't that a river in Egypt?" This time Carver's smile looked genuine. The smile faded. "It looks like smoke inhalation, but it's hard to say," he said as they watched the drama with Maude. "Something didn't seem right to me. The medical examiner will let us know."

Not right indeed.

"She's staying with me at our mother's house. If you have updates, you'll find her there." Sydney took a chance and a deep breath. "I have a new life in California. A clean life. A job. A career in high tech, actually. I'm going to get back to that as soon as possible. And take Maude with me."

"You'd be better cutting your losses with her," Carver said. "Take my word for it. You do know her license has been suspended, right?"

As Maude reached the car, she broke free of Detective Payne and threw herself into Sydney's arms, sobbing.

Sydney rocked her sister. "Okay, okay. Let's go home now." She guided the limp and unresisting Maude to the passenger seat.

As she started to open the driver's side door, Carver held out a hand to stop her. "Tell me, Ms. Lucerno, is Caleb Elway waiting for you back in California?"

This time Sydney's shock was completely genuine. "What? Caleb?" She recalled what Maude had told her the night before about Caleb.

"Caleb. Your boyfriend? He killed my father. He ran off with you. We know that."

Sydney stood with one foot inside the car. The stench of fire and death filled the air and made her want to puke.

"Sorry. You caught me by surprise. It's been a long time since I've thought about him. Caleb is . . ." She stopped and forced what she hoped was a cooperative and courteous smile. "I haven't seen Caleb since I went into that rehab program. He left before I got out, not with me."

Sydney settled her bottom into the driver's seat as if she were sitting on eggshells and closed the car door. She reached across Maude and pulled the safety belt to strap her sister in place and then fastened her own. She turned the key in the ignition and forced herself to put the car in gear.

Caleb. The sound of his name brought back the anguish Sydney thought she had buried. She felt like she'd been suckerpunched in the gut—twice—first by Maude outside Steve's office and now by Chief Carver. She hadn't lied. Caleb was long gone. He was dead. He had been dead for over thirteen years.

13

Obituary

As soon as Sydney put the car in gear, Maude stopped sobbing. Threading her way through the various emergency, fire, and police vehicles, Sydney risked a glance at her sister. Was Maude still breathing?

Maude leaned forward against the seatbelt, her swollen eyes tracking the ambulance, presumably where Randy's body awaited transport to the coroner. Her lips shuddered with each breath.

Sydney wasn't sure how to take her sister's extreme grief. As best she could tell, Maude had been blasé about their mother's death. Maybe a bit resentful, but not visibly upset. Of course, she had been raised as Randy's sister. Perhaps that attachment made the bonds stronger. It didn't seem to be a good time to ask.

At home, Maude stumbled through the mudroom and slumped onto the family room couch. Sydney trailed behind her, first removing her outer clothing in the mudroom.

The stench of unhealthy smoke on their clothes and hair followed them into the house. Sydney pulled off Maude's boots and forced her sister's limp limbs out of her jacket. She tossed all outer layers into the mudroom and closed the door with a firm click before she sat on the couch and pulled Maude down so that her head rested on Sydney's lap.

She stroked Maude's face and gave her hair a finger combing.

After a few minutes, she could feel Maude's body start to loosen and melt into her lap.

"Don't stop," Maude said, her voice barely a whisper. "It's been so long since anyone touched me like that."

Sydney bent and kissed her sister's forehead. "Would you like to come live in California? Let's get out of here. I'll take you."

Maude rolled her face into Sydney's belly. "Could we go to-day?"

Sydney tilted her chin up to rest her head on the back of the couch. "Why not?"

As simple as that, it was an option, an alternate reality. By this time tomorrow, some portion of her soul would be in Ohio in their mother's car, headed west.

Maude sat up and blew her nose in long honks on the sleeve of her flannel shirt. "I don't suppose that's very practical."

Sydney rested her hand on Maude's back and rubbed. "No, it's not. But it doesn't have to be long. About a week? We need to hold a memorial service and make sure everything is moving along with this house."

"A 'Service of Remembrance' is what they're called these days," Maude said with a half sob. "Now two of them. Both of my parents. Two estates to take care of. And what about Grandpa?"

Rats. Dual complications. Maybe triple.

"We should call Steve. He might know if Randy had a will," Sydney said.

"I suppose I'll be the proud owner of his double-wide." Maude wiped her face.

"Not much left of it, I'd say. The good news is . . ." Sydney stopped herself. She wanted to say, *The good news is the land will probably be worth more without that eyesore.*

She restarted. "The good news is that there's also the cabin. I'll bet that's worth something. If Randy did have a will, he probably left everything to you and Mom. Since she is dead, you might have full control."

"What if he didn't have a will?" Maude's eyebrows met in a frown.

"Uh. That's why we need to talk to Steve." Sydney hoped Maude wouldn't have to split anything with Lilith and Zile.

To her relief, Maude looked over her shoulder and laughed. "This place will never let us go. It's like quicksand, even in winter."

Sydney slapped Maude on the back and stood up. "Time for lunch. I think we have tuna, mayonnaise, and crackers. Then we can make some lists. I'll go to Brochu's for basic provisions and stuff for dinner. We'll figure it out."

As they consumed their makeshift lunch, Sydney put down several pieces of paper on the dining room table.

"I printed these out. I need to submit the obituary today for the *Hartwell Gazette* if we want to have a memorial at Martinson Funeral Home next week. Martinson's will place one for us for free. Did you know you have to pay for obits these days? Who knew?"

Maude lifted the top sheet and read as she struggled to swallow her plain cracker.

Leslie Helen Graham, 53, died from the complications of flu and pneumonia on January 22.

Leslie was born in Syracuse to Sydney (Brucker) and David Graham. She grew up in Oriska and graduated from Hartwell Central School. An avid linguist, she attended Brown University, graduating with her BA in French and Romance Languages, and from Middlebury with her master's in French.

Leslie married Rafael Lucerno and lived in Marblehead, Massachusetts, where she taught French, before she moved to Oriska after her divorce. She taught French at the Hartwell Central School and left to start her antiques business several years later.

Leslie is survived by her father, David Graham, her daughters Sydney Lucerno and Maude Jaquith, and her longtime companion, Randy Jaquith.

A service of remembrance will be held at Martinson Funeral Home on Saturday, February 1, at 1 p.m. Donations may be made to the Oriska Free Library.

Maude set the paper down and looked up at Sydney. "Her longtime companion?"

Sydney pulled the paper back and wiped her tears away. "I guess I should remove it even though Randy's death isn't completely official. I need to send it in."

She scribbled down the notes. "Okay. We get a B plus for a good effort."

"Does your father know she died?" Maude asked.

"Oh yes. I called him. He wanted to know if she left him anything in her will."

"Seriously?"

"Totally." Sydney rested her forehead on the table for a brief break.

"My grandfather says he's some sort of Mexican."

Sydney rolled her head to face Maude. "Not that it should matter, but he's from *Argentina*." She pronounced it the Spanish way.

Maude kept quiet for a while. "Are you part Native, like me?"

Sydney sat up and rested her chin on one hand. "No, his grandparents came from Italy on his father's side and were German Jews on his mother's side."

"You're Jewish?"

"Your grandfather Zile's favorite people to hate, followed by Latinos, as I recall. Old Sheriff Carver's, too. I guess some would say I'm part Jewish, but my father was raised Catholic, and I was raised nothing. It's kind of a moot point."

"We're matrilineal when it comes to membership. I told you, right? That was always important for my grandmother. A point of pride. I was born a disappointment."

Sydney tapped her pencil on her mother's obituary. Most of what she knew about the Iroquois or *Haudenosaunee* she learned in fifth grade mixed with a few misremembered tidbits from Randy. She could only speak to what she knew.

"Traditional Jews are matrilineal, too."

Maude stared at Sydney. "I guess we're both outsiders."

Sydney studied the end of her pencil. She never paid much attention to her ancestral roots. Her self-centered father was estranged from his family. She barely knew her father's parents living in Argentina. She had studied French and spoke only a few words of Spanish.

"I never paid much attention to religion," she said.

Maude lowered her eyebrows, turning her stare into a glower. "It's not about religion, Sydney. It's about culture and values and lots of other things. At least it is for me. I can't speak for you."

Sydney felt her cheeks glow. *Try again.* "I am sure you were not a disappointment to Randy or our mother. For what it's worth, I know Lilith loves you. And you are a true sister to me."

Maude's face was folded in on itself for a few minutes.

"Does your father think you are a disappointment?" she asked.

"My father is thrilled that I am not asking him for money anymore." Sydney reached over and stroked Maude's hand.

Maude pulled her hands back into her lap. "Does he love you?"

Sydney snorted. "He's the kind of guy who claims that saying 'I love you' all the time cheapens the emotion, and it should be obvious from actions."

Maude picked up her final cracker. "When was the last time he told you he loved you?"

"Right before he asked me if my mother had left him anything. Before that, maybe four or five years ago."

"Asshole."

"Of course. Good thing I don't count on him either way. Now, I've got to send this in and then I'll go to Brochu's. Any requests?"

"Are you kidding? Anything edible and not expired will be a gift."

14

The Kitty Litter Aisle

Brochu's lay within her line of sight from her mother's porch, down the slight incline, squatting in the middle of Oriska. It seemed silly to take the car for a couple hundred yards. The weather was milder and Sydney yearned to be outside, away from the smells of winter indoors and car interiors. She would walk. How hard could that be?

Maude was adamant that Sydney drive to the Save Lots super-market in Hartwell for shopping. Maude had a point, of course. Save Lots at least passed for a reasonable imitation of a suburban supermarket, complete with fruits and vegetables not locally in season, cuts of meat in convenient packages, and salsa in glass jars.

However, something about her sister's tone made Sydney suspicious. She slipped both sets of keys to her mother's car into her jacket pocket before she set out on foot. One unexpected road trip a day was enough.

Brochu's survival into the twenty-first century was a mystery. There was no math Sydney could figure that would sustain a tiny general store in the middle of nowhere. Brochu's did boost its inventory during the warm months, but this place lay outside the main traffic of the Finger Lakes, and most of the so-called summer people were locals who went to Florida or Arizona for the winter.

As she stumped her way along the slushy road, she passed the vacant and derelict filling station, followed by the post office, now operating on reduced hours. Thanks to the morning's event, she knew the volunteer fire department on the far side of town was still operational, and the library opened every day, also thanks to volunteers, but the blinking yellow light in front of Brochu's at the main intersection of three roads seemed to be missing a beat.

Between these musings on her walk, thoughts about Sydney's father rose, unbidden, thanks to Maude.

It was true her father was not the demonstrative type. Still, he had taken her in when she hit rock bottom and headed to California. He let her stay at his place in Santa Barbara and researched rehab places for her. Residential facilities, naturally. He hounded her to get her GED. He told her to get over blaming her parents.

He deserved her gratitude for all that. Why the jerk expected some sort of gratuity from her mother was another mystery.

Basking in sudden warmth, Sydney could see that Brochu's had not gone through any restructuring since her last visit. It wasn't organized into neat rows and columns like a supermarket. It had grown organically from a number of small buildings, loosely linked together by the narrow wooden plank floors, and was still haphazardly crisscrossed by shelving of varying vintages.

Along with the single checkout counter, the front section held frozen food freezers, beer, fizzy drinks, potato chips, ice cream, school supplies, and basic drugstore items. Toward the back lay aisles of canned goods and cooking supplies, framed by the meat counter on the near side and fresh vegetables and dairy at the far end. Hardware, guns, and fishing gear lay to the right connected by a DVD section over the bridge to the rushing river underneath the building. Dry goods like clothing, boots, and sewing supplies were upstairs.

Sydney knew staffing was kept to a minimum in the winter when customers were scarce. At the moment, there wasn't another human being in sight. It felt like she had the place all to herself, although she knew Rob Brochu would be hovering around, probably in hardware.

Sydney paused between the ATM machine and the meat counter to plan her route up and down the aisles. She located most of her items quickly and set out on a search for toilet paper, which was not to be found in its previous location.

After several minutes, she found the toilet paper at the narrow end of a dead-end aisle with stacks of kitty litter on one side and dog food on the other. She snagged two six-packs of the only brand left on the shelves, tucking them under her arm.

She turned to head back to her cart and found the way blocked by a large obstacle—a man. She started forward, planning to squeeze by, but upon closer examination, took a step back instead. The man's expression reminded her of an encounter with a rabid raccoon several summers before, but that had been from the safety of her car.

Zile Jaquith.

Even hunched over, he filled the aisle. His left arm was braced against the cat food shelf, perhaps to block her way or perhaps to prop himself up. The smell of sweat and liquor wafted around the narrow space. His matched set of canvas coveralls and jacket was filthy. Spittle, nicotine stains, and other ambiguous fluids flecked his scraggly beard and long hair. His eyes were black holes in deep sockets—fixed on her.

"I thought it might be you this morning, down by Randy's place," he said.

Somewhere in the back of her mind, she registered that Zile wasn't accusing her of having anything to do with Randy's death. *A blessing?*

Sydney stopped holding her breath. "I didn't see you."

"No, of course not, you stupid cow."

"Mr. Jaquith, I saw the fire. I am so sorry about Randy."

Jaquith swayed and leaned in closer. "I hear your mother died. Losing a parent is nothing like losing a child." He belched, spewing a fresh miasma of alcohol and some nastier fermentation.

Sydney blinked as the image of Randy's silver pendant flashed. She clutched the toilet paper packages tightly to her chest.

"Hey, Zile. Let a girl pass." A gloved hand appeared on Zile's right shoulder, turning him so that his back now rested against the shelves stacked with kitty litter.

Sydney stared at the tall African American woman with long dreadlocks who had taken Zile's place in the center of the aisle—Caleb's sister and her best high school friend, Cassandra Elway.

"Go figure," Cassandra said, staring straight at a spot in the middle of Zile's forehead. "I live on a farm, but my cat, Yarrow, won't eat anything except this canned stuff." Sydney noticed Cassandra made no move to pick out any cans.

Sydney wondered if Cassandra had grown since they were BFFs. At about six feet tall in her boots, she was still a good bit shorter than Zile, but she was several decades younger. And she was sober.

That was when Sydney noticed Cassandra carried a tire iron in her left hand. Zile appeared to see it as well, his eyes flickering toward the implement, and he took a small step back.

"Stay out of this, Cassandra. I've got an old bone to pick with Sydney. She stole from me."

"The statute of limitations has expired, Zile. Plus, you know you were repaid by Sydney's grandfather. Give it up. You should go home to Lilith. She's grieving alone."

Zile straightened to his full height, burped, and stumbled toward the front of the store.

Cassandra watched Zile until he disappeared around the meat counter. At that point, she leaned the tire iron gently against a bag of dog chow and turned to face Sydney, who slumped back against the cat food shelf to give her legs a rest.

"I wondered when you were going to call me," Cassandra said, her face still creased with worry lines. "This isn't the Garden of Eden like California. You can't afford to walk around without noticing your surroundings."

Sydney gulped. "I get your point."

"I'm on my guard all the time. You've grown soft and lazy, Sydney. It's a good thing I dropped in to get driveway salt. I saw Zile following you around the store and picked up this little item in case he needed some persuasion." She gestured to the tire iron.

Sydney stared at her old friend, absorbing everything that was both familiar and different. She had never thought that Cassandra and Caleb looked alike, but now the resemblance was striking. Cassandra had always been much darker than her brother, Caleb. She had been a bit on the shy side and wore her hair straightened in those days. She had filled out in a good way. The dreads suited her. Her erect posture radiated a no-nonsense-tolerated aura Sydney wanted for herself. No wonder Zile had backed down.

Sydney's jaw muscles relaxed. It was easier to speak now. "Believe me, calling you has been on my list, but life's been a whirlwind. It's hard to believe Mom only died two days ago."

Cassandra stepped in close and pulled Sydney into a bear hug. "Don't mind me. I missed you so much. So, what's all the stuff Zile was spouting about Randy?"

"Apparently Randy died." Sydney tried to ignore her twinge of conscience. "I guess they're still notifying next of kin, so it's not official yet, but his body was found with a couple of others at his place down the hill." Sydney tilted her head in the general direction of Randy's property.

"Is that where the fire was?" Cassandra's eyes went wide. "Damn. Will the police come tell you? You're not officially kin, but close enough."

Sydney picked up her toilet paper packages from the floor, where she had dropped them. "They should stop by to tell Maude. She's staying with me."

"That's really generous of you, kiddo, but are you sure that's smart? I teach high school math these days, remember? I know Maude quite well. She's a problem child. Let her parents deal with her."

"That's the problem. She's my sister. Don't tell me you didn't know that, either."

"How the hell . . ." Cassandra's mouth was hanging open. Sydney could see her old friend's brain working on the fundamentals. "Oh, I get it. You know, now that I'm a teacher, I'm amazed that your mother wasn't arrested for screwing around with Randy when he was a student."

"They couldn't help themselves. Hormones." Sydney scanned the surrounding aisles for signs of other customers. After close to twenty years the scandal was still a sore point. She didn't like talking about it in public. She walked toward her cart.

"These days, things would be different. Your mother was lucky Randy was over eighteen. Lucky this place is such a backwater."

"Yeah, well, her luck just ran out."

Cassandra snorted. "Ain't it the truth. You know my dad died about two years ago, right? Heart attack. Boom!" She slapped her hands together.

"I saw your post on Facebook. Did you see my message? He was always special. I owed him." Sydney tossed her toilet paper into the shopping cart.

"Okay, so now you can owe me instead. I inherited all his assets and all his debts."

Sydney grinned despite her lousy mood. Cassandra had always been her leavening agent, even as a kid. "It's a deal. How do I pay up?"

"Come to dinner tomorrow. I'm living at my parents' old place. You remember the way, right?"

"Not likely I'd forget. Okay to bring Maude?"

"If you insist. It'll be a small group. People you won't know. Except Steve."

"Steve Lee? Since when are you buddies with Steve?"

"Since a while." Cassandra's eyebrows arched as her mouth curved up at the corners. She winked.

Sydney required a few moments to process this development. "Whoa, girl. What about your mom?"

"She moved to New Mexico. Loves it there."

"That isn't exactly what I meant."

"I know what you meant. She thinks I'm a big girl and can make up my own mind. Listen, I've got to go. We'll catch up at dinner." Cassandra picked up her bag of salt and headed for the checkout counter.

"Hey. Didn't you forget something? The cat food for Yarrow?"

Cassandra turned around and grinned. "You must be kidding. Yarrow wouldn't touch that crap. See you tomorrow."

* * *

By the time Sydney picked up a few more items and made it to the checkout counter, Cassandra was nowhere in sight, but Rob Brochu had materialized and waited for her at the cash register.

The intervening years had been kind to Rob, the latest in a long line of Brochus to run the store. He looked middle-aged by the time he was twenty—tall but a bit stooped over with thick glasses and a penchant for bow ties. Now at fifty-ish, the look suited him. He had lost hair and the glasses were clearly bifocals, but unlike so many of his peers, his skin was clear, and his teeth were white when he bared them to offer her a nod of recognition.

"Good to see you, Rob." Sydney had stolen lots of little stuff from his store and hoped he didn't carry any grudges.

"Sorry to hear about your mother, Sydney. And now I guess Randy is gone, too." Rob rested his hands on the counter and loomed over her to check her basket. "Are you going to pay for all that?"

"I most definitely will." Sydney waved a credit card to prove her status as an upstanding citizen. "Listen. I'd like to settle up. All the stuff I took from you."

Rob's eyes softened a bit behind his bifocals. "Your grandfather took care of all that and then some years ago."

"Thanks," Sydney whispered.

"I'm not the one to thank."

"I hope you'll come to Mom's viewing on Sunday. Her memorial service is next Saturday at Martinson's. And if you could mention it to other people, that would be great." She started removing items from the basket and placing them on the wooden counter. No fancy rolling belts at Brochu's.

"Sunday afternoon? I'll try to make it. Hunh. Tire iron. Kind of unusual purchase at this time of year."

"You're almost out of toilet paper back there, Rob."

"So why are you taking two packs? You could leave some for your neighbors. You know managing inventory is harder for us over the winter months."

Sydney felt her cheeks grow warm. "Yeah, okay. I'll put one back."

Rob grunted and shoved one of the packs under the counter. "Nah, I'll take care of it. You want some help to the car?"

"Nope, I'm walking. I figure the exercise will do me good."

"It might. Then again, it's a strange world these days."

Sydney buttoned up her coat, pulled on her gloves, and picked up the tire iron in her right hand and her shopping bags with the rest of her purchases with the left.

She made it a couple hundred yards from the store when she heard a vehicle coming up fast behind her, its tires sending up an audible splash of slush from the road.

She cursed under her breath. Of course, she should have walked facing traffic, particularly at this time of year. The plows never cleared enough of the shoulder and the drifts narrowed the road to barely two lanes, plus she now saw that another truck was headed toward her from the opposite direction.

She glanced over her shoulder. Based on their current trajectories, she was certain that the two trucks would meet right where she stood with no room to spare. There would definitely be no room for a pedestrian.

Sydney turned to face the truck coming toward her. Was that Zile behind the wheel? With moments to spare she dropped her bags and threw herself headfirst up onto the nearest snowdrift.

She heard the truck hit at least one bag as she rolled onto her knees. "Motherfucker!" The snow covering her face and the cold wind muffled her scream, but the tire iron she flung at the receding truck shattered the back window of the vehicle and bounced back onto the road.

Sydney fell onto her side, the fury in her blood filling her body. She held her breath as the truck swerved, narrowly missed the back end of the vehicle coming from the opposite direction, careened off the opposite snowdrift, bounced back into the road, and zoomed away.

15

Almost Family

Sydney rolled off the snowbank onto the road, still screaming. Her legs folded as she hit the gritty surface of salt and sand that covered the tarmac, and she was forced to claw herself upright before she could start to run after the truck.

A short sprint convinced her that she was chasing a lost cause. The truck was rounding the corner at Brochu's, too far away to see any useful details like a license plate.

Sydney turned her attention to the second truck, an equally oversized vehicle that took up close to half the narrowed road. The driver slowed to a crawl as he passed her going the opposite direction. She could make out a faint, ghosted outline of the driver wearing what looked like a gimme cap through the heavily tinted windows. She waved and started to trot closer, but the truck leaped forward, sending slush into the air, and took off up the hill.

"Hey! What the *fuck!*" She knew the driver was already out of hearing range, but the fear in her chest needed to escape. Squinting after the receding bumper, she realized that the truck's license plate was not merely unreadable—it was missing.

Knowing Zile, he might not have intended to kill her, but he might not have cared if he had. If he'd realized she was present when Randy died, he might have tried harder.

And I'm even kind of a member of the family.

The laws of physics meant that Zile could not be driving both trucks. Distance and time had given Sydney the insight that Zile had never been a good crime boss. He was more like a wholesaler for a range of activities that happened to catch his attention—some legit, some not. He didn't have a gang so much as a loose list of subcontractors, keeping only a few trusted individuals—usually relatives—on full-time duty. She had no idea who the current cast of characters might be, but she was willing to lay money on the chances that one of them was driving the second truck.

Sydney sank down and rested against the snowbank, ignoring the chill against her backside. She turned her attention in the direction of the first truck. What if the first driver—Zile?—turned around and came back for another attack?

Keeping her eyes on the road in both directions, she brushed off the slush and picked up the debris scattered on the road with hands still shaking from residual fear and anger. The groceries were largely unscathed, although the chicken breasts had popped out of their plastic shrink wrap, spreading chicken juice over everything else, and the toilet paper had been squashed. The tire iron lay in the salty slush.

Sydney eyed the road back to Brochu's. If she walked to return her purchases, she wasn't certain that Rob would honor any kind of trade-in, plus she would be exposed to a return attack both coming and going. She should scurry home before she again risked being flattened like the toilet paper.

What then? Call the police? The thought lasted for a second and evaporated like a snowflake on a hot summer's day.

Maude must have been watching for her. She yanked open the door to the mudroom as soon as Sydney entered.

"Where have you been?" Maude said, her voice high-pitched. The unmistakable stench of liquor and cigarettes wafted around her.

Sydney set her bags down and stared. "You smell like a still. And there's no smoking inside the house."

Maude swayed on her feet. "Says you. I needed something, and I couldn't find any of Mom's stash."

"You needed something," Sydney echoed, stripping off her jacket and boots.

"My father who never wanted me and my mother who never acknowledged me are dead. I needed something."

Sydney carried her bags into the kitchen and set about unloading and scrubbing the contents while she counted her breathing.

"Just to be clear, I removed everything I could find of her *stash*. And you know that none of that solves anything."

"Oh, thank you, Miss-I've-been-to-rehab."

"Have you ever been to any kind of rehab, Maude? Counseling?" Sydney chopped the smashed chicken breasts into bite-sized pieces for a stir-fry and dumped them into a bowl.

"Hell no."

Sydney tapped the knife on the counter. "I don't suppose you have health insurance."

"What does that have to do with anything?"

"If you did, treatment might be covered under your policy."

"I don't need treatment." Maude started to leave but stumbled, caught herself, and settled into a chair. "My college policy ended this month. They cut me off because I dropped out in November."

"Why'd you drop out?"

"I was bored. It was a long commute. I had better things to do. What's it to you?"

Sydney made a V sign with her fingers. "Peace. I'm just trying to help. What was your major?"

"Something useless. Give it a rest, Sydney."

Sydney resumed chopping. How much did she owe this erstwhile sister, anyway? What would her mother expect?

Would Maude qualify for some kind of COBRA? Did that apply to college policies? Probably not. Thanks to her upcoming inheritances, Maude probably would not be able to get Medicaid until rehab had eaten through most of the money. Another headache.

Sydney decided to ask Steve for an insurance agent who

would know the ins and outs of health care coverage in New York State. A deep, unbidden chuckle escaped her lips. She had to hand it to Maude—the girl could pivot the world around to focus on her. Mere minutes ago, Sydney was steaming mad and terrified after her near miss on the road. Now that seemed like ancient history, superseded by new, more daunting problems.

"What are you laughing about?" Maude stood and swayed on her feet, pouting. "Are you making fun of me?"

"No, I wouldn't dream of it. What color truck does your grandfather drive?" Sydney asked.

"Which one? He owns about four, I think."

"Blue? Maybe dark green?" Sydney realized that with all the road slush, both trucks had been more gray than a specific color.

"You're kidding, right? They're all blue or green."

"Does your cousin Dwayne still work with him?"

"Nah, Dwayne got sent up for a good long stretch. Domestic abuse, if you can believe that."

"Imagine." Sydney threw up her hands in mock horror.

"These days it's usually my cousin Gonzo. Not very bright but extremely loyal. And there's Austin, one of my grandmother's great nephews or a cousin or something."

Sydney paused to gaze out the back window at the field that led down to the woods surrounding Hangnail Pond. "What about the color of Randy's truck?"

"His are always red. His favorite color."

"Good," Sydney whispered to the field. "That's good at least." Both trucks had been so covered in winter road slush she wasn't sure what their underlying pristine colors would be, but she was positive neither one was red. At least Randy's ghost wasn't chasing her down.

16

Official Notification

Although twilight was still a couple of hours away, a deep gray gloom settled around the house. Sydney was turning on lights in the family room when she noticed the motion-sensitive spotlight over the barn door pop on.

Maude rushed to look over Sydney's shoulder. "Cars. Damn. It's the cops." She ran her fingers through her hair. "Do you think they're going to arrest me? Or maybe it's you."

Sydney studied the two vehicles—one a Hartwell Police Department SUV and the other an Oriska County Sheriff's Department truck. Chief Carver climbed out of the driver's side of the Hartwell Police Department vehicle as Officer Payne exited from the passenger side. They both waited for the man from the Sheriff's Department. "Settle down and prepare yourself. I'm sure they're here to tell you officially that Randy is dead."

"I've already prepared myself, but it isn't helping." Maude sighed out a puff of alcoholic fumes.

Sydney was tempted to tell her sister to try to make a good impression but realized it was probably too late for that. Besides, she needed to watch her own behavior when it came to the Hartwell PD. "Sit down and let me bring them in."

She moved to the door onto the porch and flipped on the outside light. As the three officers loomed into view through the upper glass of the door, she fought the instinct to step back.

Instead, she pulled the wooden door open and pushed open the glass storm door toward the men on the far side.

"Ms. Graham," Chief Carver said as he stepped in. Sydney decided not to correct him on her name and offered to take his jacket and hat. He waved her off. "We won't be long."

Oliver Payne merely grunted and fixed her with what she took to be his best no-nonsense stare. *Once an asshole, always an asshole.* Sydney tried to give him her best I'm-an-adult-now smile.

The Oriska County Sheriff was nothing like his predecessor, Homer Carver—Chief Carver's father. This man was no taller than Sydney, which put him on the short side for a man, with a full head of snowy-white hair and eyes the color of ice.

"Sheriff Curtis Sowles," he said as he shook Maude's hand, and did the same with Sydney. If he had an agenda, Sydney couldn't read it.

The sheriff stepped around the overabundance of knick-knacks and made his way to a club chair in the sitting room area. Officer Payne followed but seemed content to stand. Chief Carver stood by the entrance to the mudroom, watching the proceedings.

Sydney took her seat on the couch next to Maude, who by then was slumped against the cushions, clipping off the dead ends of her long hair with a small pair of scissors. She looked up at the sheriff.

"Maude, I think you know why we're here," Sheriff Sowles said. "I'm sorry that we have to confirm that your father, Randy Jaquith, was found dead in his house this morning."

Staring at Maude's profile as he spoke, Sydney shifted her focus to Chief Carver's face about eight feet beyond. His face was softened with fake sympathy as far as Sydney was concerned because his gray eyes seemed to glitter with self-satisfaction. He was probably thrilled to have one less Jaquith in the world; plus she was sure he was about to drop a big surprise about Randy's death onto her unsuspecting little sister and twist the knife. She reached over and grabbed Maude's left hand, yanking it free of her hair-grooming exercise.

"How did he die, Sheriff?" she asked. "Was it smoke inhalation or the fire? What about the other two men?"

She saw Carver's eyes narrow and his jaw muscles clamp shut. He recomposed his face before he leaned forward again. Payne shuffled his feet and coughed. *Hurray for small victories.* She had stolen a bit of wind out of Carver's sails. Maude should know that something more was coming.

Sheriff Sowles cleared his throat and started again. "Ms. Jaquith, I am sorry to say that the deaths look suspicious. We will have to wait on the autopsies, but it appears that all three men were shot. In fact, they may have been moved to your father's place postmortem."

Maude sat up straight, suddenly animated. "What? Does that mean they died someplace else?"

Sydney did her best to imitate Maude's body language. "Are you sure?" she asked.

Sheriff Sowles tucked his chin, never taking his eyes off the sisters. "Until we get further information from the medical examiner, I can't say more. Do you know who the other two men are? They did not have any ID on them, and the only vehicles on the scene were a red Ford truck registered to Randy and a pickup registered to you, Ms. Jaquith."

As he was speaking, Officer Payne leaned into the group and dropped three color photos on the coffee table. Maude yanked her left hand free from Sydney to pick up the pictures.

Maude stared at Randy's picture and passed it to Sydney, who took one look and bit her lip. Randy's photo caught him from his left side, his eyes slightly open with a dribble running from his mouth. The fire or smoke had left blackened smudges over his face, and it appeared his hair had burned.

"What the hell is this?" Sydney crumpled the photograph and threw it back at Payne, hitting him in the chest. "My sister has suddenly lost her father. Is this really how you break the news?"

She directed the second part of her tirade at Sheriff Sowles, who stiffened and blushed. His raised eyebrows and pressed lips indicated he might have felt blindsided by his police department colleagues.

Sydney leaned over Maude's shoulder to look at the other two photos. The two Canadians—not that she was going to say anything. She tried to snatch those pictures away as well, but Maude pulled them out of reach.

Maude looked up at Chief Carver, her voice a low growl. "These are the assholes that killed my father?"

"We don't know that for a fact yet."

Payne leaned forward and reached for the pictures, which Maude whisked out of range in the other direction.

"They killed him. I know it." Maude placed the photographs flat on the coffee table with her left hand and stabbed with the scissors clutched in her right fist, driving the sharp point through over and over as she let out a long, low moan.

Sydney flattened herself against the couch while Carver and Payne jumped forward to wrestle away the shredded photos. As soon as the police officers had secured their precious pictures, Sydney grabbed Maude and pulled her back across her lap.

"I don't know who those men are," Sydney said. Struggling with Maude made it easy to hide her own guilty conscience. She glanced at the sheriff, who looked eager to leave.

"I'll kill them." Maude thrashed in Sydney's embrace as Sydney patted Maude's back.

"Not an option," Chief Carver said, wiping his mouth. "Do you recognize them, Ms. Jaquith?"

"No," Maude said, burying her face in Sydney's shoulder.

"And when was the last time you spoke to or saw your father?"

Despite the confusion, Sydney was aware he was watching her responses, too. She kept her focus on Maude and away from the two police officers.

"I dunno." Maude turned to face them. Her words were slurred. "Maybe two weeks ago I saw him at my grandparents' place. We didn't talk regularly or anything."

"What about you, Ms. Graham?" Carver directed this question at Sydney.

"Her name's *Lucerno*," Maude said, leaning against her sister.

"Ah. Yes, that's right." Carver tilted his head forward.

"Of course it is and you know it." Maude ripped herself free and slumped back against the couch cushions as a wave of love and devotion devoured Sydney for several seconds.

"That's all right, Chief," she said. "I haven't seen Randy for over thirteen years. If you check his cell phone records, I'm sure you'll see that I had been trying to get in touch with him since Monday, when I found out my mother was on death's door." She raised her shoulders and grimaced. "But sadly, we never connected."

"We already checked," Oliver Payne said, stepping closer into the sitting room so that he could face her. "Lots and lots of phone calls until forty-eight hours ago. Then nothing. Why is that?"

Stunned, Sydney stared at him for several long seconds. She hadn't thought of that. *Shit.* She should have kept calling.

"I . . . Well, after my mother died I tried a few more times and then gave up. It was too late for him to get to the hospital. And to be frank, I was pissed as hell."

"Pissed enough to shoot him?" Payne asked.

This time Sydney gave a genuine laugh. "You must be kidding. Would I go out of my way to shoot a man I'd put up with for nearly twenty years, simply because my mother died of pneumonia? And dispatch two other men besides?"

"I've seen stranger stuff," Payne answered in a half grunt.

Sydney stared at him until he blinked and turned to study the gas fireplace. *Jerk.*

Sheriff Sowles pressed his hands on his thighs and stood. "That's it for now. I am very sorry for your loss, Ms. Jaquith. We may be back once we know more from the autopsy."

Maude bent over and sobbed. "What about his body? When can we get that? How do I arrange for a service?"

Carver made his way to the door, followed closely by Officer Payne. Both seemed eager to leave.

Sheriff Sowles spoke as he edged his way out. "Because the death is suspicious, it might take some time before we can release the body. I suggest that you work with your grandparents on a mutually agreeable plan with a funeral home for a service. The funeral home will know how to make the arrangements."

The two sisters trailed the officers out onto the kitchen porch and watched as the three men climbed into their squad cars and pulled away.

Maude draped an arm across Sydney's shoulders, still holding the scissors like a dagger. "Did I do good?"

17

The Coven

Sydney pried the sharp scissors from her sister's hand. "I guess it depends on the desired effect. You sure scared the shit out of *me*. But that won't keep them from coming back."

"Yeah, well, they'll think twice about it first."

"A quick word of advice. Making people who carry guns nervous does not give you a tactical advantage. Not to mention you also damaged the coffee table. According to Mom, that was worth a lot of money."

Maude sputtered her lips. "I don't buy it. There must be three more exactly like it in the barn." She skidded her stockinged feet over the slippery surface of the porch and headed indoors.

"You need to call Steve. If he's not in the office, leave a long message."

"Stop nagging me." Maude shut the door before Sydney could slip through.

Sydney wrestled with the knob for several frigid seconds before the door popped inward. "If I thought it would help, I'd stop in an instant."

Her sister continued to grumble, but after pacing the entry area several times, Maude stalked off to the dining room "for some privacy" and picked up the landline phone.

As Sydney chopped vegetables and prepped a chicken stir-fry, she reviewed her long list of action items that would lead up to her planned escape, with or without Maude.

Maude's voice rumbled from the dining room, pausing for breaks and an occasional sob. That was much too long for voice mail. Steve must have been in his office.

Sydney couldn't make out the words, but Maude's tone told her that the news was not happy. She paused to set down the knife and take deep breaths. She wasn't sure she had energy left to deal with an unhappy Maude. Or even a happy one.

When Maude reappeared, she came to the opposite side of the kitchen island and eased onto one of the wobbly stools. Sydney stole a glance at her sister's face. She seemed calm and deep in thought, but that didn't mean a storm wasn't about to break.

Sydney pushed a mug of hot tea across the island and took a sip of her own. "And?"

"He split things between me and my grandparents," Maude answered. "There's not much money, but at least almost everything is in a trust. I'll get about ten thousand. If Mom were still alive, she'd be the executor, but since she's gone, it will be my grandmother. Steve thinks I'll have to split expenses for the funeral and stuff. That's the way she operates. There won't be much left after that, I figure."

"Who gets his house?"

"They do."

Sydney stifled a sigh of relief by clearing her throat. A quick visit to the funeral home for Randy, followed by a quiet memorial service, and Maude would be in the clear.

"But I get the cabin."

The knife dropped from Sydney's hands and landed with a clatter on the slate floor. By the time she picked it up and straightened, her face was composed.

"Maybe your grandparents would buy it off you. Cheap. Real cheap."

"I kind of doubt that. My grandmother hates it. She says you could get a contact high by sitting on the porch."

For once Lilith and Sydney agreed on something. "Even if you let the whole building collapse, you'll have to pay property taxes and God knows what else," Sydney said. "And that will be hard to take care of from California. It has lakefront. It's probably worth more than this house. Sell it."

Maude's eyes were wet. "Maybe I could rent it."

"Ugh. No heat aside from the woodstove, no insulation, no shower, barely running water, mosquitos, and ticks galore. And don't forget the black flies in spring."

Maude studied her mug of tea. Her voice was trembling. "I don't want to talk about it right now."

"Sure. Fair enough." Sydney walked to the opposite side of the island and rubbed her sister's upper back, relieved to have dodged another intense emotional outburst. "This is a lot to process."

Sydney reluctantly invested in clearing the dining room table of her mother's endless piles of old papers and knickknacks. It was either that or eat off one of the collection of standing trays in front of the sitting room television, or squat on a teetering stool at the kitchen island.

After she had shoveled everything into plastic bags, she wiped down the tabletop, which had probably not seen the light of day for at least ten years. Maude wandered in from the sitting room, where she had been watching the television.

"Randy is on the evening news," she said. "But they didn't mention him by name. Do you really want to eat in here?"

"Yes."

"Can we have wine with dinner?"

"No."

"Vodka?"

"No."

"I'm almost twenty-one."

"No."

"I'm not almost twenty-one?"

"Eighteen months to go, right? And no."

"Give me a break. Don't you drink?" Maude asked, slapping her hands to her head.

"Yes, I do, but not when I'm in the middle of extreme emotions."

"What about if you're really happy?"

Sydney put down the sponge and rubbed her eyes. "I don't make excuses for when I drink."

Maude stared, glanced at the ceiling, and turned away. "If that's a rehab thing, then you can keep it. You only drink when life is *meh*," she said over her shoulder.

"I didn't say that," Sydney said, trailing after her sister. "In fact, tomorrow night we're invited to Cassandra Elway's for dinner. And there will be wine."

Maude reversed course, her face bright. "Good. I'll be the designated driver and drive us home."

"What? No, not while your license is suspended."

"Okay, then. You can't drink, either. No Uber around here, you know. Not even any taxis. So there!"

Over dinner, Maude seemed to want to find fault with every-thing Sydney brought up. Case in point: what to serve at their mother's memorial service.

"How about a crudités of vegetables and some dip? Hum-mus and pita bread. Coke, Diet Coke, orange juice?" Sydney asked.

"Jeez, Sydney. No one's going to come. She was the local floozy. A pariah. We might as well save money and get a bag of Cheetos and a six-pack of Bud."

Sydney scraped at the bottom of her plate. Her stir-fry was the most delicious dish she had eaten since her last real meal in California. Sushi. Fresh fish, sharp wasabi, tart ginger. The scraping sound drowned out the whine of Maude's voice.

She stood up. "I cooked and set the table, so you clean up," she said to Maude. "And I mean dishes in the dishwasher, pots and pans in the drain board."

Francine picked up the phone after two rings. "Yup. Watcha want, Sydney?"

"How'd you know it was me?" Sydney was watching Maude balancing dishes on her way back to the kitchen.

"I've got this modern invention. Caller ID. It tells me that you're calling from Leslie's phone, but she's dead. It could be Maude, but I doubt it. How's it going with your little sister?"

"Great. We're bonding."

"Is that what you call it? So, what's your pleasure?"

"I'm worried that not many people will come to Mom's service next Saturday."

"Well, I told you to let me know. Remember? I've been waiting to send out a notice to the coven."

"Excuse me?" Sydney sat up straighter.

"Ha! Gotcha there, right? It's what we call a bunch of us who go walking together and keep in touch. We have coffee, clean up the roadsides when the snow melts."

"Why the coven?"

"It's an inside joke. We didn't want to be Stepford Wives."

"Stepford Wives?" Sydney could not quite place the reference.

"Please don't tell me you're too young. A movie about suburban housewives who get lulled into acting all perfect. Creepy."

"Do we have any suburban housewives here?"

"Never mind. If you tell me the time, I'll send out the word."

"Thanks, Francine."

"Naturally a good turnout depends on the food. Too little, they don't come. Too much and they don't leave."

Sydney picked up a pen and grabbed a scrap of old newspaper. "What do I serve?"

"Cocktail weenies are very popular. With honey mustard. Good cheese. New York cheddar, and none of that Vermont crap. Potato chips with onion dip. A bunch of six-packs of beer and some of that boxed wine. Coke."

"Diet Coke?"

"Makes my stomach turn, but if it suits you. Rob Brochu will help order it all. Tell him to get the Farewell Special for thirty to fifty people, enough for two hours. You'll have to get the wine separate because this is the wonderful Empire State. Plastic cups are fine."

Sydney sank back into the club chair jammed into the corner of the dining room, feeling the tension drain from her shoulders to her hips to her feet.

A long, sucking burble came from Francine's end of the line.

"I'm sorry, Francine. Are you eating dinner?"

"What? No, I'm drinking whiskey."

That explained Francine's jovial mood. "Was my mother part of the coven?"

"Sure, of course she was. No one's excluded as long as they're female."

"But everyone thought she was the town slut."

"Don't believe that bullshit. She made her mistakes, and she had bad taste in men, but that applies to a lot of people. She had a lot of friends."

Sydney started to say something, but the words got stuck in her throat and she could only gurgle.

"And Leslie was real proud of you, I can tell you that. The way you took charge of your life, got clean, went to school. That cute house you live in."

As soon as she hung up, Sydney was going to head for the barn and have a long cry. She needed to finish her business with Francine before the dam burst.

"One more thing, Francine. Maude and I need a ride to Cassandra Elway's for dinner and back tomorrow night. We'll be drinking."

"Oh yes. Not a bad idea. The cops are mighty pissed off about Randy, and you're part of the Jaquith gang as far as they're concerned. They'll be watching for you."

Tell me about it. "Would you pick us up at five thirty? I'm not sure when we'll finish. Maybe about ten o'clock? I could call you when we're near the end."

"Don't worry. I'll show up at eight thirty for dessert."

"I'm not sure—"

"You're taking the dessert. Am I right?" Francine asked. "Cassandra never makes dessert."

"Sure."

"So plan for one more." Francine hung up.

"In California, I just give the driver a tip," Sydney said to the dial tone.

18

Catharsis

As soon as Sydney hung up the phone, the tears rolled. She needed some alone time.

"Hey, where are you going?" Maude asked, scrubbing at the sink. She turned off the water and started to follow Sydney into the mudroom. "It's cold out there, you know."

Sydney waved her arms, driving Maude back into the sitting room. Half-blinded by her tears, she ignored Maude's questions, grabbed a heavy jacket, and headed out to the barn. For once, Maude seemed to grasp the message.

In the far left corner, she found a familiar wooden cupboard. She squeezed in and closed the door and let herself wail.

The sobbing didn't last long. It was too cold, and she had outgrown her childhood hiding spot. Drained and calm, she clambered out and wandered among the orphaned furniture and dishware, running her ungloved hands along the surfaces, conjuring up her mother's spirit.

Thanks to Francine, she could now envision her tall, willowy mother and appreciate the physical beauty and charm that drew people to her. Sydney always envied Leslie's easy access to attention and admirers. Why were her own body and temperament so pedestrian and undistinctive?

Perhaps things came too easily for her mother. Leslie was distractible, always looking for a new passion, never content with what she had. Except for Randy. She threw away so much treasure and held on to the one thing she should have given up. *Talk about bad choices.*

It was true that Randy was gorgeous, but even as a hormonal, drug-addled teenager, she could tell he was a dead end. Not intentionally evil—but headed down a dangerous path. All these years later, she now understood why her mother also stayed for Maude.

Sydney made her final tour of the first floor of the barn. She stopped at a post toward the back wall, where she knew a plank would move aside. This was not a secure place to hide the Luger, but she couldn't figure out where else to put it. Long term, she couldn't leave it behind for the next owner. Short term, Maude was scavenging for drugs and alcohol.

It was too cold to marinate in her own thoughts. She stepped into the mudroom and cracked the door into the sitting room to spy on Maude in front of the television.

Their mother had the amazing ability to make others feel as though they were interesting and special. Why was neither of her daughters blessed with their mother's sunny charm?

That went double for Maude. Where had her sister acquired her volatile temperament? Sydney feared that this was Zile's influence, be it genetic or learned. Lilith was cranky and difficult, but not crazy, and Randy was usually the kind of guy who grew calm as things around him got hot.

Maude jumped up from the sitting room couch as Sydney came through the mudroom door.

"What's with you? What's the matter?"

"Now I would like a drink. Do we have anything left?" Sydney asked.

"I thought you only drank when you *weren't* upset."

"I'm not upset now. I was overwhelmed for a few minutes. Mom dying. Losing Randy. Dealing with you."

"What about me? What are you talking about?" Maude paced and waved her arms.

Sydney grabbed her sister in a hug. To her surprise, Maude grabbed her back, squeezing the wind out of Sydney's lungs.

"I was scared," Maude muttered. She was so tall, she had to bend over to rest her chin on Sydney's shoulder. "I need you." She squeezed tighter.

Sydney tapped her sister's back. "Can't breathe," she said with a wheeze.

"Sorry." Maude loosened her grip, and she wiped away Sydney's tears.

"I'm going to have one drink and go to bed," Sydney said. "Tomorrow I need your help sorting out Mom's office."

"I don't know if we'll both fit inside." Maude handed Sydney a glass filled with dark liquid.

"No complaining. We'll clear the space, even if you have to sit on my lap. And we need to make dessert for tomorrow night. Apple crumble, I figure." Sydney settled onto the couch and motioned toward the TV. "What are we watching?"

"No idea."

19

Truck Off

By breakfast, priorities had shifted. Bad Elf Maude was back in form.

"We need to go get my truck."

Sydney dumped plain oatmeal into a bowl and plopped it in front of her sister. "Ignoring the fact that you can't drive, it's at Randy's and that's a crime scene."

"I've called the Hartwell police station and told them I wanted to pick it up. See, I can take the initiative, too!"

Sydney poured a healthy dollop of maple syrup—New York maple syrup—onto her oatmeal sludge. Maude might not like maple syrup, but Sydney couldn't stomach oatmeal without it.

"So, what did they say?"

"He said fine."

"Which *he* would that be?"

"Someone. I didn't get a name."

"I'll double-check. If they say yes, we'll ski down, and *I* will drive us back."

Sydney slipped on her cross-country skis outside the barn. This was almost becoming second nature. Not quite, but at least easier.

"I don't ski," Maude announced. She plopped down a pair of steel and plastic snowshoes. "No sliding downhill with minimal control for me. I'll follow and meet you down there." She handed a ring of keys to Sydney. "You can clean off all the snow and start up the truck. Remember to pump only twice or she'll flood."

The powder was light and fluffy on top of a solid base. Perfect temperature in the twenties with blue sky overhead. Sydney was gliding downhill, fast enough to accommodate an elegant, decorative stride but fully in control.

Sydney had dreams like this sometimes that almost convinced her she could live in Oriska again. But not quite.

Snowshoes were solid but slow. She was grateful that it would take Maude much longer to arrive at Randy's property.

Randy's red truck must have been towed away. Maude's truck sat to the right side of a glorified shed that Randy called a barn, almost hidden by the drifts and a shed door that the cops or fire crew had left hanging open.

Snow was piled up close to two feet high on all the horizontal surfaces and coated the sides of the truck thoroughly enough to hide the color. Sydney wiped a section clear above the back bumper. Midnight blue. Even with large snow tires, she and Maude would need to dig out a path for the vehicle to reach the plowed area in front of the shed.

Scratch that. Maude could dig out the path. This was her truck.

Sydney jammed her skis and poles vertically into a nearby drift. The repetitive squeak of the shed door hinges as it swung back and forth in the breeze set her teeth on edge. She found a broom and a shovel inside the door and shut it firmly.

The first layer of snow brushed off easily. The remaining topping was a nasty mix of layers of ice and crusty snow. She used the broom handle to chip away access to the driver's side door, which opened with a cracking and creaking in protest. She hoisted herself inside and pumped the gas twice before she turned the key in the ignition. The engine turned over with a roar.

Hurray for small victories. She cranked the heat and blower up to the max and climbed out. That should accelerate the deicing process from the inside.

Where the hell is Maude?

As if in answer, a black police SUV pulled up behind the truck. Even puffed up by a winter uniform, Police Chief Michael Carver looked like a leggy black widow crawling out of a den. All he needed was a red hourglass on his belly and a couple of extra legs.

Now that she thought about it, she'd never even seen a black widow until she migrated to California. Perhaps Chief Carver was the first of his species to be pushed north by global warming. Or maybe they'd been here all along, waiting to pounce.

"Nice to catch you for a little one-on-one, Ms. Lucerno," the chief said, slipping his hands into long gloves that didn't quite cover the gap over his raw wrists.

Something about that inch of flesh made her neck prickle. His father had long arms just like that.

Don't let the visions of the past blind you to the present. Despite so many familiar traits, Michael Carver was a different beast from his father. She hoped.

"Sure thing, Chief." Sydney coughed to mask her need to swallow the sudden flood of saliva that filled her throat. She leaned her left arm against the side of the truck, hoping this looked relaxed and casual. "We called about picking up Maude's truck. Hope we didn't get our signals crossed."

Carver squinted as if he noticed the truck for the first time. "No, that's fine." He clapped his gloved hands together and continued. "Funny thing about your buddy Randy and his pals." He stood with his feet very wide as if about to do a split.

Sydney didn't know what to make of his body language. Could that stance possibly be comfortable?

"As we suspected, the autopsies show they didn't die here. Their bodies were moved to Randy's trailer, and then everything was set on fire. Three bodies, three guns. Three revolvers to be precise. Want to guess what else we found?"

Sydney hated playing guessing games like this. Clearly, Carver knew the answer.

"Randy died from one or two or three shots from the guns of those other two, and they died from his gun?" she asked.

Carver snorted and moved his feet together. "About seventy-five percent right. Randy died from one of three gunshots, two from one gun and a fatal third from the other. And the other two men died from a different gun. The problem is those shots weren't from the gun placed with Randy's body. In fact, we can't find that gun anywhere."

Damn Zile. He had already screwed up by trying to restage the fight in Randy's trailer. How stupid did he think the police were? Now he'd also screwed up with the gun evidence. She'd been a fool to expect more of him.

There was no denying she had played a major role in this disaster. She had taken the Luger, and now she'd have to wiggle out of the consequences.

Sydney stamped her feet. The air was suddenly much colder and she wanted Carver to get to the point. "So, Randy didn't shoot the other two men?"

The chief wagged his head. "His hands show lots of GSR. That's gunshot residue for you *citizens.*" His professional demeanor was cracking along the edges. "He fired a gun. Multiple times. But we can't find it. Not only that, it's from a 9mm pistol, not a revolver."

Sydney decided to play dumb. "What's the difference?"

Carver stared at her. "Don't tell me you don't know. Different kind of handgun. More importantly, the bullets match a very different shooting. One from thirteen years ago. As soon as I heard these were from a 9mm, I had a hunch. I had them checked. Same gun."

"Chief, I don't know what to say. Help me out here."

Carver stepped up until he loomed over Sydney. "That same gun killed my father thirteen years ago. He was found up by Schwarzer's quarry, in his vehicle, shot in the chest and the head. As I think you know."

Sydney backed up. "I had heard some things, but I didn't know much. Not the details. It happened after I left."

Carver leaned forward at the waist. Sydney could smell coffee and something more pungent on his breath. "I'm not buying that. It's all timing with you, isn't it? You happen to leave town right before my father's body is found. You arrive in town right before Randy's body is found. Randy's body was moved, along with his 'buddies.' My father's body was moved after he had been shot. Forensics don't lie, and they are leading me right back to you."

Deep breaths. "You're scaring me, Chief. I can assure you that I did not kill your father or Randy." Her voice was soft and raspy. She hoped the chief took this the right way—sincere denial.

Carver blinked and stood straighter. "I'd like you to come down to the station and make a formal statement."

"About Randy?"

"No, about the death of my father. Sheriff Homer Carver. Thirteen years ago."

"That was so long ago."

Carver leaned in again. "There is no statute of limitations for murder, Ms. Lucerno. Or for aiding and abetting murder after the fact . . ." Carver continued to sputter, but Sydney had started to hyperventilate, and her brain began to skip over words.

"I will require a lawyer. I assure you that I don't know anything."

"I don't believe you. You ran off with Caleb Elway after he killed my father. You know where Caleb is. Now you're back, and there's another murder. In fact, three of them."

Carver's voice was loud and shrill. For the first time, Sydney worried for her physical safety. Not a single car had passed on the road. They were hidden, squeezed between the shed and Maude's truck with the chief's car blocking her way. Perhaps she had been too complacent in thinking Chief Carver was very different from his father.

"I told you already. I haven't seen him since mid-August that year. He's dead."

Sydney held her breath, and for one brief moment she thought they had reached an impasse.

"Fuck you, Sydney Lucerno." This time Carver's voice was soft and lowered to a hiss as his venom made a dart pointed at her heart. "I know you're lying. How do you know he's dead?"

Panic and anger surged forward, breaking through all her careful defenses. Sydney needed to take a risk and call the chief's bluff.

"Your father told me Caleb was dead," she said.

They stood face-to-face in a precarious balance. Carver took a tiny step back. Sydney leaned in.

"I got out of rehab. I was looking for Caleb. Looking in every spot I could think of. Caleb was my heart. I wanted to see him so bad. He had only come for short visits. I ached for him." Sydney clutched her fists to her chest and glared into Carver's face.

"Your father tracked me down. He found me walking on Hartwell Road and took me in his car to the Hangnail Pond boat access. He said he had killed Caleb in late September and dumped his body in Schwarzer's quarry."

Chief Carver's eyes opened wide. "Why would my father have told you that?"

"Intimidation, asshole. He wanted me to worm my way back into Randy and Zile's operations and snitch for him. With a bit of sex thrown in, by the way. Caleb had been a 'disappointment.' That's a quote. Your father wanted to let me know he was serious about consequences when people 'disappointed' him."

"That's total nonsense. My father was an honorable man." Carver's back had stiffened, forcing his chin upward.

"An honorable dick! I think that if you bothered to look, you'd find that this was not a unique conversation. Talk to Caleb's family. Talk to Bernie Riggs."

Sydney and Carver were now in a dance as he moved backward and she moved in his wake in lockstep. One portion of her brain warned her that this was an armed officer of the law. Another knew he wasn't his father, but she still wanted to grind him under her heal.

"He was a piece of shit, and you know it. He told me he killed Caleb Elway, and I believed every word he said."

Carver reached his vehicle. He folded his long limbs into the driver's seat and slammed the door shut.

Sydney leaned forward, her fists resting on the hood. She pounded in time to her voice. "He killed Caleb. He killed Caleb.

You want me to make a statement? I'll make a fucking state-ment. I'll be there tomorrow and I'll peel off every bit of honor you thought you wanted to preserve."

Their eyes met. Same heavy-lidded eyes. Same face with the heavy brow. But this time, the eyes were filled with tears. Old Sheriff Carver would never have cried.

Sydney lifted her hands and rocked back. The surge of pent-up emotion flooded her body, and she stumbled, drunk on relief.

Carver threw his SUV into reverse, kicking up salt sludge as he slid onto the road.

Sydney sank down on a hard block of ice that had fallen from underneath Carver's car and cried. She pounded her fists on her knees and screamed at her ankles.

Gradually her sobs turned to whimpers. She sat straighter and thought of Caleb. His body. His dark brown eyes. The smooth texture of his deep golden skin. The way he had made her feel.

She rose and kicked the ice turd into tiny pieces. A creaking sound pierced her reverie. The shed door was swinging again. Sydney pulled the door open and leaned left to look inside.

Pressed against the side wall, clutching her snowshoes and poles to her chest, Maude's face was the color of three-day-old snow after a short thaw.

"Never trust a Carver. That's what my father always said," Maude whispered.

20

The Locket

Count on Maude to show up like a bad penny at the wrong time.

"About time you got here," Sydney said. Her throat was rough and sore from all the yelling. "You clear a path so we can back the truck out. I'll keep working on the cab."

For once, Maude did not seem to want to argue. She picked up a snow shovel with a bent handle. "These shovels make clearing snow much easier," she said, waving it in Sydney's direction to show how it worked.

"The only thing that makes shoveling snow easier is when someone else does it," Sydney responded. "Let's get going."

The heat from inside the cab of the truck had been working its magic while Sydney was arguing with Chief Carver. The remainder of the ice and crust broke free easily. With a few strategic taps, she was able to clear the residual pieces with the broom. The physical movement helped put strength back into her limbs and steadied her hands.

She needed to talk to Steve. How could she have let herself be goaded into something so stupid?

"Done," Maude said. "Should I shovel out the bed?"

"Waste of time. You can do that at the house. Put these tools away and let's get out of here. And shut that stupid shed door."

As Maude put away the shovels and broom, Sydney tossed

her skis and poles into the truck bed, followed by Maude's snowshoes and poles.

Sydney settled into the driver's seat and shoved the truck into reverse. Maude barely had time to shut the passenger door when Sydney stomped on the gas.

The truck flew backward past the garage and across the icy driveway. Sydney kept accelerating until all four tires hit the road and she spun the wheel to face uphill.

"Jeez, Sydney. What kind of driving is that?" Maude's face was sweaty. "What if there'd been a car coming?" She reached for her seatbelt and buckled up.

"Shut. Up." Sydney slammed the truck into drive. The wheels spun as they headed home.

The short trip was made in silence. Sydney contemplated the buzzing in her head from all the demons she had unleashed. It never paid to lose her temper. Why was this a lesson she had to repeat over and over? Now she was going to pay the price.

She considered her options. She would refuse to answer any questions. She would make Steve do the talking. She would laugh it all off and deny she had said anything to Chief Carver. It was her word against his.

Unfortunately, there was one witness. Fortunately, Carver didn't know that.

As she pulled into the driveway and parked the car next to their mother's Subaru, Sydney glanced at Maude, sitting with her eyes glued on the road, chewing on a hangnail.

"What?" Maude asked.

"I didn't hear you arrive."

"I came in from the uphill side. That cop was already there, and it seemed like a good idea to stay out of the way."

"I guess you could hear us talking."

"Caleb Elway worked for my grandfather. Did you know that?" Maude asked.

"Yes, I knew. Randy introduced us, but his sister, Cassandra, was also my best friend at school."

"Did Chief Carver's father really kill him?"

Sydney studied the driveway. She wanted this short errand to end. "I absolutely believed it then, and I believe it now."

"Who is Bernie Riggs?"

"One of many people the good sheriff screwed over."

"Did you kill that guy? The sheriff?"

"Oh, please."

"Did you kill Randy?"

"No!"

Maude opened her door and climbed out. "I can tell you aren't being straight with me. I'm not sure what's going on, but I'll figure it out." She slammed the door and headed into the barn toward the mudroom.

Sydney rolled down her window. "Hey. Get your stuff out of the back and put it away."

Maude kept walking and flipped Sydney the bird with both hands.

"I could tell you, but then I'd have to kill you," Sydney said in a low groan. She rolled up the window and switched off the engine. "The good news is I might do that, anyway."

By the time Sydney reached the kitchen, Maude was slathering crunchy peanut butter on a piece of whole wheat bread, a glass of milk already waiting on the counter.

"That looks good," Sydney said, sliding onto a stool. "Can I have some?"

Maude tossed the bag of bread across the island. "Help yourself." She picked up her slice, which sagged in the middle under its heavy load and sent dribbles of peanut butter over the sides.

Sydney clenched her jaw muscles and her hands in unison to keep from blowing her top. She had already lost her temper once that day, and nothing good had come from it.

"Why are you being such a pill?" Sydney asked. "We're supposed to be helping each other."

"How can I help if you aren't telling me stuff? Like about Caleb? And that guy he killed."

"To be clear, even though it feels like a lifetime, we met less than forty-eight hours ago. And more to the point, Caleb did not kill Homer Carver."

Maude stuck out her tongue to catch a peanut butter drip and followed up with a big bite. After a thorough chew, she washed it down with a swig of milk.

"Okay. I'll make you a sandwich if you'll tell me about Caleb and the sheriff."

Sydney tossed the loaf of bread back across the island. "Do you remember Caleb? What does your family say?" she asked.

"I didn't see very much of him because he worked for my grandfather. My grandmother tried to keep me away from most of that. She didn't want to encourage bad influences, I guess."

Sydney pressed her lips together to keep from speaking. *Too bad Lilith didn't use good sense like that when raising Randy.*

"I also gathered his parents didn't like the Jaquiths much."

"Think about it," Sydney said. "Dr. Elway and Professor Elway. Cassandra's father taught biology at Cornell, and her mother taught biochemistry at Colgate. They had higher ambitions for their son than being a bagman for someone like Zile. It led to some tensions."

Maude appeared to consider this as she lined up her ingredients for the sandwich. "I've never met Caleb's parents. I had Ms. Elway—your friend Cassandra—in high school for math. Do you want butter and peanut butter or plain peanut butter?"

"Both. And jam—a little schmear. If Zile and Lilith hold some sort of service for Randy, Cassandra will probably show up. And you'll see her tonight. Her father died of a heart attack a couple of years ago, and her mother retired and moved away."

Maude finished the sandwich, cut it diagonally into quarters, and put the gooey pieces onto a paper towel, which she pushed across the island. Someday Sydney would have to introduce her sister to plates.

"Milk?" Maude asked.

"Hate straight milk."

"Them's fighting words in dairy country, you know." Maude poured Sydney a glass of orange juice.

"Anyway, I met Caleb because he was supposed to be working for Zile but in fact was doing stuff with Randy. And by 'stuff' I don't mean anything legal. I was fifteen. Even though Cassandra was a buddy, I didn't know him very well because he was four or five years older."

Maude delivered the orange juice and slid onto the other stool. "Love at first sight?"

"Definitely on my part. Not tall, massive gorgeous like Randy, but Caleb was put together exactly in the right way. Smart and with a wicked sense of humor and a smile that turned me inside out. He made me laugh a lot. Made me happy when I was fifteen."

"I wasn't happy when I was fifteen," Maude said.

Sydney tried to picture how much worse of a handful Maude must have been at that age. "Being a teenager is hard for a lot of people, but I was incredibly miserable. We Grahams were pariahs after the whole scandal with Randy and our mom. I only had a few friends and I hated school. Then along comes this guy who was so sweet."

Maude looked away. "Sydney, I have to tell you this is not how I hear people talk about Caleb. He was the guy who made collections, right? The one who helped keep things in line?"

Sydney squirmed. Sitting on the narrow stool, she felt like a worm on a hook. "I know he had a temper, but he was always good with me. He never hit me. Not once. I wanted us to run away together. I knew we both needed to get out of here."

"So what's the story with Sheriff Carver?"

"He was one of those hardcore types that appealed to a lot of people around here. But he didn't have much patience with anyone who didn't measure up to his standards, and when that happened, he didn't mind bending the rules to get results he thought were right. Some, like Randy and Caleb, were definitely not model citizens, but he also went after people he plain didn't like."

"Like black and brown people?" Maude asked.

Sydney wiped the counter with her paper towel. "Exactly. Even minors like me with Latino names and lots of problems.

You can ask Cassandra and Steve about that tonight. Cassandra had her share of run-ins, and Steve made a steady income representing people with unlawful arrests and complaints."

"He represented you, too, right?"

"Oh yes. The good sheriff scooped me up in a raid on Randy's cabin. Randy and Caleb made a dash out the back door with the evidence, but I wasn't fast enough. I tried to hide behind the downstairs closet. Plus I was carrying."

Maude stared. "Randy and Caleb deserted you?"

"That was the first chime of my wakeup call. It took a while to sink in, but I realized I couldn't count on my so-called friends and that maybe they weren't so good for me. Plus spending a few days processing through the system proved to me that I was definitely a junkie."

To give her sister credit, Maude didn't look away. She held Sydney's gaze and tilted her eyebrows. "And?"

"Fortunately, I was only sixteen at that point. Steve got me a deal. I went to residential rehab over by Ithaca. In return, I would have my record cleared if I stayed out of trouble."

"That must have sucked."

Sydney allowed herself a smile. "It was the best thing that ever happened to me. Not that it was easy or fun. I finished my junior year there and spent all summer cooped up. But I got clean. I also realized I was smart. And I definitely realized that if I came home, I'd be back in serious trouble in no time. My only hope was to get away from the people who were sucking me into that life."

"Including Randy."

"Randy was the chief offender. Zile, his crew."

"And Caleb?"

Sydney stood and stretched her legs, pivoting in a slow circle. She hated retracing the past. "I had a plan to escape, and I wanted him to come. He visited most weeks I was in rehab, and we talked it through. We would drive to California in his truck. I would ask my father to help us get set up. I would get my GED. He could start college."

"And . . . ?"

"And then at the very end, he didn't show up. When I got out, I went looking, which was hard because I didn't have my driver's license yet, so I had to sneak out in Grandpa's car or hitchhike."

"Don't tell me, let me guess," Maude said. "That was how the sheriff picked you up."

"Exactly. He stopped me hitchhiking on Hartwell Road and took me to the boat access. I was terrified because this could be considered violating the terms of my agreement. That was when he made it clear he had other things in mind."

Maude's face flushed. "Sex? He wanted sex?"

"That was part of it, but I wish it had been that simple. He wanted me to go back to my life as before and be his snitch."

"Why would you agree to that?"

Sydney's legs felt tired. She could feel her heart pounding in her temple. "That was when he explained what he did to unco-operative types. Like Caleb." For several seconds, her vision was clouded by the memory of Sheriff Carver looming over her, his gun in his right hand and something hidden in his left.

"He actually said he had killed Caleb?"

"He asked me if I had seen Caleb recently." Sydney paused, remembering the knowing smirk on Sheriff Carver's face. "He said if I wanted to find Caleb, I'd have to dive into Schwarzer's quarry so the two of us could be reunited permanently."

"I know that place," Maude said, wrinkling her nose. "Filled with stinky water and no way to climb out. You believed him?"

Sydney swallowed before she spoke. "He had something on a chain he was swinging around. He stopped and tossed it to me. It was half of a locket. It was a cheap thing Caleb had found— a locket that could split into two interlocking pieces. Sheriff Carver had Caleb's half. I had the other half around my neck."

"You're sure?"

"It had Caleb's initials on the back. And a little ding on one edge. It was his."

Sydney felt dampness on her cheeks. She must have been crying. Tears thirteen years old were finally coming to the surface.

Maude got off her stool and kissed Sydney's forehead. Sydney tried to swallow but realized that her mouth was filling with saliva. She broke free and rushed to the kitchen sink, arriving barely in time to upchuck the remains of her peanut butter sandwich and orange juice.

Maude came over to pat Sydney's back until her retching subsided. Sydney turned on the water and let the lunch remains flow down into the garbage disposal while she washed out her mouth. Maude soaked another paper towel and gently wiped Sydney's face.

"Is that why you stole money from my grandfather? To get away?" Maude asked, continuing to mop up new tears.

Sydney gurgled and bobbed her head. "I knew I was dead if I stayed here. I'd start using again and let myself OD because of Caleb. Or I'd screw up and I'd end up in Schwarzer's quarry. Or something even worse."

"You went all alone to California." Maude was crying now, too.

Sydney reached out to touch Maude's cheek. "I did it once. I'll do it again. This time you're coming with me."

21

Past Sins

After her second lunch—scrambled eggs prepared by Maude—Sydney announced she was going to Brochu's to discuss the Farewell Special for their mother's service with Rob.

"I'm coming with you," Maude said, shaking her hands dry after cleaning at the sink.

"No need. I can handle this."

"You think Rob is a nice country bumpkin, but he's a shrewd negotiator. We need to make a good deal. We'll play good cop, bad cop."

Sydney headed for the mudroom. "I can guess which cop you'll be."

"We aren't going to walk, right?" Maude asked. "Let me drive my truck."

"No."

"Please? You can see Brochu's from here."

"No."

As Sydney signaled to pull into the last shoveled parking slot in front of Brochu's, a Hartwell police squad car rolled past the store. She opened her mouth to remind her sister about the perils of driving with a suspended license, but Maude beat her to the punch.

"Yes, yes. I see him. You don't have to rub it in." Maude climbed out and slammed the passenger side door.

Despite the full parking spaces, the place seemed empty. Maybe all the shoppers were in the hardware section, where the selections were more exciting, assuming that browsing for fishing lures, hunting supplies, and electrical wiring was what made you happy.

Rob was hunkered down over a battered rolltop desk squeezed into a tiny office near the checkout counter.

Sydney rapped on the side of the doorframe. Rob looked up, squinting as if she were an alien who had dropped in from Mars, but once she explained she wanted to do business, his attitude brightened.

With Maude glowering over their shoulders, Sydney and Rob made their list.

"You can get hummus?" Sydney asked, amazed.

"Of course. I don't stock it 'cuz it'd go bad on the shelf, but I can order that."

"And little carrots?"

"Sure, but you get pita chips if you really want them because you'll be the only one eating those things. Trust me."

"We don't need two hundred plastic glasses," Maude said, stabbing her finger at their planning paper. "Same for napkins."

"It's the minimum order, Maude," Rob said, pushing his reading glasses up onto his forehead. "If you want to go get them yourself in Hartwell, you can save yourself all of two bucks."

"We're not going to nickel and dime you here, Rob," Sydney said, slapping Maude's hand away. "You tell me what I need to get."

Rob slipped his glasses back down to his nose and snorted. "You bring a couple of nice tablecloths and some platters and bowls. I can get the beer, you get the wine. I can't sell wine or liquor."

"Yeah," Sydney said, making some notes on her own pad of paper. "One of the nice things I forget about living in California."

"Two boxes of white stuff, one red. The vintage doesn't matter—whatever Hartwell Liquors has in stock. Chill it in your barn but don't let it freeze. I'll get to Martinson Funeral Home thirty minutes before."

He wrote a number at the bottom of the pad and Sydney blinked. It was less than a sushi dinner for four in Palo Alto.

"Is cash okay?"

Rob crossed out his price and wrote a lower dollar figure. Sydney rounded it up to the nearest number ending in a zero. Maude stalked by and slammed the front door behind her.

"Was I that crazy?" Sydney asked.

Maude was waiting in the passenger seat sorting a pile of envelopes and packages.

Sydney loaded their groceries into the backseat and dropped the crumpled party receipt into the closest bag. "What's all that?" she asked.

"Mail. Mom's mail and some of mine." Maude pointed with her chin in the direction of the Oriska Post Office, situated a couple of doors from Brochu's.

Sydney slumped into the driver's seat, mentally slapping her forehead. *Gosh for dumb.* How was it she hadn't twigged that there had been no mail delivered to the house?

"Mom preferred using a post box in case she was away. She didn't like things piling up outside," Maude said. "*I* like it because I don't want my grandparents opening my private stuff. Or anyone else."

"Like who?"

"Like Randy, for example." Maude tsked several times. "He never wanted to be a real father unless there was something in it for him."

"Such as?"

"Checks, information . . . Sometimes just to prove he could."

Sydney backed the car out and headed for the house. "Anything interesting in there?"

"Some stuff looks official." Maude tapped an envelope against her teeth. "Here's something funny."

"Okay, I'll bite."

"I know Randy was doing a big deal with some Canadians. If things had gone differently, I'd be putting stuff into little packages and making deliveries right now."

"I'm going to forget I heard that."

"Pay attention, Sydney. Randy died with two guys on the day he was supposed to take a final delivery and pay for it. So where are the drugs, and where is the money?"

Sydney pretended to think about this. "Well, we know they died someplace else and were moved, right? I'd guess where they died?"

"Yeah, but my grandfather is looking for all that, and we know he was the one who moved the bodies, right?"

"We do?" Sydney turned into their driveway, thrilled to have an excuse to bring this conversation to an end. She parked and pulled the bags out of the backseat.

"Give me a break, Sydney. Even you aren't that stupid." Maude headed inside, empty-handed as usual.

22

Overload

"How do you know Zile moved the bodies?" Sydney asked as she put away groceries.

Maude looked up from sorting the mail on the counter. "Well, for one thing, he told me, but that was because I told him what I had figured out."

Sydney stared. "When was this?"

"I called him this morning. Before we went after the truck."

"And he admitted to all this?"

"Nah, he was in a bad mood, and I figured I should hang up before he started blaming *me* for everything." Maude reached for one of the apples Sydney had piled on the island counter.

"Hey. Leave those alone. I need to make apple crumble for dessert tonight."

"It's only one more person."

"Fine, I'll tell Francine you ate her share."

Maude took a huge bite out of the apple and set it back down with the others. "Yeesh. So touchy."

"Naturally I'm touchy. Your grandfather is in a bad mood, and when he's in a bad mood, he's like a plague that hits everyone in his path."

"You don't need to lecture me about my grandfather, Sydney. I'm the one who grew up with him."

"I don't suppose he mentioned where he found the bodies."

"No, and don't worry. I know how to handle him."

"Famous last words," Sydney said to the counter as Maude left to open her letters in the privacy of the dining room.

Sydney tried to push away her concerns about Zile as she assembled the crumble. She hated to cook when she felt worried or angry—like she was putting all those bad feelings into the food—but she couldn't shake the mental storm clouds. It was bad enough that Zile hated her. Did she now have to worry about what he might do to Maude, the girl he had raised as his own daughter?

The smell of the baking crumble improved Sydney's mood. Perhaps the good vibes of apples, brown sugar, and butter could overcome nasty personal demons after all.

Most of her mother's mail consisted of flyers and junk solicitations. There were a few bills, mostly for utilities. She would have to figure out how to route those to California or handle them online until the house sold. There were two credit card bills, showing nothing significant, no suspicious charges. Those cards she needed to cut off right away.

The last envelope showed the return address of a major health insurance company and was stamped with "Your New Insurance Cards Inside."

Sydney whistled a cheerful note. This was welcome news. The hospital only had old insurance information for her mother that expired at the end of December. This new policy would help cover most of the costs of Leslie's final struggle. Minus a substantial hit for deductibles, copays, and maximum out-of-pocket expenses, of course.

She studied her mother's health cards with all their useless bits of information and realized that there were two sets of cards. She slid aside the upper set.

Maude was still seated at the dining room table, gazing at her own bills, when Sydney plopped down the insurance cards in front of her.

"What the hell?"

"Our mother put you on her health insurance, starting January first," Sydney said, and eased into a chair next to Maude.

Maude leaned forward to study the cards without touching them. "Did she do that for you, too?"

"No, I'm too old. You can only include your children up to the age of twenty-six. Besides, I have coverage through my beloved employer. At least for now."

"Does this mean I'm covered now that she's dead?" Maude sniffed and wiped her nose.

"We'll have to ask an insurance agent or the insurance company. I kind of suspect this policy will be terminated at the end of January now that Mom is gone."

Maude stroked the cards with her fingertips. "It still shows she thought of me."

"She loved you, Maude. I could never figure out why she wouldn't spend more time with me in California. Now I know. She wanted to be here for you."

"Will they let me get my own policy?"

Sydney stood and rubbed her sister's shoulders. "Maybe. But you're coming with me to California. I'll make sure you get coverage there. I'll be there for you now."

Maude leaped to her feet and hugged Sydney.

"I just wish you were a bit more clever," Maude said in a whisper.

Once finished with mail, Sydney pulled the crumble out of the oven and stretched out with a groan on the sitting room couch. Less than one week ago, she had been complaining about the rainy winter weather in Northern California. Since then every day had presented one challenge after another, and she was beat. She had no energy left for her mother, for Maude, for Randy, or even for herself.

Something was poking into her shoulder. She opened one eye and saw Francine looming over the couch.

"Hey there, Cinderella. Your pumpkin has arrived and it's time to go to the ball."

"Can't make it. Give my regards to the prince."

Maude appeared next to Francine, dangling Sydney's parka. "I've packed the crumble, the ice cream, and the six-pack of New York Red you bought at Brochu's. We're all set."

Sydney blinked and studied the sitting room ceiling. It was cracked and needed patching.

"You need to talk to Steve, remember?" Maude said. "All that stuff about the sheriff you said to his son?"

"Is that so?" Francine asked. "I'm looking forward to hearing about that over dinner."

Sydney groaned and forced herself to her feet. "You're our ride. You are coming back for dessert so you can drive us home."

"You Californians ought to check the weather report. Nice set of snow squalls coming through. No way I'll leave and come back in that kind of weather. I'm staying for dinner. Don't worry. I already called Cassandra and told her," Francine said. She waggled her eyebrows and pulled an old bottle filled with clear liquid from her jacket. "Besides, I brung the hooch."

"Glad I didn't plan on changing into something fancy to wear. Where the hell'd you get that?" Sydney let Maude shove her arms into a jacket and propel her out to Francine's car.

"I didn't *get* it anywheres. I made it."

Sydney climbed into the backseat and fell over on her side, hugging the six-pack of lager to her chest, the apple crumble on the floor beside her. Her eyes were already closing as the doors slammed.

"The whole point of hiring you was to have someone sober to drive us home."

"Don't worry," Francine said. "I'll be sober. I've got a hollow leg."

23

Bitter Stew

The suspension in Francine's backseat did not make for a restful nap. After the car jolted over what felt like the fourth or fifth major pothole, Sydney sat up, yanked back into the present.

To her surprise, she felt wide-awake, her head cleared. On the one hand, she was pleased to be back in her own skin—in control and thinking logically. On the other, she could still feel the black poison of exhaustion hovering. She had been pushed to an edge by stress and lost her resilience. This was a wake-up call. She needed to watch out for her own mental health.

"Welcome back, Cinderella," Francine said.

"That's Snow White. Or Sleeping Beauty." Sydney yawned and stretched her hands up to the roof of the car and pushed as she arched her back.

"Yeah, well, those require a kiss from Prince Charming. Which I am not."

Sydney couldn't recognize anything outside. The whole world was pitch-black as they passed along bleak white tunnels.

"So, when does this pumpkin arrive, Fairy Godmother?"

Maude snorted. "We're almost there. It's right around the corner."

Francine rolled through the next stop sign and turned left. As promised, Elway Farms loomed ahead, brightly lit, inviting them to enter.

Unexpected tears sprang to Sydney's eyes. This had been one of her only safe havens back when. If she'd been able to drive, she would have spent even more time here, under the stern, watchful rule of Cassandra's parents. They always welcomed her.

Now they were gone. Cassandra's father was dead, her mother living elsewhere, and Caleb was wherever Sheriff Carver had put him. Only Cassandra remained.

Even in the dark, lit by a few outdoor lights and shrouded by falling snow, the Elway farmhouse loomed clear as day, burned into Sydney's memory. The driveway swung past the front of the 1830s structure to a well-lit, broad, open area between the house and a set of barns. The deep summer porch beckoned for a visit, and the back door swung open, silhouetting a waiting figure. *Cassandra.*

They were swept inside, greeted by a large and enthusiastic black Lab, a mutt of uncertain parentage, a gray tabby cat, and a roaring fire. The smell of bread in the oven and something with beef and garlic filled the mudroom.

"Moon Dog, Roscoe. Down." The dogs settled onto their haunches at the sound of Cassandra's firm, low voice. "Yarrow, stop rubbing Sydney's ankles." She bent over, picked up the cat, and dropped him outside.

"Isn't it too cold outside?" Sydney asked, tracking Yarrow through the glass storm door as he raced toward the barn.

"He's got a nice, warm place out there with the horses and a bunch of other barn cats," Cassandra said.

"Aren't you down a dog or two?" Francine asked. To Sydney, she said, "Cassandra's our local pet and livestock whisperer. She takes in lots of animals in need."

"Dogs, cats, horses, and goats. Sometimes sheep. I don't do cows. I treat them, get them healthy, teach them manners, and find new homes for most," Cassandra said.

"Sounds like teaching high school," Maude said in a low mutter.

"It worked for you. You did manage to graduate." Cassandra helped Maude take off her coat, tugging on the sleeves.

Maude's mouth curved in a half grin. "The first Jaquith to do that within living memory."

"I'll take that as a thank-you."

Sydney rubbed her eyes and hid behind her coat to mask her deep breaths, listening to the good-natured banter. This was the first time she had felt warm and safe since stepping off the airplane four short days before.

Even Steve giving her the stink eye made her happy. He must have received her frantic voice mail and was now pissed off at how she had mishandled Chief Carver, but he was in her corner to help.

Cassandra raised Francine's bottle of hooch with a crow of joy. "*Eau de vie*. The best pear brandy south of Quebec. I've been waiting for this." She nudged Francine with a quick hip check.

"Are we the only ones?" Sydney asked.

"The Holmeses and the Friedels won't be coming thanks to the storm. It's great you have Francine to shepherd you home."

Sydney grabbed one of her beers and made a show of taking a couple of swallows. Maude asked for red wine, which she proceeded to guzzle. Francine had already disappeared into the living room, sipping on something gold and fizzy.

Steve jerked his head toward the master bedroom, off the kitchen, where he took up court leaning against the bathroom door.

"Suppose you tell me exactly what you said to our good police chief."

Twentyish minutes later, Sydney and Steve rejoined the women sitting around the fire. Their lively chatter stopped. They looked disappointed at being interrupted.

Sydney didn't even need to ask. Maude had been sharing her version of events with Cassandra and Francine, and a free-for-all discussion ensued.

Steve motioned to Cassandra to make room on the couch. She handed him a gin and tonic, which he accepted.

"I'm going to say this once for all of you," he said, after indulging in a long sip. "First, the investigation of Sheriff Carver's death is a county affair. His son may feel some territorial urge to contribute—which he can do—but I don't think it's likely he will engage in something so speculative tomorrow. Besides, tomorrow is Sunday."

Steve paused to swirl the ice cubes in his glass before continuing. "Second, don't volunteer to talk to the local police or the sheriff's department about this." He stopped and raised an eyebrow in Sydney's direction. "If someone does come and request a statement, tell them to call me first."

Sydney crossed her arms, and Cassandra shifted her position on the sofa. "But . . ." Cassandra said, a question forming on her forehead.

"No buts," Steve said, smacking the arm of the couch with his hand. "They may say this is off the record or something like, 'Don't you want to avoid a trip to the station?' but I want you to hold the line. Clear?"

Maude saluted with her glass of red wine and Francine straightened up. "Glad that's settled. Can we eat now? I'm starving."

Midway through her beef stew, Cassandra's spoon slipped from her hand and fell to the plate with a clatter. Sydney didn't jump like the others because she had been watching a single tear roll from the corner of Cassandra's right eye, down over her cheek, and come to rest in the corner of her mouth. Her good friend was suffering.

Sydney reached over and put her right hand on Cassandra's left as the others paused, spoons, forks, and chewing suspended.

Cassandra cupped her hands over her mouth before she picked up her spoon.

"San?" Steve asked.

"That motherfucker." Cassandra's voice was low and even.

"Which one are we talking about?"

"Sheriff Better-Than-Everyone Homer Carver, that's who." Cassandra clamped onto a piece of bread with her teeth and yanked it free as if she were ripping off the sheriff's head at the neck. "He ruined my family. He drove off my best friend. My father died an early death because of him. I didn't kill him, but I swear to God that he deserved what he got and now, even in death, he is coming back to make life miserable."

Steve took a long sip of wine. "I think you mean his son is still stirring that fire."

"Michael Carver should get an exorcism." Cassandra's voice was a low growl.

"Carver is a pretty good police chief. He's a bit obsessed about his father. No one should condone murder."

Francine raised her spoonful of beef stew. "That son of a bitch ruined the life of my nephew, Bernie. And it was all for his own personal gain."

"How'd that work?" Maude asked.

"You're probably too young to remember because this was about fifteen years ago." Francine punctuated her words with the spoon, weaving and diving. "There was all sorts of money and equipment for law agencies to fight the War on Terror, even in places like this. Sheriff Carver wanted to have his own personal SWAT team. Not that he put much into training or anything, but he did get a lot of fancy gear. And then they went on a raid that blew up in their faces. For real."

Steve spoke up. "The way I remember it was that Bernie was a deputy sheriff and a rising star. He was in charge of the unit. The sheriff decided that Gus and Harriet Adams were cooking meth in their trailer on the other side of Hartwell and he set things up for a raid with a no-knock warrant."

"They busted down the door at three in the morning and tossed in a couple of smoke grenades and whatnot," Francine said. "The problem was, there was a baby sleeping in a crib in the living room. And by the way, they never found any meth."

"What happened to the baby?" Maude asked, her voice soft.

"Survived, fortunately. Otherwise things would have been a lot worse," Steve answered. "But he required a long hospitalization and surgeries after."

"I think you represented his parents in the lawsuit, right, Steve?" Francine asked. "Quite successfully."

Steve dabbed his mouth with his napkin. "We won a good and fair settlement, but nothing could undo that damage."

"Plus, my nephew, Bernie, got forced out. Left for Colorado to do construction."

Eating resumed for a minute or so, although the stink of sulfurous emotions still hung in the air.

"My father . . ." Cassandra started to speak and stopped. "My father grew up here, like generations of Elways and other black families who came this way on the Underground Railroad. Not a lot of black people around, but he used to say that once he had a chance to get to know people and they got to know him, he never had problems."

She chuckled. "Well, I could have told him a thing or two about high school, but for the most part, he was right. That's why I'm still here, working my butt off, teaching and trying to give kids a future. But when Caleb started running with Zile, Sheriff Carver began to pull over my dad for no good reason, giving him a hard time, calling us names. Even before Caleb disappeared, Dad started to age. My mother was from Virginia. She was hurt, but she had lived like that before. For Dad, it was like his life had been built on a lie."

Sydney picked up the beer bottle she had been nursing all evening for another swallow. "Lots of people hated that man."

Cassandra swiveled to face Sydney. "That's why my dad believed you when you came to tell us about what Sheriff Carver did to Caleb. He knew you were all screwed up, but in his heart, he heard the truth."

Steve spoke up. "You could both be suspects in his death. You too, Francine. I want you all to be certain to contact me if you are questioned. Remember that."

"Dad is dead," Cassandra said, a smile flirting at her mouth. "But on the night before the sheriff was killed, we were on our way to Philadelphia with Sydney in the backseat. Right, kiddo?"

Sydney waved her spoon over her chest. "Cross my heart. Cassandra and her parents took me to Philly in the back of that rusty old Taurus. Why Philadelphia, I don't know. We stayed one night in an awful motel that seemed like a palace and ate at

Burger King, which was a real treat. The next morning, he put me on an airplane to California with Cassandra as my guardian. He saved my life."

"By the time I came home, Sheriff Carver was dead," Cassandra said, and thumped the table with the flat of both hands.

"Couldn't have happened to a nicer guy," Sydney said, and drained her beer.

Francine licked her spoon clean of beef stew on both sides. "And here I thought I knew everything that went on in this place. Not bad for a first course. Bring on dessert."

24

The Barn

Sydney bent to pull her apple crumble from the oven, where she had put it to warm, while Cassandra stacked bowls and pulled out the vanilla ice cream from the freezer. As Sydney straightened and set the pan on the counter, she felt Cassandra press behind her. She turned and the two women squeezed each other tight in a wordless embrace.

Once the crumble dishes arrived at the table, for several minutes the only sounds were the scraping of spoons and murmurs of enjoyment. Steve retrieved five small cordial glasses from a nearby corner cupboard and poured everyone a dose of Francine's hooch.

Maude helped herself to a second pour. "Is it true you stole ten thousand dollars from my grandfather?" she asked Sydney.

Sydney swizzled a sip of *eau de vie* around her mouth, savoring the burn of the high alcohol content mixed with the perfume of pear. "It was more like six thousand, and I didn't steal it. I took it."

"There's a difference?"

"There was to me. He owed me the money for peddling his poison, and he wouldn't pay up. Said I had forfeited access to it when I went to rehab. Randy wouldn't dare get in the middle of that argument. I knew where Zile kept some of his cash, out at his lumber yard. I didn't take all of it. That would have been stealing."

"That was . . ." Maude paused and scratched her head. "Brave. It must have been exciting."

"Easy peasy," Cassandra said with a snort and poured more hooch into her glass. "Sydney knew when everyone would be away, and we strolled in like we were shopping at Brochu's."

Steve's eyes went round. "You actually helped?"

"Oh, for Pete's sake, Steve." Cassandra's voice was full of dismissive laughter. "I was seventeen, I had access to a car and a driver's license."

"It's a good thing Zile never found out you were a willing accomplice," Sydney said.

"Damn straight. And I don't intend to let him know about it, even after all this time."

"Didn't your grandfather pay him back?" Steve asked Sydney.

"Yup, with interest. But it seems like he's still determined to take it out of my hide one way or another."

"That's because it's personal," Maude said. "It's not really about the money. Trust me."

"Oh, I trust you," Sydney said. She slumped against the back of her chair. "When it comes to Zile and personal insults, there is no such thing as over and done."

"Ah. Speaking of personal insults, that reminds me," Maude said. "My father's memorial service is going to be on Wednesday afternoon. At the Grange in Hartwell."

Francine looked up from her second helping of crumble. "That's a hell of a time. A weekday night."

Steve grinned. "I suspect that was the only time they could find a place that would let them do it."

Francine smacked her lips in agreement. "I can't say I blame the funeral home. They've buried Jaquiths before, and there was always a fight. And none of the churches are going to allow a liquored-up shindig in their fellowship halls."

"I assume we should all go," Cassandra said.

The five diners exchanged glances.

"Well, *I* have to go," Maude said. "And I'll have to stay long enough for the service or whatever. My grandmother says I'm supposed to say something."

"We'll all be there," Francine said, and patted Maude's hand. "Come late and leave as soon as possible. Shake hands but don't touch the drinks."

"Our mother's viewing is tomorrow, and her service is on Saturday," Sydney said, feeling very discouraged. "Will anyone come to the service if Randy's is first?"

Francine snorted. "Everyone should be out on bail by then. Besides, I don't think she'll draw the same crowd."

With some trepidation, Sydney climbed into Francine's car. Her concerns were more about the weather than Francine's sobriety. Despite her bravado, Francine had only indulged in one glass of wine during dinner and a small glass of her own "hooch" with dessert. Meanwhile, the swarm of snowflakes had grown into a steady squall.

"Maybe we should stay here," Sydney said as she tried to get comfortable on the lumpy front seat. She eyeballed the evil seatbelt while Maude crawled into the backseat with leftovers.

"Don't be silly. I'll have you home in two shakes of a lamb's tail. Buckle up."

By the time they passed beyond the lights of Elway Farms, Sydney was hyperventilating. The snow smacked against the windshield in a solid assault. Visibility around the car was about one foot in any direction.

"What in tarnation are you doing?" Francine asked, her voice a sharp bark.

"I'm rolling down the window so that I can see the snow plow markers on this side of the road."

"Roll up that stupid window. I know exactly where I am."

"What are you talking about? It's a whiteout."

"Stop sign in fifty feet. Right turn. Go two miles. Straight at the next stop sign. Third stop sign in one mile. First streetlight about three miles after. That's Oriska. You'll see. I could drive this blindfolded. Now buckle your seatbelt and stop pumping your foot. There's no brake there. You're making me nervous."

Sydney submitted to the strangulating tug of the seatbelt and leaned back in her seat. An unfamiliar quiet settled around her head and shoulders as she made a concerted effort to relax and count her breaths. She was flying through a tunnel with no control over the past or the present, headed blindly into the uncertain future.

True to her word, going fifty miles an hour, Francine glided under the first Oriska streetlight like a 747 coming in for a perfect landing. Without slowing down, she swung smoothly around the twisting curves through the village and into the Graham driveway.

Lit in the blaze of the car's headlights, Sydney could see the rear ends of her mother's car and Maude's truck sitting in the barn. She blinked and frowned. Something wasn't right.

The barn doors should be closed.

No sooner had the thought entered her brain when the barn door began to slide. The hair on the back of her neck bristled. She couldn't see anyone inside, but Sydney didn't believe in ghosts. Someone was pushing the door shut.

"What the . . ." she said, still processing the scene.

"Hey. What's with the door?" Maude asked from the backseat, resting her arms on the two front seats.

"Shit," Francine said. She reached under the dash and pulled a lever. She was out of the car and heading for the back bumper by the time Sydney heard the trunk pop open.

Sydney struggled with the seatbelt and thrashed herself free to join Francine, rummaging in the car's trunk.

Francine finished loading a shotgun and handed it to Sydney. "You know how to handle one of these?"

Sydney took possession of the shotgun and hefted it a bit to test the weight. "It's been a while." She froze as Francine pulled out a large-ish looking revolver and proceeded to jam in a speed loader filled with bullets. "Holy shit. What are you doing with all this firepower in the trunk of your car?"

"In case you haven't noticed, Sydney, the countryside isn't necessarily all wood smoke and pumpkin spice."

"I do know that, but—"

"Normally, I keep these for when I'm out in the woods. Coyotes are a nasty business around here, and there are some other varmints. But sometimes the two-footed ones come poking around, too. I protect myself."

By this time, Maude joined them and took the shotgun from Sydney. "I know how to use this."

"We should call the cops," Sydney said.

"How the hell are we going to do that?" Francine asked, her voice lowered to a vicious whisper. "Your cell phone won't work here. Your landline phone is in the house. Your neighbors are all away for the winter, and it's snowing to beat all get out. I am not driving ten miles to Hartwell in this crap to tell them someone is in your barn."

Sydney wiped the slush building up on her face. "Keep in mind we don't lock the barn door, but we did lock the house. We left some lights on inside. Those look the same. Let's go in by the kitchen porch door and do a sweep inside. I'll call nine-one-one from the house phone once we're in."

Francine seemed to be itching for a fight, but she nodded. "Makes sense. Then Maude and me can check out the barn."

"Francine, is that handgun registered?"

"What? Don't be silly. It's practically impossible to get a permit."

"So, let's avoid calling attention to that. Don't fire unless you really need to." Sydney turned toward her sister. "Maude?"

"Shotguns are legit," Maude said.

"Yes, but we want to go to California, remember? Not get stuck here fighting legal complications."

"Okay, okay," Francine said, sounding resigned. "Let's sneak up to the porch, nice and quiet."

"No," Sydney said. "We're going to make lots of noise and advertise where we are because we would rather not find anyone around, inside or out. Right?"

Francine grunted and slammed the trunk shut. Maude and Sydney closed the car's side doors with as much noise as possible, and the three women trudged to the kitchen porch. Sydney stamped her feet to shake off the snow and unlocked the door.

Francine pushed her aside and rushed in first, holding her gun out in front of her in a two-handed grip.

Sydney bit her lower lip to keep her frustration in check. The 911 operator seemed exceptionally dense, but perhaps Sydney's nerves were getting the best of her.

"You say there is someone in your barn at the moment?"

Standing in the darkened dining room, Sydney tapped her foot and stared out the French doors facing the backyard. The snowfall had lightened enough that she could make out the unmarred pure coat of white covering the open space, hemmed in by the black bulk of the barn to the left and a dark smudge of trees to the right. She could hear Maude and Francine moving through the house, checking every room and closet.

"They may have left by now. We tried to make lots of noise."

"So, there is no one in the barn?"

Sydney suppressed a sigh. "I don't know. We don't want to risk checking."

"And the barn door wasn't locked, I assume."

"Uh. No, I guess that was an oversight on my part."

"No one locks their barn doors, dearie."

Sydney blinked and squinted. The side of the barn had changed shape. A bulge of black poked out from the barn siding, grew, and moved toward the yard. A chill radiated across her back as she realized someone had left the barn by the side door. She leaned forward and flipped on the backyard floodlights.

The black bulge transformed into two creatures. Varmints of the two-legged kind, to quote Francine.

Zile turned his face to the light and turned away. The other man—a massive presence—stood transfixed by the lights, like a moth drawn to the flame. Sydney had time to get a good look, but he was only vaguely familiar. Zile smacked the bigger man on the shoulder, and the two slogged their way across the far end of the yard and disappeared into the trees and the veil of falling snow.

"They're gone," Sydney said into the phone.

"Excuse me?"

"They left. I'm looking out the back, and I saw them leave the barn by the side door."

"Did you recognize these individuals?"

Sydney paused. "No."

"Stand by. A car will be there shortly. Please do not touch anything."

"Shortly" was not very specific guidance. Once Maude and Francine determined that the house was safe and untouched, they stood in the sitting room shuffling from foot to foot.

"Are you sure it was Zile?" Francine asked.

"Absolutely. The other guy looked sort of familiar. Huge, even compared to Zile."

"Gonzo," Maude said, stamping her feet in a nervous rhythm. "My cousin. Scary stupid."

"Oh. Gonzo," Francine said. "Sad case. Abusive upbringing and all. And he's not very bright. It's not his fault, but he grew up mean. He's not someone you'd want to meet on a dark night."

The three women studied the windows facing the road. Francine leaned one way, then the other.

"No sign of our friends in blue," she said.

"We need to be patient," Sydney said.

"No, we don't." Maude was already headed for the mudroom, carrying the shotgun Francine had loaned her. "Motherfucker. I'm his granddaughter."

Francine followed close behind.

"Wait . . ." Sydney said, and sank onto the couch as headlights swept the driveway. Her fears had materialized—the cops had arrived and were about to find Maude and Francine, illegally armed and in the barn.

25

Old Friends

Sydney found herself caught between running to meet the police or running to the barn to tell Francine and Maude to hide their weapons. She took two steps one direction, then the other.

Deep breaths, please.

Francine and Maude were not stupid. Or deaf. They would hear the police had arrived. Sydney's job was to give them a bit of time.

She stepped out onto the kitchen porch and waved.

The officer who climbed out of the squad car seemed familiar. Sydney squinted into the veil of falling snow twinkling in the car's headlights.

"Why, it's my old friend, *Monsieur* Fox," she said, and clapped her hands.

The officer bounded up onto the porch. "Apologies for being late. It's been a busy night." He gave her a hug. "Welcome back to the armpit of Central New York, Ms. Lucerno."

Peter Renard hadn't aged a bit. His red hair was styled in a brush cut, but he still had the youthful red cheeks and the same clever foxy grin like his name in French.

"I'd heard you were back. Your mother and all."

"Apologies for not reaching out, Peter. My goal is to get out of here as soon as possible."

"I used to love sitting in front of you in French. And trig."

"You were one of the good guys, Mr. Fox." Sydney rocked back on her heels. "I wish I had more friends like you still living here."

The two shuffled their feet as Sydney considered how dramatically different her life might have been if she had accepted Peter's offer for a date rather than going into the woods with Caleb Elway all those years ago.

"So. I've got a problem here. A break-in. Sort of."

Peter bowed and waved her through the kitchen door. "Let me guess. The barn wasn't locked. Or your cars. I gather the house was locked up. What's the story?"

Peter turned down Sydney's offer of hot tea, but he looked like he was about to settle in for the rest of the evening as he took off his heavy coat and sat down on the couch.

"That is a hell of a lot of stuff hanging around your waist," she said, pointing to his gun and other accessories. "Doesn't all that get in the way of crime prevention?"

Peter seemed suitably amused. She figured he must have heard that a million times a month, but he mustered up a sly grin and even a bit of a blush. "When you add in a bulletproof vest, it's a lot of weight. But if you come over here, I'll allow you to take inventory."

Sydney was half tempted. She hadn't realized how much she longed for a friendly face. In fact, if Francine and Maude hadn't been freezing in the barn, she might have even succumbed. They must have stowed their weapons long ago.

"I'd love to, but I'd like you to check out the barn. My sister Maude and Francine are out there poking around to see if anything is missing."

Peter bolted to his feet and snapped back into professional mode. Had he really thought she was here alone, what with Francine's car running in the driveway? *Ah well. Hormones are a powerful drug.* She should know.

He grabbed his jacket and gloves after he jammed his official winter hat back over his cute crewcut. "By all means. I need to check on that right away. I may need to come back tomorrow, once it's light."

"Let's go through the mudroom."

"Did you say Maude was your sister? You don't mean Maude Jaquith, do you?"

By this time, Sydney had opened the door from the mudroom to the garage.

"One and the same."

Maude and Francine were sitting in Maude's truck with the engine running and the heat blasting. The music blared so loud that Sydney had to pry open the passenger door to get their attention.

"Hey, guys. Please climb out and help Officer Renard with his assessment."

Maude turned off the ignition and climbed down. "Sure thing."

"You aren't supposed to be driving," Peter said, pointing a gloved finger at Maude.

"I wasn't driving. The truck was sitting perfectly still as I avoided hypothermia while you were canoodling with my sister."

Peter wiped his face. "Okay. But don't drive. You've only got a month or so to go before you have your license again."

"Two weeks. But who's counting?"

Francine oozed from the passenger side in slow motion, like a slug hitting cold air. Sydney noticed that Francine's eyes narrowed and her mouth pressed into a line when she checked Peter up and down. Not a member of the Renard fan club apparently.

Peter walked toward the back of the barn, keeping to the outside edge. The three women trailed behind. The visibility wasn't great. Two low-wattage bulbs high above lit the interior sufficiently to avoid obstacles, but not enough to reveal many details.

"It's always a mess back here," Maude said. "But it's an organized mess. Things are normally all stacked up into piles."

The little pack stopped to survey a pile of smashed furnishings. Peter ran the light from his flashlight over the devastation and over the floor.

"Are these your boot prints?" he asked.

The three women gathered in close.

"Some of these are too big," Sydney said. "The only people

back here recently have been me and Maude and the real-estate ladies."

"In winter these prints might have been made weeks ago," Peter said, scratching his chin.

"So true," Maude said. She looked at Sydney and raised her thumb and forefinger to form an L in front of her chest. *Loser.*

Peter turned his attention to the open sliding door on the side wall.

"It looks like the person might have left this way," he said. "Or come in that way."

"Good guess," said Francine, as Peter leaned out to peer into the tracks across the backyard. She seemed a bit impatient as well.

"I think there were two," he said, pulling his head back inside. "Unfortunately, I can't get a crew here until tomorrow, and all that will be mostly filled with snow by then. But we'll come by to make sure. Meanwhile, you be sure to lock up these doors with chains and take an inventory tomorrow when it's light."

"Sure thing, Officer. Thanks so much." Sydney offered Peter a bright smile to compensate for Francine's scowl.

After a tip of his hat, Peter sauntered out the front of the barn. Before he had driven away, Francine was leading a search party for heavy chains and padlocks.

"I think we should try the basement," Maude said.

Sydney could hear a low growl coming from Francine as they walked back through the house and traipsed down the rickety stairs to the lowest level. Sure enough, there did seem to be some padlocks and chains.

"Sydney." Francine's voice was sharp as she pulled out a thick coil of steel. "When you lived here you were still in high school. All the boys were single. Available."

"Yeah. So?" Sydney held a rusted padlock up to the light and tested its key.

"So, I can assure you that there is not an unmarried or unattached man over the age of twenty-three living in this county worth two cents. All the good ones have either permanently relocated or been scooped up."

Sydney hefted the lock from one hand to the other. "Are you saying Peter is one of the dregs or that he's 'scooped'?"

"His wife, whose name is Wendy, by the way, is pregnant with their third."

"What about my dad?" Maude asked, her hands filled with heavy chains.

"Oh, he was 'scooped,' but part of him never quite got that message. Sorry to say there are a lot more interesting women around here than there are men worthy of them."

"Sounds a bit harsh," Sydney said as they climbed the basement stairs. "What about Steve? He's not scooped and he isn't the bottom of the barrel."

"He's divorced. Two years now. And your friend Cassandra has got him all roped in, I hear."

"His mother must hate that," Sydney said, half under her breath.

"Don't presume to think you understand Mrs. Lee, Sydney. She dislikes lots of people because she sees their bad sides, what with running Steve's business. But she's no bigot. She'd love a couple of grandchildren, no matter what color."

As the three of them secured the barn doors with chains and padlocks, Sydney found a small, warm glow in her belly, which grew and forced up a smile. Her friend Cassandra had an important, worthy job, a solid life, and had scooped up one of the last free-range good guys still roaming around Oriska County.

Francine and Maude retrieved their firepower from the hidden corners in the barn, and the three women locked themselves into the house. Francine stripped down to her long underwear and crawled under a comforter on the sitting room couch, her shotgun on the coffee table and the revolver tucked under the skirt of the sofa.

"All those loaded guns don't make me feel much safer," Sydney said. "What if I need to come downstairs during the night?"

"Turn on a light and make a lot of racket," said Francine as she pulled up the comforter. "Don't pussyfoot around. Soft noises are a dead giveaway."

26

Sunday Brunch

Sydney rolled over at five a.m. and stared at the corded landline phone next to her bed, barely visible in the gray predawn light.

Over the past day or so, Maude had been talking. She had been talking to her grandparents. She had probably been talking to friends.

Why should this be a problem? A girl should have friends. Sydney may have lost most of her old contacts, but Maude grew up here, and she knew lots of people.

Lots of people who are junkies and worse. That was the problem. Despite her time away from this place, Sydney knew that some fundamental things simply do not change.

It seemed like she and Maude had spent every single minute together, but that was not completely true, and it had only been over a couple of days. *Hard to believe.*

Sydney mentally enumerated the ways communications were not limited to the phone line. Cell phone text messages seemed to get through, albeit unreliably. More likely Maude was using the same things Sydney used from her cell phone and laptop to keep in touch with her California life. Things like Skype and other online phone apps. And email, Facebook, and more.

Sydney rolled back to her other side, away from the phone. She knew she needed to get online and reach out to friends, but that would be later. It was too early to get up. Besides, she might risk being shot by Francine. Better to let sleeping dogs lie for a few more hours and get a bit more rest.

Francine did not hang around in the morning. Her guard dog duties were over. "I need to get to church by nine," she explained, and dashed out the door to scrape the snow off her car and disappear in a cloud of vapor.

"Which church?" Sydney asked after Francine had slammed the door.

"No idea," Maude answered with a loud yawn. "Do I have to go with you to get Grandpa?"

"Absolutely. We'll have lunch with him, and then we'll come back for Mom's viewing. After we can have dinner in Hartwell or with him."

"Back at the OPH."

"OPH?"

"Old people's home," Maude said. "That's what he calls it. Why are we having a viewing and a memorial service? Doesn't that cost more money?"

Sydney poured herself some coffee. "Don't give me a hard time, Maude. Please. I have no idea what to do when someone dies. Mr. Martinson said that some people will want to see Mom in person, in a casket. They feel like they can pay their respects directly. Other people like coming to a celebration of life."

"By which time, she'll be a pile of ashes."

Sydney poured another mug of coffee and handed it to her sister. "Does that bother you? Do you want her buried with her feet facing west?"

Maude strode to the kitchen window facing the backyard, mug in hand. "Not so much that. I guess she doesn't feel dead to me."

Sydney watched two Oriska County Sheriff's Department vehicles roll into the driveway. "That's exactly what the viewing is for—people like you who need to know. I saw her die. I told the Martinsons not to make her look young and beautiful with all their magic. She suffered, and I wanted her to look dead."

Maude took a deep swig of her coffee. "This is going to be grim."

Sydney headed toward the porch to greet the dedicated members of law enforcement who were forced to come out on a Sunday morning. "I'm not talking about zombie hideous. I'm talking about realistic death. No fancy makeup." Even as she uttered the words, she could feel her own trepidation swell. She must have been in shock when she made the arrangements straight from the hospital. The prospect of seeing her mother's body again filled her with an achy sense of uneasiness.

"I think I'd prefer the fantasy version," Maude said.

Supported by Peter Renard from the Hartwell Police Department, the members of the Oriska Sheriff's Department made a serious and dedicated effort to figure out who had broken into the unlocked barn the night before.

Sydney watched from the kitchen window as a team followed the half-buried footprints across the backyard, presumably to the location of a parked vehicle. Another team was taking impressions of boot prints by the side barn door that weren't filled in by snow. She was curious about how that process worked in cold and snowy conditions, but she suppressed the itch to get a little closer and stayed out of the way.

After half an hour, she and Maude bundled up and went to the barn to see if they could assist. Peter gave Sydney a brief nod and returned to helping the barn team members, huddled over key places checking for fingerprints.

The two sisters moved around the edges. Sydney wrote down notations of damage to furniture and crockery on a pad of paper, noting that Maude was looking into cupboards and drawers that weren't damaged. Was she looking for something? Perhaps whatever Zile was looking for?

After a few minutes, Sydney saw Maude's back stiffen. Her head came up and swiveled back and forth. Why was she being so furtive?

Sydney approached her sister and looked around. All she

could see was the dirty wooden floor with some scuffed boot tracks. "What's up?" she asked in a whisper.

Maude fixed Sydney with a look that read as a warning. When Sydney didn't back away, Maude looked down at her feet and very slowly swiveled her left boot on its heel. Beneath her boot lay two cigarette butts.

Sydney looked around for Peter, only to be interrupted by a sharp grunt from Maude. Maude shook her head and bent over to retie the laces on her left boot. When she straightened, the cigarette butts were gone.

Sydney felt the blood rise to her cheeks. She moved away to stand at the front of the barn, where Peter joined her.

"Not much in the way of fingerprints," he said with a quick grin that brought a smile to her face. "That is to say, there are lots of prints, but most are smudged and many could be as old as these—uh—wonderful collectibles."

"Do you need fingerprints from Maude or me? To rule us out?"

Peter's eyes lost their twinkle. "I think we still have yours on file." He coughed twice. "And we definitely have Maude's."

"It seems like if a person can change her entire life, she should be entitled to new fingerprints."

"Not the way it works, Sydney." The gleam made a reappearance as he turned to gesture to the interior of the barn. "Hey, before I forget. There's a party tonight at Denny Jenkins's. Remember him? Off of Cooper Road." He gave her a wink.

As one of the technical investigators approached, Peter's face returned to a deadpan. "We can confirm that they came and went through that side door from your backyard. They had parked a truck three doors down at the Mallons'. No one there in the winter, of course, but the Mallons keep their driveway plowed. Two sets of prints, one large, one huge."

Peter offered Sydney a sideways glance. "Not too many people around with feet as big as character number two. You got any candidates?"

Sydney snorted. "I've only been around a couple of days, remember? I saw two large shapes leaving last night from the dining room window, but no details."

A lie. Why was she not confiding that she had seen Zile? Something locked her tongue to the roof of her mouth.

She wanted to talk to Maude first. Her sister was protecting Zile and Sydney wanted to know why. She knew she was rationalizing, but her mind was made up. The guilty pang in her gut faded a bit. She could always call and tell the police later that her memory had been miraculously restored.

After the police and sheriff's team left, Sydney changed into a black skirt, black tights, and a gray wool sweater, topped with one of her mother's red and white scarves. Despite some prodding, Maude seemed content to wear her jeans, tartan flannel shirt, and Hartwell Central School hoodie. So be it.

As soon as they got into the car, the argument started.

"Why did you hide those cigarette butts?" Sydney asked. "We called the cops, and all those guys came out and worked on a Sunday morning, and you go and hide evidence."

"Hey. I didn't call them. You did. You were the one who didn't mention seeing Zile, remember? And then you had to dance with Officer Renard. I would have left it alone. Besides, we looked like idiots—leaving the barn unlocked." Maude slumped down in her seat and pulled out a cigarette.

"Not in here," Sydney said, and slapped the cigarette to the floor. They were on a straightaway. It seemed safe to take one hand off the wheel.

"Jeez, Sydney. Give this some thought. We don't want to make things worse. My grandfather was there for a reason. He was looking for something. You don't want to get on the wrong side of him."

Despite her protests, Sydney's gut agreed with her sister. "I'm already so far on the wrong side of Zile, I'm going to meet him coming the other direction." She returned her focus to the road.

The sight of their grandfather waiting for them in the lounge of Valley View Senior Living left Sydney breathless. How had he aged so much in only a few short days? Or perhaps her own memory refused to accept how he had changed.

Once tall and spare, he was now hunched and scrawny. As he hugged her, Sydney could feel every bone in his back and rib cage. She choked with guilt. She should be here every day.

"How do I look?" he said, waving to his apparel. "I don't go to many formal functions these days."

He wore brown corduroys with a brown checked shirt, a brown striped tie, and a brown plaid sports coat.

"I like brown," Sydney said.

"I see I could have worn my normal stuff." David waved toward Maude, beckoning her to come in for a hug, too. "Nice sweatshirt. My alma mater. Your mother's, too. I guess for all of us. Plus where I taught for so many years."

"I never graduated, Grandpa. Remember? I ran away," Sydney said.

"So you did." Her grandfather stared at her as if he wasn't quite confident how she was related to him.

They moved at a steady shuffle toward the dining room, where a special table had been set aside for their family gathering. Sydney knew Valley View boasted locally sourced products in the summer, but winter didn't offer many options. The food was wholesome, inoffensive, under-salted, and forgettable.

Halfway through eating his potatoes, her grandfather set down his fork and stared at Sydney. "I couldn't run away. I tried when I went to college and grad school, but I had to come back. I had to."

Sydney paused with her mouth open. She inserted a chunk of meat, chewed, and swallowed. "I wouldn't have made it without you," she said in a whisper.

"I wanted to leave when the whole thing with Randy bubbled up. It cost me my job. But you needed me." He looked at Sydney as if she were still ten. "And then there was Maude." He rotated to stare at his other granddaughter. "So, I stayed and stayed and now it's too late to run."

Maude tucked a piece of broccoli into her cheek. "Chief Carver wants to talk to Sydney about the death of his father. Got a whole thing up his butt about that."

Sydney choked and grabbed for her water glass. Her grandfather continued to cut his meat.

"I knew a Homer Carver," he said after a while. "He was the sheriff, not chief."

"Chief Michael Carver is Homer Carver's son," Sydney said. He should know this. Watching her grandfather struggle to remember made the food turn to ashes in her mouth.

"Ah. Right. I'm not allowed to talk about that." He stared at Sydney as he wagged his head back and forth. "No good would come from it."

Sydney sucked in her breath. Maude didn't seem to notice, and Sydney exhaled a silent prayer of thanks. "No good at all."

27

The Viewing

Sydney was so preoccupied with the prospect of seeing her mother's body, mixed with concerns about her grandfather's tendency to reveal old secrets, she barely noticed the drive from Valley View Senior Living to Hartwell. Her grandfather and Maude managed to keep up some kind of patter without her participation.

The human brain is remarkable. She made the entire drive on automatic pilot to Martinson Funeral Home and didn't put the car into a ditch or run into anyone.

Once at Martinson's, Maude and David continued into the viewing room as Sydney dallied at a table outside to lay out a guest book and a couple of pens. After a deep inhale, she stepped inside.

The room was smaller than she had envisioned based on her phone conversation with Bruce Martinson, the funeral director, with about twenty chairs arranged lengthwise across the space. Her mother's coffin was sitting in front with two vases of calla lilies, one at either end.

"What do we do?" Maude asked. "Sit here and contemplate the universe? Receive guests? For three hours?"

"Be glad we aren't Jewish," David said. "We'd have to sit shivah at the house for a week."

"That would be lame," Maude said. "We'd get, like, one visitor a day."

A slight commotion at the door provided Sydney the distraction she needed. As her grandfather and Maude went to greet visitors, she moved to the open casket.

There she was. Leslie Helen Graham.

She was dead. There was no mistaking the sunken cheeks and eyes. As Sydney had requested, any touchup was minimal.

And yet her mother was still lovely. Her red-blond hair spread out in artful waves, her delicate features unmarred.

Sydney bent to kiss her mother's cheek. It was so cold that she straightened immediately.

This is what they mean by closure.

Sydney turned to greet guests and sit in mourning.

Attendance was low but steady. Francine showed up wearing a shapeless denim dress and lipstick, accompanied by two women who did not look familiar. Part of the coven, no doubt. Cassandra and Steve put in a short visit.

Maude had the brilliant idea of taking selfies with the visitors and sending copies to their email addresses. Despite the solemn event, there were a few smiles, and Maude assembled a less anonymous record for posterity. The final total of attendees came to thirty.

Number twenty-nine was Lilith.

She slipped in when Sydney went to the bathroom and was standing by the casket, staring as Sydney returned. She met Sydney's eyes with a wooden gaze and turned her attention to Maude. She jerked her head to one side, and Maude followed her out of the room like a puppet on a string.

Sydney followed them to watch, staying about a foot inside her mother's reception room. Lilith looked once in her direction with a glance that said, *Stay back*.

The viewing was finally over. Sydney collected the sign-in book and went to settle up in the main office.

When she came out, Maude was talking on her cell phone as their grandfather stared at his hands on a padded bench in the lobby. Maude looked up and terminated her call.

"What did your grandmother want?" Sydney asked.

"She reminded me to bring food for Randy."

"You mean food for the guests at his funeral?"

"That's all taken care of." Maude waved away Sydney's words. "Guests are supposed to bring something for him. Something he'd really like. And talk to him about that. Encourage him to move on. It's an Iroquois thing. You're supposed to bring something, too."

Sydney rubbed her eyes. "He liked weed, but I'm fresh out."

"Well, you should think of something. She also said big trouble might find us because we're going to cremate our mother and not give her a proper burial."

"Hasn't it found us already?"

"She's serious about this stuff, Sydney."

"My apologies. I do respect her advice, but it's too late. Are you ready to leave?"

"I'm going to a party. You should come, too."

Sydney forced herself not to react right away. She helped her grandfather into his winter coat and boots. "Where is this party?"

"On the other side of Hartwell. Denny's."

"Peter mentioned this party. I'm not sure you should go."

"Shit, Sydney. You are not my mother. I am not a child." Maude pulled on her jacket.

Sydney tried to appear cool and collected. She handed his padded hat to her grandfather. "I do worry about you because I know you are tempted to use."

"Fuck you."

"I know how that goes, Maude."

"I am not a junkie."

"Great. How are you going to get to this party?"

"Matt will pick me up. Here."

"Who is Matt? And how will you get home?"

"Shit. Matt. Denny. Someone else. Leave that to me."

Maude turned her back and walked outside—presumably to wait for her ride.

Sydney squinted at the door. "Note to self. If I ever have adorable little children, please remember that this day will come again." If the stakes weren't so high, she might have appreciated the irony.

By the time Sydney escorted her grandfather to the car, Maude was gone.

"Do you want to come to the house for dinner? Stay the night?"

David Graham pulled open the passenger door and lowered himself onto the seat before he swung his legs over. He fumbled for the seat belt before he gave up and let it slap back against the doorframe. "No, I want to go home." He turned to look at Sydney. "That place is home now. I have friends. I have a routine."

Sydney squeezed his arm. "That's fine. How about getting an early supper at the Hartwell Diner? A little change of pace."

"No, it's omelet night at Valley View. With fries. That's what I want. Home." He leaned in close. "And don't worry. I will never tell."

On her way back from Valley View, Sydney stopped at the Hartwell Diner and ordered meatloaf takeout. Thrilled with full data access on her cell phone, she checked messages, news, gossip—fully engaged. *Civilization.* She wouldn't have noticed or minded if her order had taken an hour.

When her order was called, she reluctantly put aside her phone and looked up. Zile was sitting mere feet away. He wasn't eating. He was staring.

Sydney fumbled with her dollar bills. Somehow she managed to come up with the correct amount along with an outrageous tip. All she could think of was to get away. Back to the house. Back to anywhere.

Once she was locked inside with the barn secured, Sydney felt her breathing slow. The meatloaf was as good as she remembered. Better. *How many childhood memories meet that test?*

After dinner, she took her beer to her mother's quasi-office, sandwiched between the formal living room and the half bath.

What was she going to do with all these boxes and files? At least her mother's laptop was small enough to stuff into a backpack.

Where is the password?

Sydney sorted through papers and tossed piles out the door as she pawed through decades' worth of nonsense. She wanted to take a break and take care of her own business. She had friends, contacts, a job.

As she finished one pile of useless old utility bills, a corner of the small area rug curled up, released from the oppression of so much paperwork. Sydney pressed it down but at the last moment caught a flash of yellow.

A sticky note.

Sydney bent over. She lifted the edge of the rug and peeled off the note.

S1dney&Maud3

She fired up her mother's laptop and entered the password. Applications appeared, starting of their own volition.

The phone rang.

WTF?

Maude didn't even wait for hello. "Sydney, I need you now. It's bad. It's really bad. Come now."

28

Rescue Mission

Sydney took one step toward the door, returned to get her coat, returned to get her wallet and her cell phone, searched for the car keys. At last, she sat down on the couch and collected her thoughts, holding her head in her hands.

There was no point in leaving without knowing where to go. Dialing *69 led to a busy signal. Wherever Maude had called from was occupied. She tried Maude's cell phone number in the dim hope that service was available at "Denny's." No luck. What had Peter said?

Using her own cell phone, she texted Maude's cell and prayed the message would get out:

Send address. I'm coming.

Returning to the landline phone, she called Cassandra.

"Who the hell is this?" Cassandra's sleepy voice rasped. "It's after midnight."

"Don't hang up. This is Sydney. Maude went to a party, and she's in trouble. Do you know Denny Jenkins? He was in our class, but I barely remember him."

Cassandra's voice now came through as someone who was wide-awake. "Denny. Oh yeah. He lives in his parents' old place about three miles east of Hartwell on Cooper Road. Did she say what was wrong?"

"No, she said to come right away, and she sounded high."

Sydney heard a murmur of a man's voice from Cassandra's end of the line.

"Hold on. Steve's saying something," Cassandra said, her voice faintly muffled. More murmurs followed.

"Okay. We think it's probably an overdose or something like that. Denny's a good enough guy, but this crap is touching everyone these days."

"Should I call nine-one-one? I'm not sure Maude was able to do that. What if this is a false alarm?"

"Something tells me it's the real deal. Tell the nine-one-one operator about the call and that it could be drugs. We'll meet you there. I'll bring my naloxone."

"You've got that stuff in your house?"

"We've had a few ODs at school, and we've had calls from kids at home when a family member overdoses. I'm grateful they feel they can call us. Anyway, I have a small supply."

"Give me directions. I'll call nine-one-one and take off."

Sydney was not a religious person, but she did whisper a thank-you as she drove well over the speed limit toward Hartwell. The roads were clear of ice and snow, and the sky was bright with stars cheering her on. Following Cassandra's directions and a hazy memory of the back roads, she slowed as she drew closer to where she thought her destination lay.

As it turned out, the place was hard to miss. She crested a ridge and headed pell-mell for the valley below, where a distinctive glow lit up the bottom. Lights blazed from every room in a large farmhouse, and floodlights bathed the driveway and snow-covered pasture in a cold glow. She could see people running into the field. The strobe of two police cruisers made her stomach tighten.

More vehicles converged on the farm, several with flashing lights.

Sydney turned left onto Cooper Road and drove past the house so her car wouldn't be in the way of the official responders. She slid to a stop as close to the snowbank as she could manage. She left the car running and the keys in the ignition, and sprinted toward the house, only to bump into Chief Carver as he climbed out of his car.

This was not good. In her experience, police chiefs did not show up for run-of-the-mill problems.

"Whoa. Watch it!" he said. He stepped back and took a better look. His back straightened with recognition. "I hear you called this in."

Sydney tried looking around his shoulder. *Where is Maude?* "My sister called me. It sounded bad, and then the call was cut off."

"It's bad," Carver said, his voice gritty and low. "Stay out of the way and let us do our jobs. The EMTs will be here in a moment."

Sydney heard a shout and looked over her shoulder. Cassandra and Steve were dashing up the driveway right behind her. The three of them followed in Chief Carver's wake into the main hallway.

The scene inside was surprisingly quiet aside from a couple of Hartwell cops, who were assessing two people sprawled on the floor of the living room, to the left of the front door. The rest of the partygoers were milling around in the dining room across the hall and toward the back of the house. Only a few faces looked familiar. Some were still holding their drinks. Others were gathering their coats and starting to push for the back door.

Sydney forced her way into the living room, confident she would find Maude on the floor. She realized that both victims were men, and she exhaled in relief. That was when she recognized the second man as Peter Renard. The shock ran through her body like a gut punch. She could see Chief Carver's face sag, and he staggered back into the hallway.

As she allowed Cassandra to pull her away, she heard the cop working on Peter say, "Wooden chest. That's fentanyl."

"You go look for Maude, Sydney. Steve will help you," Cassandra said. "I'm going to tell these guys that I've got naloxone if they need it."

"Where are the EMTs?"

"Coming. I'm certain. With some fire department folks. Go find Maude."

Sydney wandered through the kitchen to a back room that looked like a combination of man cave and family room. A couple of small children stood in their pajamas, eyes wide. Maude was slumped against the far wall.

For several long seconds, Sydney was sure her sister had OD'd, too. She yanked Maude's head back by her hair. When Maude blinked and grunted, Sydney sank to the floor in relief.

Maude let her head fall back against the wall as a slow grin spread across her face. "Hey, Sydney. You came to the party after all."

Maude's pupils were pinpricks despite the poor light in the room. "You called me, remember?" Sydney said. She gestured to Steve, who was squatting next to the children. "You said you needed help. Steve and Cassandra came, too."

"Oh. I guess I did."

"Let's get out of here. I'm taking you home."

Once she was vertical, Maude seemed more alert and stable, giving Sydney hope that the danger of an overdose was over. *For the moment.*

"Do you think one of the EMTs would take a look at her?" she asked Cassandra, who had joined Steve by the two children.

"I think they've got their hands full," Cassandra answered. She checked Maude's pulse and looked at her pupils. "Her pulse is good, her nails and lips aren't blue, and she's breathing fine. Hey, Maude. How're you feeling?"

Maude scowled. "I *was* feeling quite fine, thank you very much."

"Do you know what you took?"

Maude pursed her lips. "Not exactly. Blue pill."

"How long ago?"

"I dunno. What time is it?"

"One o'clock."

"I guess about two hours ago. More or less."

Cassandra patted Maude's shoulder. "Okay. You're going to go home now, as soon as the police say you can leave. I'm going to give Sydney some naloxone to take with you, just in case."

Sydney watched Steve help Maude into her coat. "Should I drive her to a hospital?"

Cassandra handed Sydney two naloxone inhalers. "I don't think she's going to OD. At least not tonight. She needs treatment, but not the kind the ER can help you with. You know how this goes, right?"

Sydney fought back nausea that flooded in along with her own memories. "I was lucky. I never overdosed."

"You were lucky the stuff back then was more benign."

"Will the police let us leave?" Sydney asked Steve.

Steve rubbed his chin and looked at the remaining partiers. "I'm guessing all the interesting stuff has either been flushed down the toilets or disappeared out the back door. Once things are calmer, they'll collect a list of guests and addresses, and ask who brought the drugs or was selling them. Stuff like that."

"If Peter doesn't make it, there will be hell to pay," Cassandra said. "Maude, were you giving out stuff?"

"Hell no," Maude answered. "If I had anything I wouldn't have had to come to the party. That was Peter."

"Peter? No." Cassandra's voice was a hiss.

"Said he'd robbed the cookie jar."

Steve leaned in between the three women. "I'm going to take the kids upstairs. Their mother's in the kitchen. She doesn't look great, but at least she didn't OD. Her mother is Sally Banks. I'll call and tell her to get over here."

The cops had turned over saving lives to the EMTs and were in the process of bringing order to the rest of the scene, taking names and statements. Cassandra, Sydney, and Maude pushed their way to the front of the house, fighting the tide of people who preferred to avoid the police.

When they reached the living room, Sydney could see the first victim had revived somewhat and was sitting in a chair, prodded by a young woman in a Hartwell Fire Department jacket. Peter was gone.

"What about Peter?" Sydney asked.

Cassandra's face was expressionless. "It didn't look good. They took him in the first bus. At least Denny revived a bit."

Sydney felt the air leave her lungs. *Peter.*

Detective Oliver Payne gestured for them to come into the dining room, waving a notepad and pen. "Ladies? I have some questions."

Before she put the car in gear, Sydney leaned her head back and let starlight bathe her face through the sunroof. Another disaster averted for their family of two. She sent mental hopes toward Peter, somewhere on his way to the hospital.

"Are we waiting for something?" Maude asked, wrestling her seatbelt buckle into submission.

"Hopefully not for the other shoe to drop." Sydney put the car into drive and did a slow U-turn. "I don't know if you can wait for rehab until we get to California."

"Hey. Would you do it with me?"

Sydney snorted. "At this rate, it's not a bad idea, but I'm betting that would be very expensive."

"Well, Ollie Payne was less than thrilled when I told him Peter had supplied the drugs. I could tell he was itching to put that on me."

"Stay tuned. I don't think we've heard the last of this, particularly if Peter doesn't make it."

The car rumbled over a patch of ice and slid. Sydney turned into the swerve, and the car resumed its journey as if nothing had been amiss.

"I want you to know that I'm not a junkie," Maude said.

"What was all this about?"

"It's only an occasional thing."

"Well, at this rate, one of these occasions you'll be dead."

"So I've been told. Can we give it a rest for tonight?" Maude asked.

"I'm not letting this go." Sydney inhaled cold air and puffed out a cloud of warm white vapor. She leaned forward to wipe condensation off the inside of the windshield. "You mean too much to me."

29

In the Crosshairs

The next morning, Sydney broke one of her cardinal rules and turned on the television as she was tinkering with breakfast. Most mornings she much preferred the steady tones of NPR, a source that did not require her visual attention.

She made exceptions for extreme weather events—rarely an issue in California—or disasters. Peter's death was a disaster of the man-made kind. His passing was announced as part of every local news summary.

"In an era where drug-related deaths have become almost commonplace, the death of a young law enforcement officer strikes a very special fear and sorrow. Peter Renard was a ten-year veteran of the Hartwell police force and leaves a pregnant wife and two children," the perfectly coifed woman stated, her face appropriately solemn.

But not distraught. Distraught was for the victim's family and friends—friends like her.

Each summary of the situation brought more tidbits of information: Peter's background, the party . . . the likelihood that Peter was the source of the drugs, taken from the police evidence room.

The enormity of the opiate contagion hit her with a visceral slap. This was not a simple matter of stopping a couple of Canadians or thwarting the Jaquiths.

Time to take a trip.

Sydney filled a mug with coffee, two scoops of sugar, and a liberal dose of half-and-half. Placing one foot deliberately in front of the other, she made her way across the house and up the stairs to her mother's room. She kicked the door until Maude opened up, her hair a tangled mass and eyes still swollen from sleep.

"Here," Sydney said. "Be ready to leave in half an hour. We're going on a field trip."

Maude accepted the coffee with both hands and took a deep swallow. "Huh?"

"Peter's dead and that means the cops are going to be interviewing everyone from the party. They'd probably like to start with you."

"Shit. Why me? I told them everything last night."

"Lack of credibility? Maybe because they know that Zile and Randy have been major suppliers around here? I'm betting they'd love to find out that someone other than Peter brought those drugs to the party. We'll talk to them. No problem. However, let's not be first on the list."

Maude raised the mug to her lips and turned toward the en suite bathroom. "Got it."

Back downstairs, Sydney assembled breakfast sandwiches from English muffins, eggs, and cheese, and loaded other snacks and bottles of water into a bag. She poured the remaining coffee into travel mugs. She called her grandfather at Valley View to let him know they would join him for lunch.

A faint crunching sound caught her attention. Icicles falling from the roof? Tires on the driveway? She turned to face the door and met Zile's baleful stare. He had pulled open the glass storm door and was turning the doorknob of the door into the kitchen. If the upper half of the door hadn't been glass, she wouldn't have seen him.

Sydney felt a wave of prickling run across her scalp as every hair on her head stood to attention.

She assessed the distance to the nearest telephone—about twenty-five feet in the dining room—and the tire iron she had bought at Brochu's, resting on an antique settee to the right of the door. She could see the little thumb latch on the doorknob was turned to the locked position, but the deadbolt lock was not. How had she forgotten to lock the deadbolt?

Zile rattled the doorknob and scowled, but he didn't seem to be deterred. She could see that Zile was leaning against the locked door. Probably testing whether it would stand up to a shoulder strike.

Sydney swung around the island, moving fast. Her brain was headed for the dining room and upstairs to lock herself in the master suite with Maude. Her body seemed to have other plans. She ran toward the door, picking up the tire iron on the way.

She turned the thumb lock with her left hand and allowed the door to open. Zile stepped back. She reflipped the lock and closed the door behind her.

Lord, it is cold. She was standing in her padded slippers, draped in no more than a sweater, with a locked door behind her and an angry dog of a man facing her in ten-degree weather. She had spent a lifetime avoiding confrontations with Zile, and now she had trapped herself. She turned so that the tire iron was hidden behind her right leg.

"What the hell are you doing here?" Her voice built to a low roar.

Zile took another two steps back. "I want Maude."

Despite the danger, Sydney followed him, keeping him close—much too close. Her heart pounded so hard she could barely hear.

"She's hiding things from me," Zile said. "I keep calling, but she won't talk to me."

Part of Sydney's mind registered the question: When had he been calling? The other part surged forward.

"Why would she talk to you? You break into our barn with your thug? You hound her with calls? You show up like a maniac on our porch? Do you honestly believe this will make her inclined to talk to you?"

With each breath, Sydney took a step forward, and Zile backed up. Until he didn't.

He held his ground. She had to stop. He was way too big. He leaned in close enough for her to smell his stench even in the cold.

"She was there when Randy died. I know it. She took the drugs and the money and left his body there for me to clean up." Zile's eyes were slits, their color subsumed by the embers of hate radiating from his soul. "Those are mine, and I want them."

Sydney's tongue locked. She wanted to say that she had been the one with Randy, but the words stayed in her throat. She had put her own sister in danger.

"Get out," she said, leaning into Zile's face. "You aren't welcome here. You leave us alone."

Zile straightened up. His scowl relaxed and allowed his face to sag into a twisted smile.

"You remind me of your grandfather. A very stupid man, but he did have his principles."

"He's not dead. Just for the record."

"I saved your fucking life, you little shit. And you don't even know it, do you?"

Sydney blinked. "If you're talking about the money—"

"Fuck the money. You still owe me. With interest. You ask your grandfather who pressed the trigger that night. Remind him there is no statute of limitations for some crimes and no age limits on life sentences."

Sydney was transported back over thirteen years. She could smell the rancid mold in Randy's cabin and taste the same fear in her mouth.

Zile pushed out a belly laugh that came straight from Hell and yelled, "Now give me Maude. Maude! Get out here. Now!"

His right arm came up from his waist in a backhand blow aimed at Sydney's head. She ducked to her left and aimed a quick snap from the tire iron in her right hand at his left kneecap.

As the tire iron made contact, Zile's punch caught her high on her head and spun her around, unhurt but disoriented. A gratifying howl filled the air. She used her momentum to spin on her left foot and slash again at Zile's left ankle as she came around. She flipped her wrist and flicked the tire iron over to tap Zile's right wrist as he reached for the doorknob.

The two backed off, Sydney trying to regain traction in her slippers, Zile holding his right wrist and hopping on one foot.

Sydney raised the tire iron over her head and brought it down with both hands, smacking the flooring of the porch, sending frozen spikes into the air.

"Go. Get the fuck out of here and don't come back." Her voice rose from the center of her chest as it swelled to fill her entire body. She flipped the tire iron so that the prongs were facing out at the far end.

Zile turned and stumbled to his truck, parked in the driveway. Sydney followed in her own lurching stupor and let him climb in but smashed the left headlight before he backed away and disappeared toward Brochu's.

Now what? Sydney hobbled back to the porch. She was stuck outside a locked house without a key. The barn was chained shut. It was well below freezing.

And yet, she felt great. She had confronted the biggest bogeyman in her life on his own terms and survived. She wanted to lift her chin to the sky and crow, but she was too cold. She hefted the tire iron, considering the best way to break into her own house.

The door to the kitchen burst open. Maude pulled Sydney inside and wrapped her in a bear hug.

"Oh, my God, Sydney. You are some crazy bitch. No one has ever done anything like that for me. Ever."

30

Slip of the Tongue

Sydney's limbs were filled with fizzy energy, buoyant, lighter than air. She swayed in her sister's arms, savoring the warmth of the kitchen and the clean, nutty smell of Maude's skin and hair.

"Time to go," she said, unwinding her embrace. "A few minutes ago, I would have loved the sight of a patrol car. Now I'd still rather postpone the conversation."

"Tell me about it," Maude said. She looked Sydney up and down. "You're still shaken up. You should let me drive."

Sydney was back at the kitchen island, packing their breakfast and snacks. "You really do not think things through, do you? The cops are probably on their way here right now to talk to you about the party. The chances of crossing paths are quite high. This is a small place, and they know exactly what you look like *and* the status of your suspended license."

Maude picked up two bags of provisions. "Well, if you put it like that . . ."

"I do. Give it a rest and don't ask me again until your license is valid. If I need you to drive, I'll tell you."

"Bitch." Maude headed toward the mudroom.

Sydney picked up the remaining bags and her purse. She wanted to make sure that all the doors were locked before they left.

* * *

The weather had warmed to a balmy twenty-five degrees, the sky was blue, the roads were dry. It was the perfect day for a road trip.

"You know," Sydney said, glancing at Maude slumped in the passenger seat, "up in the Sierras this is what winter is like all the time. It does snow like crazy, but when the snow stops, it's warm and bright and wonderful."

"I thought you said you never go there."

"I feel an exception coming on." Sydney grinned at the salt-streaked windshield and gave it a futile squirt of wiper fluid. Her confrontation with Zile had imbued her with a sense of power. She recognized this was temporary. Zile was an unrelenting maniac. Normal people like her couldn't sustain his level of paranoid intensity.

They passed two patrol cars going the opposite direction. Maude swiveled in her seat to watch them.

"Are they turning around?" Sydney asked.

"Not yet, but you might want to drive a bit closer to the speed limit. Just saying."

Sydney grunted and eased her foot off the accelerator.

"What did Zile mean about calling you?" she asked. "I never heard a call come through for you."

Maude examined her hair for split ends. "Sometimes he uses text. You know how it is around here for coverage. Those come through on my cell phone, but not always. So mostly he uses Skype."

Sydney pondered this as they slowed for the stop sign at the top of the hill above Hartwell. Ordinarily, low-hanging clouds and weather wrapped the town in obscurity, but on this day, the valley stretched out like a picture postcard of wholesome opportunities in a winter wonderland.

"Zile as technology maven. I never would have guessed."

"It took me a long time, but at some point I realized the problem isn't that he's not smart. He's plenty smart. He's just twisted," Maude said.

"Yup." At least her sister had some street sense after all.

Sydney glanced in the rearview mirror and down the two side roads as well as at the road ahead. No cars from any direction.

"So, what's all this about Randy and whatnot?"

Maude sniffed and wiped her nose. "Shit, I don't know. Yeah, I was supposed to help with distribution, but I have no idea where they were meeting or what happened to the merchandise. Or any money."

The winter sun was low in the south, hitting the streaky windshield and dispersing a blinding haze into Sydney's eyes. She could barely make out the road.

The fizzle in her blood drained away. This was the time to tell Maude that she was the one who had been with Randy. She was the one who had put her sister in Zile's crosshairs.

As she opened her mouth, a truck pulled up behind them and honked. Still half-blinded, she lifted her foot off the brake and rolled down the hill into Hartwell. She needed to give this more thought—phrase it precisely the right way. *Soon.*

Patricia Atwood was hovering by the reception counter as Sydney and Maude signed in to Valley View Senior Living.

"Your grandfather says he's not feeling well. He may have another cold or something else. We're going to bring lunch to his apartment for you."

Sydney introduced Maude. "Patricia is the director of services here. This is my sister."

"We've met. I heard about your policeman who died. Such a shame."

"There won't be a cause of death listed in his official obituary, I'm guessing," Sydney said, finishing her signature with a flourish.

"They ought to put one." Patricia gathered up some papers. "It might make people realize how bad this epidemic is. Drug victims are not a bunch of losers. They are the people we love."

David Graham rubbed his hands together, stood, sat, stood.

"Sit, Grandpa. Your food is getting cold," Sydney said.

The three of them were seated around a drop leaf table next

to the pass-through to their grandfather's kitchenette. It made for a cramped and intimate eating experience.

"I like to eat in the dining room," he said. "It feels like home now. The food's good. I have my favorite table."

"You weren't feeling well. You don't want to expose other residents if you're sick."

"The food looks great. Let's eat some," Maude said, tucking into the baked chicken. "Ketchup?"

David rubbed his hands on his thighs. "Something isn't right."

"My grandfather—my other grandfather—told us to tell you something," Maude said, placing her knife and fork neatly across her plate.

David stared at Maude. "Go on."

"He said, 'Remind him there is no statute of limitations for some crimes and no age limits on life sentences.'"

"Syddie had gone to that damn cabin. She was sleeping with Randy."

A silence descended on the room like dense fog. Sydney swallowed her last bite of chicken. Her grandfather was using her childhood nickname. He was wandering deep into the past. "Not true, Grandpa."

"Only because I caught the two of you in the living room," David said, mopping away tears. "I'm glad your mother was away."

"She ran off to Montreal or Quebec City so she could speak French and pretend she was in another world," Sydney said.

"Dealing with you was stressful, Syddie. It was hard for your mother. She wasn't cut out for that."

"You slept with my father?" Maude's eyes were round. At least she wasn't jumping up and down. Not yet.

"It didn't quite come to that."

"But only because of Grandpa."

Sydney raised her hands high and lowered them to pull her hair. "It was a terrifying time. Caleb had disappeared—killed by Sheriff Carver, if he was to be believed. Caleb was the love of my life. I've never felt anything like that since. It ached so bad. I started using again. Randy was there."

"Not exactly a unique excuse."

Sydney found Maude's calm more unnerving than her tantrums.

"Carver was a son of a bitch," their grandfather said, talking to a spot on the opposite wall. "He had killed people. Legally. That little boy in the drug raid. They burst into that trailer and opened fire."

"The boy survived, Grandpa," Sydney said. "He was hurt, but he made it."

Her grandfather didn't seem to hear. "I didn't expect to find Carver at the cabin when I followed you. I thought it might be Randy or Zile, but I was glad I brought my gun." He shifted his focus to Sydney. "He would have killed you. I heard him say it. I couldn't let him."

No one spoke for several long beats.

"I'm not a killer," David said. He stood and favored each of his granddaughters with a pat on the head and a kiss. "I'm very tired now. I wonder if I have a cold. I'll see you soon."

Sydney followed him to his bedroom. She could see his gait was unsteady as he shuffled in and closed the door.

31

Fessing Up

"Sydney—" Maude said.

"Shhh. No talking until we're in the car. Let's clean up. I'll ask the desk to send an aide to check on him. Tomorrow he won't remember."

"I am not going to *shhh*," Maude said. She dumped the dinner plates and utensils into the sink, raising a loud clatter. "He can't hear a thing once he takes out his hearing aids, and I don't care if *he* remembers or not. *I'm* going to remember what he said today."

Sydney shouldered Maude away from the sink and turned the water on full blast. Maude leaned over and turned off the water. Sydney tried to pry her sister's fingers off the faucet, but Maude kept an iron grip on the valve with one hand and pushed Sydney against the counter with her other.

"Don't be such an infant. We are going to have this conversation," Maude said.

Sydney studied the kitchen floor. Maude picked up a dishtowel and gave it a crackling snap against the refrigerator.

"You do know that protecting a murderer is a crime, right?" Maude asked in a hiss.

"Hmm," Sydney non-answered.

"At the very least you withheld information about the death of Sheriff Carver. That's obstruction of justice or whatever."

"Thank you for your legal advice. I'm glad you aren't my lawyer."

"Does Steve even know about this? No wonder you don't want to talk to Chief Carver about his father. Shit, Sydney. Our grandfather killed that guy and you protected him."

"I didn't lie," Sydney said. "I had already left for California by the time I found out the chief was dead."

"Sounds like hairsplitting to me."

Sydney turned her back on Maude to face the sink. This time she turned the water on low, and she picked up a sponge. "It was in early November. After the mess with Randy, I knew I had to leave or I'd be dead soon. That was when I went to Zile's lumberyard with Cassandra. He owed me money, and I took it. After, I went to the cabin because I knew Randy always kept a bit of his stash there, and I needed enough Oxy or something to tide me over until I could get to California. I was hoping Randy would be there, but he had run off someplace."

"You found something?" Maude took a rinsed plate from Sydney's grip.

"Yeah, there's a little door with a hidden spring in back of the woodstove. Hard to get to when the stove's hot. Which it wasn't. I found a couple of bags of stuff in there. That was when I heard footsteps on the porch. Someone big and heavy. I hid in the back of the coat closet under the stairs."

"Sheriff Carver?"

Sydney handed Maude another plate. "He wandered around the place. I think he was taunting me, giving me hope he'd go away. But instead he yanked open the closet door and pulled me out by my hair. He handcuffed me to the front leg of the woodstove."

She bent over and rested her forehead against the cheap Formica countertop. "Shit. I've got to sit down."

Trailed by Maude, Sydney shuffled back to the main room and took her seat at the table.

"He reminded me that he had tried to be nice and gain my cooperation. I was supposed to be his girlfriend and to take Caleb's place as his snitch. But I squandered that opportunity and my time was up. I was going to join Caleb in Schwarzer's quarry."

"People who go in there don't get second chances." Maude eased into a chair.

"Man, I was breathing so hard, I was about to faint. And I was ready to chew my hand off to get out of those cuffs," Sydney said. "Then I heard a creak. I thought I'd imagined it. Carver didn't seem to notice. The door to the side porch opened so fast it made both of us jump. And there was Grandpa, holding that old Luger."

"The sheriff must have been a bit upset."

Sydney wiped the sweat from her upper lip. "Yup, one warning shot from Grandpa took care of that. By that time, Carver was all smiles and chuckles. He had just been trying to frighten me, you know?"

"Sounds like he did a good job of that."

Sydney grunted. "Grandpa disarmed him and made him cuff himself to the stove. Grandpa took me outside and told me Ron Elway, Cassandra's father, was going to drive me to Philadelphia. I had a one-way ticket to my father in California and the drugs from one bag to last me until I could get into rehab."

She looked up and met Maude's eyes. "He told me to throw the sheriff's gun into the Hangnail and run home, no matter what I heard."

"He waited until you left?"

"It's funny. I asked him if he was going to kill Carver and he said no, he wasn't a killer. He was just going to wait until I was far away. So I took off."

"But?"

Sydney leaned back with her eyes closed. She could feel the dank chill of that November night, smell the moldering leaves, and feel the sumac and poison ivy brush against her. As she passed the mask she had carved into the maple tree, she could see the lights from her mother's house ahead, peeking through the trees. *Almost home.*

"There were two shots. I almost went back, but I chickened out."

Maude snorted. "Sounds to me like you finally did something smart."

They finished the dishes in silence. Maude took over washing while Sydney dried and put away leftovers. They grabbed their coats and Maude closed the door to their grandfather's apartment with a soft click.

The parking lot was almost empty. The sky was the color of faded denim. The moon had already risen. Clouds filled with the promise of snow were moving in from Canada.

"I've never told anyone that story," Sydney said. "Not even Cassandra. Not Grandpa, either. It's on our list of taboo topics. But I think his tongue is starting to slip."

"Don't worry. I won't tell and I don't think anyone else would believe him at this point."

"He saved my life, Maude. I know he'd do the same for you if he could. But it's okay. I'm here and I will protect you."

"Jeez, Sydney. Button up your coat. You can't protect anyone if you catch pneumonia. Where are your gloves? Put your hat on." Maude fussed with Sydney's hat and wrapped her own scarf around Sydney's neck. She leaned forward and gave Sydney a light kiss on the cheek. "We need to look after each other now. That's what families do."

32

Money Makes the World Go Around

A deputy sheriff with the last name of Cox had left a message on their answering machine, saying he and Detective Payne from the Hartwell Police Department had come by to talk to Maude. They would be back around nine a.m. the next day and hoped to find her at home.

"It doesn't sound like attendance is optional," Maude said. "Should we call Steve?"

Sydney wrote down the deputy's phone number. "They aren't saying you have to go to the station. Yet. That would be more ominous. Call Steve while I fix dinner."

"My turn to be talked down off the ledge," Maude said.

Whatever Steve said seemed to work. Sydney allowed herself a glass of wine for dinner and offered one to Maude.

"Nah, I'm not much of a drinker."

"You could have fooled me. You did go through Mom's entire liquor cabinet that first night."

"I was upset. It's not my usual go-to thing."

"Yes, I know what your usual is," Sydney said, and poured another glass of cheap red stuff. She pushed the dishes to the far end of the dining room table and set Leslie's laptop on the corner, where they could both see the screen.

"It's as good a time as any to dig into what is on this beast," she said, pressing the power button.

"Earth to big sister. We don't know the password." Maude leaned back in her chair until it groaned in protest.

"The good news is, our mother wasn't exactly a cybersecurity role model."

Maude leaned forward. The front legs of her chair hit the floor with a bang. "Show me."

Sydney tilted the laptop screen back and forth so that it caught the light from the overhead chandelier at different angles. She pointed to a little section at the bottom of the black bezel surrounding the screen.

Maude leaned in. "Is that it in pencil? S-something-something-d-something-3."

"She also wrote it on a sticky note. 'S1dney&Maud3.'"

"She wrote it right on the computer? Unbelievable. What kind of secure password is that?"

"Brace yourself," Sydney said as she entered the password on the login screen. "I'm betting she never backed it up either."

"Let me look." Maude rested her fingers on the trackpad.

"Hey." Sydney shoved Maude's hand away. "I'm doing the driving here."

The fight for the cursor was short-lived. "This is boring," Maude said, and rocked to the back feet of her chair, gazing over Sydney's shoulder.

"Hang in there," Sydney said. She paused for a sip of wine. "I want to make sure we have the overall picture and where all the edges are before we dig into the fun stuff."

"You sound like you're constructing a jigsaw puzzle. Edges first, like Mom." Maude yawned. "What kind of fun stuff?"

Sydney hunched forward to study a report of the hard disk usage. "Email. Browser history. Do me a favor and check her office for USB drives."

Maude groaned and left the room.

Sydney made her mental inventory. Older version of Windows, no recent patches applied. One hard drive with the usual things. A directory with income tax information going back at least seven years could be helpful. Most of the pictures seemed to be from her antiques and collectibles inventory. There were a few baby pictures of Sydney that made her throat close. She squinted at the ones of Maude. Even at three, her sister had a maniacal gleam in her eye. *Go figure.* One entire folder dedicated to pictures of Randy. *Too much of a bad thing.* Still, seeing him seventeen, twenty years ago, took her breath away. No wonder her feelings about him were so conflicted.

By the time Maude returned with a couple of USB drives, Sydney had started on email.

"I cannot believe a woman in her fifties lived such a dull life," Maude said after about thirty minutes. She rested her forehead on the table.

"Okay. We can come back another time. Let's move to browser mining."

"Wait, wait, wait." Maude pointed to a folder. "Why are there so many unread messages in *Drafts?*"

Sydney felt her stomach turn over once. "Uh-oh." She clicked.

Sure enough. The Drafts folder was filled with conversations between Leslie and Randy.

"What the hell?" Maude asked.

"Primitive security thinking," Sydney replied. "Rather than send email to each other, it looks like they both had access to this account. They would compose a message to the other person and rather than send it, they'd save it to the Drafts folder. These days encryption is so cheap and easy if you want to communicate in secret."

"This Drafts folder hiding is a thing? Really? Why would they do that?"

"I'm guessing they wanted to hide something. And I don't think it was family Christmas gifts."

Maude and Sydney stared at each other. Sydney blinked first. "Do we really want to find out?" she asked.

"Do we have a choice?"

Aside from an occasional hiss or groan, neither sister spoke a word as Sydney clicked through the messages. After close to half an hour, Maude sat back and rubbed the back of her neck. "It's a good thing they're both dead, or they'd be looking at some serious time."

Sydney closed the email application and opened the browser. "All those drug deals." She stopped. "I shouldn't be shocked about Randy. I mean, we knew Randy has been hip-deep in dodgy business for a long time. But Mom. I think I might be sick."

"At least it was only about financing on her side," Maude said.

"Cold comfort."

"Should we delete all of that?" Maude asked.

Sydney tapped her fingers on the edge of the laptop. "Based on my television law experience, no. We'd be guilty of tampering with evidence. More important, this is all stored on servers someplace 'out there.'" She waved her fingers in the air. "We'd be caught in no time if someone decided to take an interest."

Maude ran her fingers through her hair, forcing it to stand up at odd angles. "Okay. Where's the money? According to Steve, she had modest checking and savings accounts. Add to that her less-than-massive IRA. Not exactly chicken feed, but not big money. This shows she was coming up with twenty or thirty K at a shot and getting back more than that most of the time."

Sydney opened the browser and started checking history and bookmarks.

"Here we go. Drumlin Bank. Who the hell are they?"

Maude squinted at the screen. "Never heard of them. Small and local, that's for sure. Looks like it's over near Ithaca. Let's hope her username and password are saved."

The two sisters leaned forward, their heads close to touching. Sydney squealed when her mother's user credentials autopopulated the log-in screen.

"Holy shit," Maude said.

"I'm guessing she didn't tell Steve about it."

"Couldn't the cops or the Feds claim all this?"

"If they find out about it. I'm keeping my fingers crossed she paid taxes." She scrolled through more transactions. "Looks like she did."

"Over $300,000 in this account. How would she manage to file taxes? Based on what?"

Sydney waved her hands toward all the piles of furniture and knickknacks. "All this crap. The perfect money-laundering scheme. How do you think Zile does it with his lumber yards and woodlots?" She clicked through various tabs and screens.

"Good news. It looks like I am an official co-owner of the account." She offered Maude a Cheshire smile. "I think that means it doesn't have to go through probate. I'm guessing that means *we* don't have to pay taxes on it." She paused. "I'd better check with Steve. And a CPA."

Maude scowled. "I sure hope you're right. Why am I not on the account? So typical. She didn't love me enough."

Sydney patted her sister's hands. "It looks like she set this up when you were about fifteen. She loved you plenty. You were too young. This belongs to both of us."

"So. We're rich, right?"

Sydney closed the browser and shut off the laptop. "It's a lot of money, but not enough to make us rich. Plus, I don't know how I feel about touching this."

"You pick an awkward time to get all moral. Think of this as money for my rehab," Maude said. She stood and stretched her arms to the ceiling.

"That would be a nice ironic twist." Sydney remained seated. "Here's a thought. Do you think Zile knows about this money?"

A scowl of irritation flashed across Maude's face, followed by a thoughtful squint. "Tricky. Based on the emails, I don't think so."

"Right. It looks like Randy hid Mom's participation from your grandfather. Why would he do that? Any theories?"

Maude eased back into her seat. "To protect us? You and me?"

Sydney grunted. "I'm sure Randy cared for you, but he had no love for me. He wanted to protect Mom. In case he was sent away or even died, her money would be safe. I don't think he was so secretive because of the law. Not entirely. He wanted to make certain she was shielded from Zile."

"You don't think my grandfather knows about this account?"

"Given that he is hounding you for a lot less money than this, I'd say no. And we need to keep it that way."

Maude studied her lap.

"Maude?" Sydney grabbed her sister's hands. "Do you understand why it is so important that your grandfather doesn't know about this?"

Maude yanked her hands away. "Duh. Don't lecture me. I'm not stupid. He'll want it all."

"Not merely 'want' it, Maude. He'll demand it. I believe he could be capable of killing for it."

"I know how to keep my mouth shut," Maude said. "You worry about your own mouth. Don't tell your precious friends Cassandra and Steve." She stood and strode toward the kitchen.

Sydney decided one more glass of wine wouldn't hurt. Maude opted for beer. The two sisters slouched on the sitting room couch and sipped.

"Where's Randy's part of the money?" Sydney said.

"Got me. No idea."

Sydney sat up straight. "Tell me about his will. What did Steve tell you?"

Maude slouched lower. "He left his double-wide property to my grandmother. He left the cabin property to me. No money to help pay taxes and whatnot, thank you very much."

"No money at all? I thought there was a few thousand."

"Yeah, that won't go far."

Sydney stood and made a quick trip around the coffee table to chase her swirling thoughts. "Nothing to Zile directly?"

"Nope."

"So, if our mother managed to squirrel away over $300,000— after taxes—where is Randy's share?"

Sydney could see the cogs in Maude's brain were turning, albeit slowly.

"Huh," Maude said. "I hadn't thought of that. And my grandmother didn't mention it."

"Well, I can guarantee you that Zile has thought of it." Sydney reached over and yanked Maude's beer bottle away. "Listen to me, Maude. Your grandfather is on the hunt."

Maude scowled and made a swipe to reclaim the bottle. "Gimme that. I don't think my grandmother knows where the money is. Or even that it exists." Her face brightened. "If we can find it, this time I really will be rich."

Sydney handed Maude her beer. "Don't be sucked up by greed. Your father and two men died for the equivalent of pennies. Greed is poison."

"Thank you so much for your concern, Sydney. And don't be a hypocrite. Money makes the world go around. I know that much."

"You should warn your grandmother. She needs to find that money and move it to a safe place."

"You do know my grandfather would kill her if he found out she cheated him out of something like that, right? He would ferret out any place she put it. My grandmother is no dummy. She'd be better off letting him have it all." Maude blew a solemn note across the top of her beer bottle.

"If that's the case, I don't think you should count on anything of Randy's."

Maude peeled the label off her bottle, one strip at a time. "Unless we find it first."

33

Community

The clock beside her bed said 7:30, but it was lying, Sydney decided. Too dark. Besides, the winds were howling. Thanks to the creaks and groans from the old structural timbers, she didn't even need to look out the window to know that snow was flying parallel to the ground. Accumulation might be minimal, but visibility would be close to zero. She wondered if the cops would put off their visit. *Probably not.*

She flung back the covers and made her way to the bathroom, banging on the bedroom claimed by Maude on the way.

In the shower, Sydney decided she needed a day off from Oriska County. She wanted to spend hours and hours online, immersed in email and work and twittering and Facebook and every Internet-enhanced indulgence that would take her away from this place.

Practically speaking, she did have a couple of critical things to accomplish. She composed her to-dos between her shampoo and conditioner cycle. Communicate to HR at her company that she was sad about her mother, but things were going swimmingly. Log in and pretend to do some work. Figure out with her development team how to continue to cover her ass. Get some emotional support from people who had no idea what it was like to be sitting in the middle of this mess. Let her housemates know that Maude was about to arrive.

She needed to fake it until she could make it.

*   *   *

Sydney was making pancakes when the black Ford Explorer pulled into their driveway at exactly nine a.m. She figured it had to be the cops. Who else drove big, shiny cars with no road salt rust?

Bless their pointed little heads.

The car was unmarked, so she wasn't sure if it was a county vehicle or police department issue. It featured a welded steel grill guard in the front, multiple lights and sensors hanging from the sides, and big snow tires that churned through the ice up the unplowed driveway like a lawnmower clearing dandelions in spring.

She ran to the bottom of the stairs. "Maude!" Her voice was one small decibel level below a scream. "The cops have arrived. Get down here. Now."

Maude arrived looking serene and unrushed just as the two officers climbed onto the kitchen porch and knocked on the door.

"Hey, Chris. Hey, Ollie," she said, and waved them into the sitting room.

Detective Oliver Payne was a too-familiar sight. Sydney was surprised to recognize Deputy Sheriff Christopher Cox, one or two years ahead of her in high school.

Chris accepted a cup of coffee, black, but said no to pancakes. Payne's face was stony and expressionless. He took his coffee with half-and-half.

Chris Cox ignored his coffee and seemed content to talk to Maude standing up. Sydney noticed that Payne deferred to Deputy Cox in this as well. That suited her fine. She had no history with Cox aside from a few awkward high school slow dances in the gym back when he had wrapped his long arms around her waist and kept his body a respectful, barely touching distance away. Oliver Payne was a different story.

Sydney stayed behind the kitchen island, trying to be as invisible as possible. She busied herself finishing up pancakes and washing at the sink, listening attentively.

Cox opened with a casual statement. "I hear that Peter Renard brought bags of pills to the party. Is that true?"

Maude answered straightaway. "He said he'd gotten access to a stash in the evidence room."

Payne jumped in. His voice sounded shrill. "How do you know that was true?"

Sydney glanced over her shoulder from the sink. Cox and Maude both stared at Payne.

"I don't," Maude said after Payne stopped pacing. "He could have been lying."

Cox turned toward Maude, blocking Payne to one side. "Maude, I need to ask you this. Did you bring anything to the party that night?"

Maude shuffled her feet and looked at the ceiling. "A bottle of rum. I'm under twenty-one. So arrest me. I stole it from here."

Sydney leaned across the island. "I will attest to the fact that my mother had a bottle of rum here and it's now gone."

Cox gave her a polite smile. Her input did not seem to be important, and she returned to the sink. Maude was holding her own.

Minutes later, Sydney heard the kitchen door open and close, and turned her attention back to the sitting room. Officer Payne was already outside. Chris Cox stared at her from the other side of the island. Sydney looked left and right. No sign of Maude.

"Do you know how many overdoses we have here every month? Every week?" Cox asked.

Sydney studied the last pancake in the frying pan. "I know this is an epidemic. My mother was addicted to Oxy and pills. I was a heroin addict. I know my sister uses. It's too late for my mother. I managed to kick my habit, and I'm trying to save my sister." She looked up at him. "Tell me what to do."

Cox patted the countertop and rubbed his hands along the soft wooden surface. "If I knew, I'd be made King of the County. I do know I need your help. I'd say 'get out of here,' but I don't know where you could go that's far enough these days. Meanwhile, keep Maude away from Zile. Same for you. And help us. Please. Don't hide anything."

Sydney rescued the last pancake and watched him leave.

* * *

Sydney caught up on email and social sites. She found herself staring at the screen of her laptop, waiting for the next hit, the next response.

She left the dining room and found Maude in front of the TV in the sitting room.

"Are you watching that?" Sydney asked.

"Background noise."

"Let's label a few things." Sydney handed a pad of colored dots to Maude. "I've looked up renting a van. We can haul stuff out to California if we want."

Maude studied the dots. "You've got enough room?"

"We'll rent storage. We should only take the stuff we really treasure. Green we take. Yellow maybe. Red is interesting but not critical."

They started upstairs, moving room to room. Fortunately, most of the decisions were easy, but a few were hard.

She pointed to the bed in their grandfather's former room, now surrounded with boxes and stacks of newspaper. "That bed frame was a rope bed," Sydney said. "Generations of Grahams were made there. Maybe even you and me."

As she placed a green sticker on the frame, a soft noise caught her attention. She turned to see tears streaming down Maude's cheeks.

Oh shit.

"What?" Sydney asked, in what she hoped was her nonjudgmental voice.

Maude wiped her face and sank down onto her haunches. "All I ever wanted was to live in this house as a family. Now I'll never have that." Her shoulders shook.

Sydney stared out the window at the snow flying sideways, taunting her. Every time she made progress, something pushed her back.

"It's a great house," she said. She winced. She had hated living in this house since the age of ten. "And we're living here together for a while."

Maude made a gagging sound. "You never would have lived here again with my father."

Sydney lowered herself to sit on a narrow patch on the bed not covered by collectibles. "My issues with this place are much bigger than Randy."

Maude sank onto the floor into a loose cross-legged tangle. "But you're cured. You aren't a junkie anymore."

Sydney patted Maude on the head and turned it into a stroke. "I've tamed the urge to use. But the reasons I did will never leave me." Her hand stopped, midstroke. "It was so sweet. That feeling when it kicked in. Heroin for me." She resumed stroking her sister's hair. "But I was ready to leave it behind."

Maude grasped Sydney's hand. "I'm not a user. Not really. It's a sometimes thing."

"If you were talking about wine, I might buy that. Not opiates." Sydney swallowed. Her chest ached. Was her sister ready? As Deputy Cox had said, there was no place they could run to without this taint. What good would moving to California bring to Maude?

"My people are here. I pull my strength from this earth," Maude said.

Sydney let her hand grow limp and studied Maude anew. Golden brown skin, light eyes, sun-streaked dark hair, long limbs. A unique person with her own internal setting.

"You're so lucky," Maude said. "White people fit in everywhere."

Sydney snorted. "It's not as easy as it sounds. You're lucky to have a center."

Maude looked up at Sydney, her eyes now dry. "My grandmother wants me to go to her people—my people—for a cure."

"Is that what you want?"

Maude's mouth puckered, her eyes squeezed shut. "I'd have to consult with a seer first. The seer would figure out what type of treatments I'd need." She glanced up at Sydney. "Seers are scary. They really can see everything about you."

Sydney stroked her sister's hair one last time and gathered the colored stickers. "I'm not saying it wouldn't help, but there's no miracle cure for addiction. Herbs and drugs might help with a few symptoms and get you clean. For a while. But getting clean is only the start. It requires hard work—deep in the soul—to cross over for good. And more to stay there. You're going to have to go through that process no matter which path you follow."

Maude stood and stared at Sydney. "You wouldn't stay here with me?"

"I'm envious," Sydney said. "To have a community that really cares about you and wants to help is a gift. I never had that. I can only offer you what it took for me. I managed to go through rehab all alone. Once I got to California, my father dropped me off and didn't talk to me for over a year. I could make calls, but Grandpa and Cassandra were back here. Mom might as well have been on the moon. She was always in denial. I couldn't get her to talk about anything but the weather. When I called, Randy wouldn't even speak to me, and he never sent email or anything. Not that I expected it. And I was convinced Zile would have killed me if I came home."

"You might be right on that score," Maude said. "I'm scared of him, and I know he actually does love me. Or at least he used to."

"Let's give this sorting project a rest. It's making both of us more sad, and I've had enough of sad," Sydney said. She headed for the hallway. She stopped at the door and turned to face Maude. "I can't stay here. Just can't. But I can't make you come with me. If you do, I'll help you get through rehab and beyond. And the good news is, you have a 'people' to come back to if that's what you want. If you don't come, I'll do my best to help, too."

Sydney spent the rest of the day connecting with friends and colleagues online. When she needed to stretch, she moved from room to room, making her own choices on what items would merit green stickers.

Much as she craved resolution with Maude, she decided that pressing hard would not help. *Less is more.*

The two drifted back to the kitchen when their stomachs told them it was time for food. Exchanging few words, Maude made real macaroni and cheese, not from a mix, and Sydney assembled a salad from the simple bits that were about to wilt in the refrigerator. Sydney was pleased that Maude didn't appear grumpy or sulking, merely deep in her own thoughts.

Once dinner was served, Sydney broke open a bottle of red wine labeled Premium California Red Blend. It was inoffensive and drinkable, she decided, and preceded to guzzle a couple of glasses before she was halfway through the meal.

The wine didn't make her any happier, but she was more relaxed. She had to get over trying to control every outcome, she decided. *Think outside the box.*

The hard facts were that her grandfather was determined to stay and her sister needed her community. Meanwhile, the ground under her own feet was growing softer and softer. The harder she tried to push off and leave, the lower she sank.

Deep in her private thoughts, a new plan started to form. They would clear out most of the house, but not sell it. It wasn't worth much, anyway. They could rent it until Maude was healthy enough to return. She could go to heal with her Mohawk relatives. Sydney would not come back to Oriska, but she could manage to fly into Syracuse every four to six weeks and stay up there, or maybe Ithaca, and visit Maude and her grandfather.

"I've been thinking," Maude said, breaking out of her own reverie. "Did Grandpa ever tell you he killed the sheriff?"

Sydney looked up from her wineglass. Was this her second or her third? It was definitely her last. "He said we could never talk about it. But I heard two shots as I was running home from the cabin. I knew he had a gun."

"I was only six, but we know the sheriff's body wasn't found at the cabin, correct?"

"They found him in his official SUV on the back road to Schwarzer's quarry."

"Where the sheriff was planning to dump you, right?" Maude asked.

"Not just me. It was where he dumped Caleb. Others, too, probably." Sydney drained her wineglass and smacked her lips.

"Someone was sending a message?"

"Or had an ironic sense of humor," Sydney said as she gathered the plates.

"Since when did Grandpa have an ironic sense of humor?" Maude asked. She followed Sydney into the kitchen. "Listen to me. Even if you believe he was desperate enough to kill someone, do you really think an old guy like Grandpa could wrestle a rather large body into a huge SUV, drive—what?—at least ten miles to the quarry, wipe everything clean, and then walk all the way home?"

"He was a very spry seventy-six," Sydney said.

"It still doesn't fit. He's so moral. He'd call the cops and claim self-defense. Or dump the sheriff in Hangnail Pond. Not go hauling a body all over the back roads and walk all the way home to make a point."

"You think he had an accomplice?"

"Just saying. It doesn't add up," Maude said.

"He was alone. I'm sure of it."

Sydney rinsed, and Maude stacked the dishwasher. Each went back inside her own thoughts.

"Do you want to watch something on TV?" Sydney asked. "I've got the streaming thing all set up now."

Maude waved her away. "I've got to plan what I'll say tomorrow."

"Oh, right. Randy's memorial."

"My grandmother says I must speak and it should be respectful."

"Try to keep it simple and very short. Even if they're sober, only a few people will remember what you say."

"You'll remember, Sydney. You're the retentive type."

Sydney smothered a laugh. "In that case, write it for me. Tell me what I need to know about Randy. Convince me he was a person I should remember fondly."

34

Forgiveness Can Wait

Sydney could tell something was off as soon as she and Maude drove past the Hartwell Grange, the location for Randy's service.

For one thing, the lot was packed with trucks. Large trucks. Very few cars. Many trucks took up more than one slot, and several were parked askew. Men dressed in what looked like winter hunting gear stood in clumps. She could see bottles of brown and clear liquids being passed around, and an abundance of shared joints as well.

As she passed by, several men turned to watch her with stares that did not strike her as friendly. She guided her mother's car back to the street and parked around the corner. She noted two horse-drawn buggies farther up the same block. Mennonite and Amish farms had flourished over the years, and she had seen the warning signs to watch out for slow-moving vehicles on twisting roads in the area.

At least someone had plowed the sidewalks around the Grange, making the walk back to the hall much safer from oncoming traffic and not as sloppy as walking in the street. If Maude was bothered by walking the gauntlet past the crowd in the parking lot, she didn't show it. She even nodded amiably to several men and called them by name. Sydney didn't recognize any of them. She tried to ignore the cold chill running up her back.

Propped against the siding next to the front door, a hand-lettered sign read:

MEMORIAL SERVICE   2:30–5:00

RANDAL IORAHKOTEH JAQUITH

Sydney sounded out Randy's middle name. "*Io-lah-go-deh.* Is that right?" she asked.

"Close enough," Maude answered.

"Does it have a meaning? Is it an animal name?"

"Names are usually picked based on the environment of the clan animal. Randy was a turtle, so names would be about things like water or rain. *Iorahkoteh* means 'the sun shines.'"

A memory of Randy basking on the rocks near his cabin on a hot summer day flashed behind Sydney's eyes. She opened her mouth to ask if Maude had a similar name, but her sister had already disappeared through the door.

Sydney wondered if she and Maude would be the only women at the service, but it turned out a contingent of community women and girls were inside, along with a larger gathering of men and boys. She noticed the faint smell of fresh liquor breath and a distinct scent of lingering marijuana, even though no one was smoking indoors.

Randy's coffin lay in front of a large fireplace at the far end of the room, angled askew so that his feet faced the door. The top section was open, revealing his face and upper chest. She could see piles of food and presents on a table beside the coffin.

Cheap, dreary flower arrangements were clustered here and there, in no particular pattern. At the other end of the room, in front of the pass-through to the industrial kitchen, a table had been set up with what appeared to be pictures and memorabilia. The space between these was filled with metal folding chairs that made her back ache just to look at them.

She knew a few of these people by sight but only a couple by name. Most of the attendees appeared to be contemporaries of Randy's—in their mid-thirties, or considerably older. Cassandra, standing on the far side of the room with Steve, waved to

Sydney and Maude, pantomiming that she had saved them two seats.

"Why is the coffin askew?" she asked Maude.

"The building isn't lined up quite right. His head needs to be in the east."

"And his feet facing the west," Sydney said, recalling her conversation with Randy at the cabin. "Probably not going to be cremated, right?"

"My grandmother says no way," Maude said in a low voice. "We're expected to put in an appearance at the coffin."

Sydney trailed Maude to the front. Maude had made an apple crumble for Randy. Sydney had settled for a set of maple sugar snowmen from Brochu's.

While Maude spoke to Randy and showed him her crumble, Sydney took a mental inventory of the items on the table: packages of venison, sausages, cakes, bourbon, something that might have been marijuana . . .

Maude tilted her head to indicate it was Sydney's turn. "I've got to talk to my grandmother. Stay out of trouble."

Sydney studied Randy for a few moments, planning her speech. From what she could see of his waxy face, his spirit was long gone.

"I know you had a sweet tooth, so I brought you these maple sugar candies. I'm sorry we didn't get along better. I'm sorry you didn't get the life you deserved."

Done. Sydney turned and moved toward the back of the room.

The dress code seemed to be business casual, Oriska-style. Men wore clean flannel shirts—tucked in with white T-shirts showing—and blue jeans. Surrounding the casket and scattered throughout the room were people wearing what Sydney recognized as Iroquois clothing.

Sprinkled in clumps were men with long beards and women with lacy hair coverings. She decided they were Plain People—Amish or Mennonite—from the local farms.

Sydney dumped her coat on the chair Cassandra had saved and headed to the table covered with pictures, located next to more tables covered with food and drink for the guests. It took her several minutes of squeezing past enthusiastic eaters to reach the photographs.

The pictures appeared to have been tossed onto the table in random clumps. Or perhaps people pawing through them had pushed them around. She did her own sorting and studied the pictures of Randy as a baby, young boy, and high school student.

One edge of a vividly colored photograph peeked from under a stack. She was sure that was her mother's face, barely visible.

She pulled out the photo and held it up to catch the light. A teenage Randy sat on porch steps and grinned into the lens, a baby propped up on his lap. Sydney's mother, Leslie, sat next to him, looking impossibly young. Sydney could see why Randy would have fallen in love with the willowy, strawberry-blond beauty with lanky limbs and a sweet smile. Sydney brushed away tears.

Leslie must have been in her mid-thirties. Only a few years older than Sydney herself now. Sydney recognized the porch. It was the side entrance to their house in Oriska. The baby was Maude, although her hair was lighter.

Based on the bright leaves littering the ground and her mother's heavy jacket, the picture must have been taken in late autumn. The baby looked to be about four or five months old. Maude appeared to scowl off to her left. Probably trying to figure out how to get into trouble already, fascinated with a future she couldn't reach yet.

A thumb and finger snatched the photograph from her hands. Sydney followed the photograph and came face-to-face with the twisted features of Lilith Jaquith, inches from her own.

"This isn't for the likes of you." Lilith's spittle sprayed Sydney's face.

Startled, Sydney brought her hand up to wipe away the dampness. She opened her mouth to respond, but her attention was pulled to the double doors leading to the parking lot. A large man in camouflage canvas clothing struggled and flailed his arms, trying to free himself from a clump of men in similar attire. *Zile.*

Lilith wheeled, following Sydney's wide-eyed stare. "Shit." She appeared to forget about Sydney and pushed her way to the opposite end of the hall, toward the casket. The photograph fluttered to the floor, forgotten.

Zile fought his way up to the casket. All eyes and most of the guests in the room moved in the same direction.

Sydney picked up the photo from the floor and turned back to the table. She shuffled through the awards and pictures, stuffing several that seemed promising into her bag. Shifting her gaze to the developing mêlée at the opposite end of the hall, she edged her way down the far side, where Cassandra and Steve had circled the wagons, pulling chairs around them in a protective barrier.

"My boy. My boy." Zile was shouting over and over, his face streaked with tears and unwiped snot. "He's mine as much as yours, Lilith. He's a Jaquith. My precious boy."

A throng of men congealed around the front of the hall and separated into two factions—those trying to keep Zile from reaching the coffin and those trying to help him gain access. A massive man in canvas coveralls who dwarfed everyone else was clearing the way for Zile. It was hard to get a clear view through the chaotic mêlée of bodies, but Sydney assumed that was Gonzo, Zile's factotum and mischief enhancer.

Lilith was a good foot shorter than Zile, but she appeared to be sober, which gave her an edge. She blocked Zile's path to the coffin with a wide stance and a determined glare.

"*Ohnorah:kowa:. Tsi-tohk.*"

Sydney's rusty Mohawk vocabulary consisted primarily of profanities. It sounded like Lilith had just called Zile a big prick and told him to go eat shit. Sydney held no special love for the woman, but she gasped and covered her mouth, assuming Zile was about to pummel his wife or have Gonzo do the honors.

Instead, Zile pouted and stomped his feet but rocked back and let his group of supporters drag him away from the confrontation. Sydney thought he looked more confused than angry by that point.

On the other hand, Lilith was just getting warmed up. She screamed obscenities in English and Mohawk, and ran after Zile, throwing herself into the thick of the fight. Face-to-face with Zile, she reached out and slapped him, hard.

"You did this to our boy, you son of a bitch. *Rariwaksen*," she said, screaming loud enough for all to hear. "He did everything to please you. He danced to your tune. And this is what we have reaped."

Zile stopped struggling. His face crumpled. Sydney figured the fight was over, but Zile rallied and launched himself with a roar at the coffin. The table holding the coffin swayed, teetered onto two legs, and crashed to the floor, taking the coffin with it.

The shouting stopped, and a soft, murmuring silence filled the room, punctuated by sobs from Zile.

Men and women halted animosities and rushed to right the table and replace the coffin. Sydney was relieved to note that the coffin seemed undamaged, although Randy appeared to have rolled onto his side.

Lilith and a man in a dark suit—a visibly unhappy Bruce Martinson from the funeral home—opened the top and reset the body and draping. Zile sat down on a chair and moaned.

The drone of conversation resumed a normal volume and came to a halt once again at the appearance of Chief Carver and another Hartwell police officer in the doorway. They were followed by two additional officers. Carver was the only one Sydney recognized.

Carver and his team moved toward the coffin. Sydney noticed that they positioned themselves smoothly between the previously fighting groups. Even though she had seen the struggle, she would have been hard-pressed to identify more than one or two individuals in each cluster. These were people who knew one another well, and that included the police.

Sydney swiveled her head. Zile and Gonzo had slipped away, presumably through the kitchen at the back. She edged forward until she reached Maude, cowering against the wall by the fireplace.

"Lilith, you don't look so good," said the chief. "We got a call about a disturbance. Do you need some help here?"

"Oh, fuck you, Michael Carver," Lilith answered with a snarl. "Like father like son. I know what you think of the likes of us. You've got what you wanted."

Sydney scanned the faces ringing the crowd at the front and around the room. Some hid smiles, entertained by the spectacle. Others scowled and muttered. From what she could tell, most had united in their dislike of the police presence, and several nodded along with Lilith's accusations.

"Now, Lilith. No one wants to see you hurt. I'm only here to make sure you're okay," Carver said.

"Your lot has already cost me everything. Your father beat me bloody once, and you know it. Randy too."

Carver's face paled, and his mouth formed a thin, grim line. "That was a long time ago."

"Not long enough. You want us to forgive and forget, but I can remember everything like it was yesterday. No forgetting means no forgiving."

Carver wiped his face, shiny with sweat. "If you'll let me, I'll pay my respects to Randy right now. I do have an obligation to uphold the peace."

The combined throng retreated a few steps, signaling a truce. The chief stepped forward and leaned over the casket, holding on with both hands. Sydney could hear him murmuring something, but she couldn't make out the words. He didn't bring a gift.

Done with paying his last farewell to Randy, Carver and his men edged their way to the door. Sydney noticed they were careful to keep their backs to the wall.

Once they had left, a collective sigh filled the hall. Sydney looked down and realized that Maude had sunk onto a chair and placed her hands over her ears. Sydney bent over to rub her sister's shoulders as Maude lifted her face, full of pain and confusion.

Sydney made her way back to her seat, and the ceremony commenced several minutes later.

Lilith spoke first, but the noise level in the hall was too loud. Sydney caught very few of Lilith's words. She left her seat and edged forward to hear more of the service. Most of the testimonials spoke about Randy being a standup guy, a pal, someone his friends could rely on. At least two women mentioned how good-looking he was, and several other women were weeping. Someone told a raunchy story.

When it was Maude's turn, she stood and put one hand on Randy's coffin. Her eyes searched the room until she found Sydney.

"When I was small, I understood that Randy was my brother. Only later I realized he was my father. But one thing was never in doubt: He loved me. When I am upset, I remember the way it felt to be cuddled in his arms, and I feel safe.

"When I understood the truth, I found I had a bigger family. I also had a strange and cranky sister, who lived in California. She never came to see us, but my father would say, 'You need to be like Sydney. She's smart and making her own way. If you ever really need help, you go to her. She'll be in your corner.'

"My father was always in my corner. I know he cherished me and I will always cherish him."

Once Maude finished, Sydney slipped back to Cassandra and Steve, making use of her tissues. She could sense the emotional temperature in the room remained high. The Plain People had left, as had most individuals she would have classified as "friendly."

Cassandra leaned across Steve's lap. "Time to get out of here. Now."

"I want to give my respects to Lilith and look at Randy," Sydney said.

"Don't be stupid. Stand up and move toward the door, right now," Steve said.

"Go get Maude," Cassandra said, pulling on her coat. "There's going to be more bad times here, and we need to be far away."

Cassandra took the lead, bumping others out of the way, fighting against the crowd until they reached the parking lot. Sydney grabbed Maude hovering near the door, pleased to see the drinkers and fighters were moving inside and the parking lot was nearly empty.

35

Thwarted

Sydney stayed up late planning her mother's service. After witnessing the chaos of Randy's memorial, she was determined to give her mother a sedate and organized event. She propped her laptop on her knees and set to work right after dinner as Maude curled up next to her and stared blankly at a series of mindnumbing television shows. She had said almost nothing since they left Hartwell.

At midnight Sydney reached for the remote and turned off the television. "All set. You don't have to give a speech if you don't want to. Do you want to check this out?"

Maude stood and walked toward the stairs. "I trust you. I'll look later."

Upstairs, Sydney paused as she brushed her teeth. Was she really becoming so inured to violence? Or was a massive case of PTSD building up inside? Despite the ridiculous scene at Randy's service, she could detect no lingering nerves.

She needed to leave Oriska and soon. A few more items to take care of and she'd be headed to California.

For once Maude was up early. Stretched out in bed, Sydney heard her sister head downstairs, and a few minutes later the smell of fresh coffee wafted into the room. She swung her feet to the floor and headed to the shower.

She was almost done dressing when she thought she heard Maude yell something.

"Can't hear you," she shouted. "I'll be down in a minute."

As she padded downstairs in her stockinged feet, she felt a cold breeze whistle past her.

Where the hell is that coming from?

"Hey, Maude. Are you trying to heat the outdoors?"

Sydney charged through the dining room and into the kitchen. Sure enough, the door to the kitchen porch was wide open. Maude was nowhere in sight.

Stepping farther into the room, her view to the driveway opened up. She could see Maude—kicking and screaming—being shoved by Zile and Gonzo into a truck with a shattered headlight.

A shot of energy raced up Sydney's spine and filled her limbs with fire. She sprinted for the door.

Her feet in their soft socks skidded as she hit the icy sheen on the porch flooring, and she landed hard on all fours. Regaining her footing, she grabbed the only item she could see that might be useful—the ice chopper she had used the day before. A five-foot iron rod was attached to a flat, tapered flange at one end. Good for pounding through ice and scraping underneath, but perhaps not the best tool for fending off two large trolls that had crawled out from under their bridge.

Yelling as loud as her lungs would allow, she leaped off the porch and swung the flange end down on Gonzo's exposed wrist so hard that her feet left the ground.

Gonzo yelped and dropped Maude's legs. His voice was high for such a large man. Ignoring the intense cold under her feet, she flipped the chopper and lunged forward, trying to catch Gonzo on the side of his throat. The blow might have been crippling, but Gonzo's feet slipped and he landed on his well-larded backside.

Sydney followed up with another blow with the flange to the top of Gonzo's head and turned her attention to Zile.

By this time, Maude had squirmed her way out of Zile's grasp.

"Get inside and lock the door. Call nine-one-one." Sydney's voice was ragged from her screaming.

Gonzo hauled himself to his feet and scrabbled into the passenger side of the truck's cab. Zile took a step toward Sydney. She kept the blunt end of the ice chopper pointed at Zile's face, a few short inches out of the range of his hands. As he stepped forward, she did, too, and thrust the chopper at his eyes.

He stepped back, then forward, taunting her, a wide grin plastered on his face.

"You tell your grandfather to keep his mouth shut. Our deal is still on," he said in a soft hiss.

Once Gonzo was seated on the passenger side, Zile slammed the door and backed around the front of the truck and climbed into the driver's seat. The engine roared to life as he closed the driver's door. Sydney barely had time to swing the ice chopper down on the passenger side mirror before the truck sped backward out onto the road. Zile twisted the wheel to face the truck downhill and roared off toward Brochu's, the mirror dangling like a broken wing.

Sydney made sure the truck was out of sight before she hobbled back to the porch. Her feet were so frozen she could barely feel them.

Maude opened the door, and Sydney stumbled into the kitchen.

"Run hot water in the tub," Sydney said, bending at the waist to catch her breath. "Did you call the cops?"

"No, I was looking for something to kill my grandfather," Maude said over her shoulder as she ran to the downstairs bathroom.

Sydney limped after her sister. She put down the seat on the toilet and scrunched up her face, trying not to cry as the blood started to flow back into her frozen extremities.

Once the tub had several inches of water, Sydney transferred her bottom to the side and submerged her feet—socks, jeans, and all—into the warm water. Gradually the pain eased, and she slipped off her clothes and sank into the tub, letting the water rise.

"Go get me some coffee. Black, no sugar," she said to Maude, who was hovering at the sink. "I'm going to lie here for a while."

Her feet turned from white to pink. They were tender and a bit puffy. Sydney decided that a trip to the doctor would be indulging her wimpy side.

"Do you still want me to call nine-one-one?" Maude asked when she returned with the coffee.

The water had reached Sydney's chest. She sank down deeper into the calming warmth. "Yes, they need to know about Zile." She blew a few bubbles into the rising water and took a long sip of the coffee. "Tell them the truck has a smashed front headlight and a dangling side mirror."

"Don't you think calling them might make things worse?"

Sydney sat up so fast that water splashed over the side. "Worse than what? Holy shit, Maude. They were going to haul you off and do God knows what to you. We need to call in the cavalry here."

Maude offered one of her pouts. "Okay, but in my experience, the cops don't help much. Just saying."

"How'd he get inside? Wasn't the door locked?"

Maude blushed. "My grandfather knocked. He didn't seem angry. He was smiling. When I opened the door, he pushed inside, and Gonzo rushed up from around the corner of the house."

Sydney balanced the coffee mug on the narrow side of the tub, closed her eyes, and sank back into the water. "Go call. Let me think."

By the time she climbed out of the cooling bath, Sydney was thoroughly warmed and wrinkled like a prune. She wriggled her glowing pink toes on the purple bath mat. They were throbbing a bit but with no remaining white tips. Even if she went to the hospital, they would probably want to wait and see. She might be prone to frostbite for the rest of her life.

No problem. She cursed steadily as she hobbled on her heels upstairs for dry clothes. She never intended to frequent cold-weather climates after this visit.

It was time to leave. The confrontation with Zile made that clear. If she and Maude needed to stay in Central New York a while longer, they could hole up someplace safer than this house. Once dry and re-clothed, she packed a bag.

Downstairs she made her way to the tiny room filled with papers and junk her mother had called an office. Somewhere under all this, there had to be a printer.

She found an antiquated printer under a thick stack of folders. She clucked in dismay at the old style paper with perforations along the side. She wasn't sure she could even buy that anymore, but her mother seemed to have several boxes stashed away, just in case.

Sydney leafed through the folders before she continued her search and sat down abruptly. The folders were filled with her old high school assignments and report cards. Painful memories of those awful years flooded back with a vengeance.

Sydney pressed her fingers to her eyes. She set the folders on the floor and continued to excavate the office. After another five minutes, she found a brand-new, fancy all-in-one device tucked behind a file cabinet.

She balanced her laptop on a box and connected it to the printer. She sorted the photographs she had collected from Randy's memorial debacle and proceeded to scan each one to her hard drive and print out two copies on photo paper.

"What are you doing?" Maude asked, plunking down peanut butter on toast. "Here. This is for you."

"Making sure you have a heritage," Sydney answered, sinking her teeth into the toast with a deep moan of gratitude. She shoved the pictures and the copies over to Maude. "I rescued these from the service yesterday so they wouldn't get trampled. I'm making scans and copies of all these before I give them back to Lilith."

Maude looked at the pictures, lingering over each one.

"What's this one? Is that Caleb?" she asked, and pointed to a picture of Randy with his arm around a young black man. Each held a can of beer and grinned into the camera.

"The one and only," Sydney answered. "Randy was celebrating his first big drug deal all on his own, without any help from

Zile. He asked me to take that picture." She winced at the memory of her complicity in the event.

"They look happy," Maude said, running her fingers over her father's face. "Still, he should have known better."

"That should be his epitaph," Sydney said, restacking the prints. *Mine too.*

After all the scanning and printing was done, Sydney put the originals into a manila envelope. She tossed all the high school folders her mother had saved into a large plastic bag.

She trotted upstairs to her bedroom, relieved to note her feet felt much better. She retrieved the chain with Randy's ring from the drawer next to her bed and looped it over her head.

Maude was pacing in the kitchen. "I've been thinking about Randy's money," she said.

"You know my thoughts on that pile of poison." Sydney stuffed her manila envelope into a shopping bag, ready to leave on her errand.

"He must have stashed it someplace. It would be too much money to keep as cash."

"Leave it alone, Maude. You've got troubles enough with your grandfather."

"Finding Mom's bank account got me thinking. Where's his laptop? I know he had one. He always seemed to have it with him."

"Well, if it was in his double-wide, it is now either burned to a crisp or ruined by water damage. Maybe it's at your grandparents?"

"Nope, not according to my grandmother."

Sydney wanted to slap Maude, but she slapped her own forehead instead. "Jeez Louise, Maude."

Maude scowled. "You said I should warn her. I called her on Tuesday. She wasn't home, so I left a message. At the service, she told me she'd looked but couldn't find it."

Sydney thought the top of her head might pop off. Every nerve was tingling in alarm. "Are you crazy? You left a message? What are the chances your grandfather listened to the message?"

Maude stopped pacing. Her eyes darkened. "I didn't think of that."

Sydney stalked to the mudroom. Maude tried to join her, but Sydney pushed her sister back into the kitchen.

"I will swing by Randy's place and see if there's any chance the laptop is in there."

"Isn't it still a crime scene?"

"Since when would you care about that? Screw protocol," Sydney answered. "The cops will be here sooner or later. You need to talk to them about Zile and Gonzo. I'd bet anything Zile has a police scanner. He'll know they're coming here and that might keep him away. Be certain to keep the doors locked. And if you call anyone, don't leave a message. Meanwhile, I want you to pack a bag. When I get back, we're going to drive to Ithaca or Cortland or Avalon and find a motel where we can stay for a while."

"Where are you going?" Maude asked.

Sydney winced as she forced her swollen feet into her roomiest boots. "Off to see a woman about a horse."

36

Fool's Errand

Sydney had her choice of parking places in front of Brochu's. She would have the store to herself.

Rob was crouched over paperwork in the tiny office next to the checkout area, his reading glasses perched on his nose. The office door was wide open, as usual, but she knew that didn't mean he was open to receiving visitors—only that he didn't expect anyone to be in the store.

Sydney gave the doorframe a sharp rap. Rob's head snapped up, and he gazed at her over the top of his glasses and grunted. He didn't seem thrilled to see her. Sydney heaved a mental sigh. She could accept that she would never be one of Rob's preferred customers, but it was hard to be reminded of her past every time she shopped.

"I have a quick question," she said.

"If it's about the memorial, don't worry. We have all your items for Saturday. We'll have everything delivered by twelve thirty." Rob turned back to his paperwork.

Sydney ignored the cold shoulder treatment. "That's great. I know you might be shorthanded so let me know if you want me to transport stuff."

Rob sagged in the chair and swiveled to face her. "Elizabeth wouldn't have it any other way. She wants to go, and I go where she wants me to go."

Sydney could recognize a backhanded slap when she heard one. Left to his own devices, Rob would rather stay in this drafty old store. She felt her cheeks burning bright red. Rob had struck home, and she was mortified she couldn't deny him the additional satisfaction of knowing it. Rob's wife must be a saint, but maybe he had other redeeming qualities.

"Rob, I know I was a complete jerk to you, and I'm sorry. But this event is not for me. It's for my mother. You went to high school with her. I know she did most of her shopping here. It might not have amounted to much, but in her mind, she did it to help you stay in business. She always stood up for you when people whined. She stood up for me when I was a complete mess. The least I can do is to honor her. I know she would want to see you there."

Sydney paused. *Stand up taller. You did your best.*

Rob raised his hands and let them drop with a grunt. "Okay. I hear you."

"Anyway, that wasn't my real question. I'm headed out to talk to Lilith. What's the story out that way?" she asked.

Rob scratched his balding head. "Do you think that's wise?"

"Let's say I think it's necessary."

"You could ask your sister."

"I'm on a secret errand. I don't want her to know."

Rob stood and rested his hands on his bony hips. "More like a fool's errand."

"All the more reason to keep it secret."

Rob took off his reading glasses and polished them on his shirt. "Don't know that you'll find Zile there. He went by about an hour ago, headed toward Hartwell. You will find a nasty dog. Banger or Bubba or something. And then there's Lilith, of course." He grinned. "You might find the dog more welcoming."

"Forewarned is forearmed," Sydney said, and turned to leave Rob in peace.

On her way past the checkout counter, she picked up a box of breath mints from the candy display. "How much for these?" she asked.

"Three bucks."

Sydney dug out a five-dollar bill from her pocket and placed it on the counter. "Keep the change."

She popped the box open, pulled out a handful of mints, and stuffed them into her mouth. She left the opened box by the cash register and walked out.

The cold breeze outside combined with the burst of minty freshness to clear her head and kill the taste of eating crow.

She was on her way into the belly of the beast—Zile's compound. All her senses needed to be on full alert. Even if Zile was not there, Gonzo might be keeping an eye on the place, and Lilith wasn't exactly a friend.

As she approached Dugway Road, Sydney made an abrupt right turn. She had promised Maude she would check the burned-out shell that had been Randy's house, and she should take care of that first.

The double-wide was still festooned with crime tape, but she suspected that was an empty warning. Based on the piles of virgin snow, she could see no one had been investigating here for days. Parked across the road, Sydney assessed the damage.

Properly fixed up, double-wide trailers could be efficient and attractive alternatives to traditional housing structures. Randy had done nothing to upgrade the aesthetics of his unit or the surrounding landscape. No big loss. Some might even consider the fire to be a blessing.

The blaze and the attempts to fight it left a gaping hole in the side closest to the road, and the former front door entrance area was an empty chasm.

Randy's laptop wasn't at her mother's house and not at Lilith's, if the cranky woman was to be believed. He wouldn't have left it in his truck in the bitter cold, and without access to the Internet at the cabin, it was unlikely he took it there.

Sydney climbed out of the car and made her way over snow-covered lumps and hidden hazards to the charred entrance. Clearing aside yellow tape, she stepped inside and considered the former combined living room and dining room. Caked in soot and ice, some of the furnishings were still recognizable, others less so.

She didn't dare step into the middle of the room—the flooring looked too fragile. Edging her way around the living space, she stayed as close to the walls as possible.

Halfway around, she reached what had been the sofa. At her feet she saw a thick cord snaking its way underneath and out of sight. Sydney bent over and tugged.

Something moved. She kept tugging until she saw the black corner of a laptop poke out.

Had Randy put it there? Perhaps one of the first responders had kicked it, or a blast from a hose had pushed it under the sofa. She figured she'd never know the answer.

Sydney yanked the cord free from the wall socket and snatched up the laptop. Time to go.

Halfway across the floor, she heard a crack. The floor collapsed under her right foot, and she sank up to her knee. In an instant, she was twelve years old again, trying to cross Hangnail Pond on soft ice.

She remained frozen in place. She could feel the floor under her left foot sink and bounce back as if she were stepping on a sponge.

Sydney bent over and scooted the laptop toward the ragged entrance before she placed her forearms on the floor and leaned to her right. She stretched out so she lay flat on the crunchy black surface and crawled forward until both feet were free. When she reached the location of the former front door, she eased to a standing position and picked up the laptop.

She hoped Lilith would agree to talk to her. One fool's errand a day was her limit.

37

A Few Truths

The road leading to the Jaquith homestead twisted down a steep hill that made Sydney's heart thump at the thought of lurking black ice at each curve. After three hairpin turns, she passed a sign warning her to watch for a horse and buggy, and she caught sight of a tall mechanical rig poking over the trees ahead.

That would be ground zero for Zile's lumber operation—the supposed source of his legitimate income.

She slowed down as she passed the large, open lot, stacked with tree trunks and lumber, to study the surrounding barn-like structures. She hadn't been this way since she had liberated the money from Zile to fund her escape to California, but she assumed his office was still in the smaller building at the far end. The place appeared deserted. No smoke came from the office building chimney, and the trucks were all covered in several inches of snow.

Around the next bend, she came upon a familiar sagging two-story frame house covered in gray asphalt shingles. A Confederate battle flag was flapping in the breeze off the front porch. Sydney thought that was an odd home décor choice given several Jaquiths had marched off to fight against the Confederacy in the 1860s. On the other hand, it did go well with the barbed wire fence that carefully delineated the boundaries of the yard. A large, shaggy German shepherd was curled up in the snow near a small hutch that did not look like it offered much in the way of shelter.

The gate hung open. Sydney swallowed, swung into the plowed driveway, and came to a stop about halfway to the house. She turned off the car and waited.

As she anticipated, the barking and snarling dog raced at the car, only to be yanked to a halt when he reached the end of the long chain that stretched back to a stake in the ground next to his hutch. She wondered how many times a day he did that. She turned on the car and backed up a few feet. She felt sorry for this poor animal, but she still wanted to be safely out of range.

Sydney leaned forward to study the trucks parked at odd angles alongside the house. She wasn't sure what kind of vehicle Lilith drove these days. She honked the horn.

After about a minute she caught a slight movement at one of the front windows. She stared to see if the curtains moved again.

The front door opened, and Lilith stepped out. She called to the dog, which slunk back to his hutch and crouched, muscles coiled, ready to spring.

Sydney got out, leaving the keys in the ignition and the door unlocked. She followed a curved, icy path that appeared to follow a radius matching the length of the dog's chain—plus or minus a few feet—to the front door.

Lilith had never been a stylish or fancy dresser, but on this day she looked exceptionally disheveled in a filthy sweatshirt, and her long gray hair was in a loose tangle. Still, her eyes glittered hard and dark.

"What the hell have you been up to?" Lilith asked. "You stink to high heaven like a barbeque. Don't track any of that black crusty stuff into my house."

Sydney paused at the bottom step and dug into her shoulder bag to pull out the large manila envelope.

"These fell to the floor during the scuffle at the memorial service. They were being trampled, so I picked them up." She held out the envelope.

Lilith beckoned with a slight twitch of her eyebrow for Sydney to come closer. When Sydney reached the top step, Lilith grabbed the envelope with a snap. She left the door open and stepped back inside the house to dump the contents onto a table by the door. Sydney tried to see inside, but Lilith blocked the view from the half-open doorway.

Lilith spread the pictures out like playing cards, quickly pawing through them. She grunted and her mouth relaxed. Several moments later, the older woman's body stiffened, and she straightened up.

"You didn't need to take those." Lilith waved her hands over the pictures. "And you definitely are not welcome here. *Sahten:ti.* Go away."

Sydney heard the dog's chain rattle, but she kept her gaze on Lilith. "I'm not here for your welcome. I learned long ago not to expect anything from you. I'm here because Maude needs your help in a very bad way."

"And why would that be?" Lilith's eyes were narrow slits, her voice low.

Sydney pressed her lips together.

She waited in vain for Lilith's glare to fade and tried to ignore the sounds of the dog, pacing in the snow behind her. "She's your granddaughter. You need to step up. Zile and Gonzo tried to force Maude into a truck this morning. Zile's been after her for days."

The light in Lilith's eyes softened. She blinked, and the hard look returned. "Maude's been holding out. She knows where Randy hid that stuff. And some money."

"She doesn't know, Lilith. And even if she did, does that mean Zile can do God knows what to her?"

"He's the boss here. She knows how things work in *our* family."

"What makes him think she's holding out?" Sydney stepped closer. She heard the dog growl, but she didn't think his chain could reach her.

Lilith looked away and took a step back. "The place where

Zile found Randy and those men. The real place. There were footprints. Evidence. Evidence that doesn't lie. There was a girl there. It was Maude. Now she needs to pay up."

Sydney felt a numbing chill move down her spine and along her limbs.

This was the moment of truth, on this cold porch, facing a woman who hated her guts. Sydney's brain raced through her options. If she knew what had happened, Lilith might kill her, and if Lilith relayed the information to Zile, *he* certainly would. But if Sydney stayed silent, she couldn't save Maude. She needed Lilith's help.

Sydney shivered the length of her body and gasped for breath. "It was me. It wasn't Maude."

Lilith snorted. "What are you talking about? You were up in Syracuse with your mother."

"No, you've got the timing wrong. My mother died on Wednesday morning, and I got here in the afternoon. Those two guys—Bernard and Pierre—they were waiting at the house and gave me a package for Randy. They said they'd see him at the cabin the next day."

Lilith's face went blank, her eyes hooded. "You're lying," she said, but her voice betrayed her.

"I was so pissed off at Randy. My mother was in the hospital, and he wasn't picking up messages. He let her die alone. I was furious. I skied to the cabin that night when it was forty below so I could give him a piece of my mind. And his stuff."

Lilith tilted her head to one side, a bird of prey studying its next victim.

"Those guys tried to sneak up and surprise Randy. I hid at the back of the closet. He put his money and the drugs someplace. I honestly don't know where. They're someplace in that cabin." She stopped to gasp for air.

"It all started nice and friendly, but they began arguing. I heard gunshots."

Lilith believed her now, based on the cold hatred radiating from the woman's body.

"And was he still alive when you crawled out from your little den?" Lilith asked, her voice a low hiss.

"Barely. He was gone in minutes, I swear. Lilith, he told me to save Maude. He begged me to get her away from here. He made me promise."

"He sent a text message."

"It said, '*shot at cabin bad news.*' I sent that." Sydney reached down inside her shirt and pulled on the silver chain that held Randy's ring. She dangled it in front of Lilith's face. "He gave me this."

Lilith lunged for the ring. Sydney leaped backward and found herself in midair, falling off the porch. She wheeled her arms and managed to land on her feet at the bottom of the porch stairs, now within reach of the dog.

The dog surged forward as Sydney's momentum carried her around to face him. She swung her booted right foot as hard as she could, catching the dog squarely in his throat, under his jaw.

The dog yelped and backed away a few feet, leaving enough room for Sydney to move out of range. She turned and faced the furious wraith on the porch.

"Lilith! Your granddaughter needs your help. You cannot stand by and let Zile hurt her."

"Give me that ring. It doesn't belong to you."

"This ring represented the love between my mother and Randy. You don't deserve it. You haven't earned it. You let Zile screw up Randy. You are letting Zile do the same to Maude. Maybe even worse. This ring belongs to Maude now."

Sydney's voice was raw. She stumbled along the curved path back to the car, trading curses and middle fingers with Lilith over the frantic barking of the dog.

As she rounded the rear of the car, she heard a vehicle approaching from the direction of the lumberyard. Gonzo rolled by in a truck. He slowed to stare but kept going.

Fifty feet later, she saw his brake lights, and he put the truck in reverse.

Time to go.

Sydney jumped into her mother's car, glad she had left the keys in the ignition. She backed out of the driveway as fast as she dared, praying for no oncoming traffic. Once the car reached the road, she swung the wheel to point the car away from Gonzo's truck, now backing up at a brisk pace, and stomped on the gas.

She took the first right even though she couldn't recall where it led, followed by a left and another right. After a few more turns she was calm enough to get her bearings. She pulled over and threw up into a snowbank.

This day was not going well, and it was still early afternoon.

38

Reunion on the Hangnail

Sydney drove in intricate patterns, crisscrossing Oriska, consumed with bitterness, fear, and a bit of self-loathing. She could feel Gonzo hovering around every corner as she drove through little intersections she didn't recognize followed by long, open stretches that brought familiar memories and tears to her eyes.

She might as well have been the only person alive in Oriska County. Not a single car or truck crossed her path.

A red light on the dashboard caught her eye. She was almost out of gas. Days of driving around and she hadn't needed to top off the tank until now. She pulled over and leaned against the steering wheel to sob. Her mother had been the last one to fill up this car. It was probably one of her last tasks.

Sydney wiped her eyes and headed for Brochu's. It was the closest source for cheap, generic fuel.

Gassing up at Brochu's required parking by the pump, followed by a trip to the cashier to present one's method of payment—cash or credit card. Sydney parked and stomped inside.

The counter was manned by Elizabeth, Rob's wife, who was sorting receipts and other papers. A bit of a phantom presence, Elizabeth spent most of her hours upstairs in the dry goods department.

Holding out her credit card, Sydney waited for another judgmental glare, but Elizabeth leaned forward with what looked like lines of genuine concern creasing her face.

"Sydney! You look like you've been rolling in charcoal. Are you okay?"

"Fine. I was doing a bit of reconnoitering in a bad place." Sydney cleared her throat and held out the card again. "I need some gas."

Elizabeth seemed to snap back to the present. "Of course, of course." She took the card. "Rob and I are so pleased you asked us to help with your mom's service. She was a precious member of our little community. We used to go walking together."

"Oh. You're a member of the coven!"

Elizabeth looked over her shoulder toward Rob's office. "Well, we only call it that as a joke. Technically we're the Lady Walkers. Anyway, I miss your mother so much. Oh dear. I'm sorry I made you cry."

Sydney took the tissue offered by Elizabeth and wiped her face. It came back streaked with black soot. "I should go home and clean up."

"I guess you've just missed Maude. I was surprised to see her drive by a few minutes ago. I didn't think she was driving again."

Sydney froze in place. "She's not supposed to be. Are you sure?"

"Oh yes. My little seat upstairs gives me a great view of the intersection."

"Which way'd she go?" Sydney leaned across the counter.

"Ah. Well, straight north. Toward Route 20."

Sydney ground her teeth as she filled the car. She couldn't go looking for Maude without gas. She collected her credit card with a nod to Elizabeth and headed home.

Sure enough, Maude's truck was gone.

Sydney pulled into the driveway, mentally kicking herself for not taking the keys to the truck when she had the chance. Maude had appeared to be willing—if reluctant—to wait until her license was reinstated. Now Sydney dreaded what she would find inside.

Maude did not disappoint. Food was flung around the kitchen, the sitting room sofa was lying upside down, lamps rested on the floor.

It could have been worse. Nothing seemed to be broken, not even Sydney's laptop, sitting in the kitchen trash compactor, but uncompacted.

Determined not to panic, Sydney plopped Randy's laptop on the kitchen island and paced in circles around the kitchen and sitting room. A blinking red light caught her attention: the answering machine. There were three messages.

The first was a robocall. The second was from Francine. She had something important to discuss. The third was Lilith.

"Maude. This is your grandmother. Pick up. I know you're there. There is something very important you need to know about your sister. Your sister and Randy. You need to know—"

At that point the message stopped. Maude must have picked up the phone.

"Lilith, you filthy bitch," Sydney said.

She noticed a flapping motion outside the kitchen porch door and went to investigate. It was a note from the Hartwell PD. They had stopped by, but no one was home.

She pulled three energy bars from the vertical pantry unit and wolfed them down. She could not afford a low blood sugar brain fog.

Even if Lilith had given Maude a sanitized version of Sydney's role in Randy's death—which seemed unlikely—Maude now knew that Randy died at his cabin. She probably also knew the drugs and money Zile was so keen to find were hidden there.

Great. A scavenger hunt tailor-made for a junkie.

She picked up the phone and set it down. Who was she going to call? The cops? She didn't have anything that clearly required their help. They might be pissed off, not inclined to go on what they would think of as a wild-goose chase. Especially for this particular wild goose.

She also didn't want to cause any more trouble for Maude than necessary. Maybe she could lure Maude home.

She wasn't sure that Maude had gone to the cabin, but it was the most likely spot. There were several other hidden locations that Zile's family used. All of them would require a bit of hiking at this time of year.

The clock in the kitchen read 3:45 when she picked up the phone and called Lilith.

"What do you want?" Lilith said, her voice a low growl.

"Listen to me, Lilith. Maude is a junkie. She has run off. I'm betting she's gone to the cabin to find Randy's drugs. And the money."

Lilith's breathing rattled over the line.

"Do you think she can really resist a hit of fentanyl?" Sydney asked. "Do you know how little it takes to OD on that? That delivery was pure poison."

"She's a grown woman. I can't control her."

"If she dies, I'm holding you responsible, Lilith. She loves you. She thinks you hate her because she can't be your daughter anymore. She aches for this land and her people and your love. You are the one who killed Randy as far as I'm concerned. You sat by and let Zile ruin him."

"It's your fault. You lied."

"I lied to protect Maude."

"You lied to protect yourself. You're still lying."

"I might be a liar about some things, but you are a coward. I'm going out to look. Starting at the cabin."

"I hope she spits in your eye." Lilith hung up.

Sydney dialed Cassandra's number. The call rolled to voice mail. Of course. Cassandra would still be doing school activities.

"Hey, Elway. Things have gone upside down here. Maude has run off. She's in a state. I'm going to go looking. I think Randy's cabin is the best first stop. If you don't hear from me—from us—by tomorrow, you'll know where to send the cops."

After a quick change into cross-country clothes, Sydney loaded her skis and poles into the car and took a detour to the back of the barn. She slid aside the boards for her secret hiding place and reached in for the antique Luger.

Gone! Sydney smacked her forehead with both hands and groaned. Maude was much too resourceful for her own good.

She raced back inside and upstairs. In the closet in her grandfather's old bedroom, she found his shotgun. The shells on the upper shelf were probably ancient, and she wasn't sure the gun would even fire. It might even blow up in her hands instead. Still, she didn't want to run the risk of bumping into Zile without some kind of intimidation factor.

Sydney could feel time slipping away from her. She had to go right away.

She slung the loaded shotgun across her back and stuffed additional shells inside her jacket pocket.

This time she pointed the car north, drove past Brochu's, continued straight until she hit North Lake Road, and hung a left. The sun was low in the sky to the west, blinding her as the rays hit her filthy windshield. She didn't have much daylight left.

Once she made another left onto West Lake Road, she slowed to a crawl. Due to winter plowing, turnouts were carved into the snowbanks on either side of the narrowed road at haphazard intervals to allow vehicles to pull over and let a car coming from the opposite way pass. Some people used them for temporary parking, too. Sydney knew one such turnout sat at the top of the unplowed lane down to Randy's cabin.

She hoped she would find Maude's truck there or in one nearby. If it wasn't, she would have to decide whether to double-check the cabin anyway, or continue on to her next candidate— a maple sugaring house closer to Hartwell.

From the top of a small rise, Sydney could see Maude's truck in Randy's pullout, and she whispered a thank-you. As she coasted closer, the thank-you turned to a curse. A second truck was parked next to Maude's—a familiar dark blue Ford with a dangling passenger side mirror and a broken headlight.

She stopped and processed the scene. A movement caught her eye. Gonzo was standing close to the trucks, a few feet inside the tree line. He had his back to the road. From his posture and gestures, it looked like he was taking a piss. He didn't appear to have noticed her stealthy approach.

She threw the car into gear and sped forward. Caught with his hands full, Gonzo was still in the trees by the time she rounded the next bend.

39

Cabin Fever

Sydney found the next pullout and backed in with the nose of the car ready to push into the road and the keys in easy reach under the driver's seat, in case she needed to leave in a hurry. She kept looking over her shoulder to see if Gonzo had followed her as she pulled out her skis and poles, the shotgun, and her small backpack from the backseat.

She wondered how Gonzo and Zile traced Maude to the cabin. Had they seen her driving or stumbled across her truck parked on the road? Perhaps Lilith had shared Sydney's secret.

She clambered over the snowbank in her skis and checked her cell phone one last time. *Maybe one bar.* She typed a text message to Cassandra's cell phone: *Maude at Randy's cabin. Gonzo Zile here too. Call cops.*

She pushed into the woods, grateful for the gentle downhill grade that added speed to her feet. She skated past two cottages, lying cold and dark for the winter. The last stretch required an uphill climb and left her above Randy's cabin, on the edge of his clearing.

Sunlight still kissed the upper branches of the trees around the cabin, but twilight had reached the ground. Lights were on downstairs. All was dark upstairs. Wood smoke wafted from the chimney.

Sydney studied the stretch of snow in front of her. It was

unblemished aside from a few animal tracks. Even if she could sneak up to the structure unseen, a quick glance out a window would show any marks she made in the snow unless she waited until it was fully dark.

She opted to ski uphill along the edge of the woods toward the summer parking area in back of the cabin. She could see traces of snowmobile tracks and boot prints, some fresh, others half-buried by recent snowfalls.

Sydney removed her skis and hid them along with the poles behind a dense patch of cedars. She edged close to a window that afforded a view of the kitchen and into the living room. It seemed the pounding of her heart must have been audible to anyone inside, but Gonzo passed by the window and didn't seem to notice.

Through the kitchen door into the living room, she could see Zile and Maude close to the woodstove. Their voices sounded loud and punctuated with sharp syllables, but she couldn't catch the details.

Zile and Maude were both waving their arms. Maude leaned forward and must have spat out a particularly pointed comment based on the venom in her face. Zile swung his right hand up from his waist and caught her hard under the jaw.

Sydney yelped and ducked down, pressing her gloved hands into her mouth. After recovering, she stood again. She could see Maude's legs on the braided living room rug. Zile was yelling, and the legs moved. She stifled another whimper.

Maude jumped to her feet and moved out of Sydney's sight. Zile lunged after Maude and returned to view holding the Luger. Sydney hoped Zile would spare his own granddaughter from a serious beating, but she wasn't ready to lay money on that.

Sydney checked the shotgun and contemplated her options. Four doors led into the cabin. The first was a glass door with large windows on either side that led from the living room onto a deck overlooking Hangnail Pond, 180 degrees from where she stood. No way she could sneak up unnoticed.

The second was off the side porch to her left, leading from the living room out into the yard. Randy had died right inside that door after shooting his attackers as they stumbled away to die in the snow. It was probably not locked, but it also had a large glass pane.

The third lay around the corner to her right, leading from a small porch into the kitchen. The boards on that porch squeaked like the devil. If the door were locked, she'd be caught while jiggling the doorknob.

The fourth doorway was a set of French double doors, also off the front deck, leading to the dining room. The benefit of those doors was that she would only have to walk on the decking for a few steps, but it was probably locked as well.

Sydney ground her teeth in frustration. She was cold and getting colder, and she was terrified for Maude.

A shadow in the kitchen made her jump. She shrank against the siding and watched as Zile joined Gonzo in the kitchen. Their small talk did not look jovial.

Zile pulled out a pack of cigarettes and unlocked the kitchen door. Both men stepped outside, presumably to smoke and conspire out of Maude's earshot. They didn't seem concerned that Maude would run—she'd be easy pickings in the deep snow.

Seeing her opportunity, Sydney pushed through the snow on the opposite side of the cabin, toward the secret light switch. She hoped Maude knew about this old trick of Randy's—or at least would figure out that someone was here to help.

She lifted the cover on the switch and entered the code for *friend—up long, down quick, up long, down quick*. She could see the overhead light in the living room flash.

She was tempted to enter her personal code, but Maude probably wouldn't recognize it. Sydney also didn't want to risk any more flashing lights that might catch Zile's attention.

The silhouette of a figure appeared at the side door facing the yard and seemed to be looking out the glass pane. A hand raised. Sydney stepped from behind the cedar and waved, then stepped back. At least Maude knew she was here.

Sydney made her way back across the yard to the side porch, hoping the light was dim enough to hide her movements. Peering over the edge of the porch railing, she had a good view into the living room.

Maude was in an armchair facing Sydney. Gonzo was stuffing another log inside the woodstove. Where was Zile? She craned her neck.

As if to answer her question, the sharp stench of drink and body odor cut through the cold. "Right in back of you, sweetie," said a voice that she knew all too well.

She turned with her hands chest high and looked straight into the Luger, pointed by Zile.

"Give me that shotgun. It looks kind of heavy," he said.

She complied, and he tossed the shotgun out into the deep snow of the hillside down to the Hangnail. "Now step up onto the porch and let's get out of this cold."

Sydney kept reminding herself that she wasn't dead yet. If her death were Zile's top priority, he could have done that already. He rapped several times on the door window until Gonzo turned the key from the inside and let them in.

Maude jumped up and let out a cry. She ran to Sydney's arms. Sydney could feel her sister shaking—or maybe that was her own body.

"Holy shit, Zile," was Gonzo's comment. A man of few words, Gonzo was a bit dim, but she knew he would do whatever Zile wanted. He was a loyal servant.

She looked Maude over, checking for broken bones. Maude sported a shiner and a bruised cheekbone, and her lips were bloody, but she seemed otherwise intact.

The living room was broiling hot within ten feet of the woodstove. Beyond that radius, the temperature dropped dramatically. With her back to Zile, Sydney guided Maude to the armchair. Making sure she had steady eye contact with Maude, she draped her jacket over the back of the chair along with her backpack.

Zile paced around the living room with a little skipping step. He chuckled and rolled the Luger around in his hands. Sydney could see the handle of a second handgun—a revolver—tucked into the front of his pants. *Please shoot yourself, asshole.*

"I haven't seen this gun in a long time," he said, waggling it in front of Sydney's face. "It's an antique, you know."

"Maybe it won't fire," Sydney said. She edged her way over

to the couch, opposite Maude. Her knees were quaking, but she resisted taking a seat. *In the off chance this really isn't the end.*

"Ho ho, I'll bet it will. It fired thirteen years ago. Didn't it?" Zile leaned in so close, Sydney could count his long, matted nose hairs. She tried not to gag at the smell of his breath. He had definitely been drinking.

"I wouldn't know about that."

Zile stopped and squinted. "Ah. That's right. You left. Only your grandfather and that asshole sheriff were here."

Zile resumed his pacing. "I was headed down here. You stole from me, and I knew this was where you'd come. Sniffing around for Randy. I'd had enough of you." He halted and pointed the gun at her. "That damned Sheriff Carver got here first. That was a stroke of luck."

"That's not what *I* thought," Sydney said, keeping her eyes on the gun.

"No, I guess you wouldn't. If I'd killed you, at least I would have been quick. He had something much nastier in mind, didn't he?"

"That he did."

Zile waved the gun toward his granddaughter. "Can you believe it, Maude? Here were the two people in the world I most wanted out of my life, waiting for me." He paused for a deep sigh. "But then David Graham, PhD, and principal asshole, showed up with this pea shooter and saved his granddaughter. Chained up the sheriff. Sent her home. Home to run away. I settled for removing the bigger thorn in my side."

Sydney's careful control fell away. She knew her face showed her shock and surprise. "*You* killed Sheriff Carver!"

"Of course I did," Zile said with a smirk. "Your grandfather planned to sit with that son of a bitch Carver until God knows when and then let him go. I fixed that."

"All these years," Sydney said, and sank onto the couch.

"You thought your grandfather pulled the trigger?" Zile tsked. "I did him a favor. Your grandfather was an idiot. Sheriff Carver would have come after him. What a dunce."

Sydney blinked, seeing her grandfather standing in this same place. He wasn't a killer, and he hadn't merely saved her life. Knowing he had put his own life on the line pushed aside a tiny bit of the terror that filled her being.

Zile seemed pleased. "There, there. Don't cry. We struck a deal after I marched Homer out to the woods. And I stuck to it. Your grandfather paid me what you'd stolen. He even helped me move the body to Schwarzer's quarry, and he hid the gun. I promised I wouldn't go after you. It would have been so easy all these years, but I didn't. He said he'd make sure you never came back, and I wouldn't tell Leslie that you and Randy were an item. And I wouldn't send Maude away so your mother would never see her again."

"For the record, Randy and I were not an item." Even to her own ears, her voice sounded weak, indecisive.

"Ha. Well, it figures that *you* didn't think so. Coldhearted bitch."

Zile stopped pacing. "But then you broke your part of the bargain. You came back."

Sydney started to protest and stopped. "You should let Maude go now," she said instead. "She wasn't here when Randy died."

Zile studied the Luger in his hands. "Yeah, it took me awhile to figure it out, but when I saw the flashing lights and you showed up, the penny dropped."

"The deal's still good," Sydney said. "I'll be leaving in a few days."

"Not good enough."

Sydney pulled off her hat and ran her fingers through her hair. It was time to play her aces.

"I'm a bit surprised you are so focused on the small stuff," she said.

"Excuse me?" Zile leveled the gun.

"Randy made a lot of money over the years. You should be trying to find that, not wasting your time on this piddly deal."

"Sydney!" Maude sat up straight in protest.

Zile looked from one sister to the other. He lowered the gun. "Tell me more."

"He had a secret bank account. A rather large bank account."

"How do you know that?"

"He managed it from his laptop. I have his laptop," Sydney said. She hoped she was too scared to reveal her lie by blushing.

"And how did you come by that, may I ask?"

"I took it with me. After those assholes killed Randy, I sent you a text from his phone. I didn't want him to rot here, and you'll appreciate that I did not call the police. When I left, I put his laptop in my backpack."

Sydney did not dare look at Maude, afraid her sister's reaction would reveal this part of the lie. Instead, she stayed focused on Zile. He leaned against the wall closest to the stove and studied her in a way that did not ease her anxiety. Still, she could see the wheels were turning.

Zile pushed forward into the middle of the room. "So where is it?"

"Hidden. At the house. Maude doesn't know about it, and she doesn't know where it is. Let her go and I'll take you to it."

Zile grinned. "Not likely. She'd call the cops." He scratched his chin with the barrel of the Luger. "See, I'm a bird-in-the-hand kind of guy. You tell me where Randy's stash is. After that, we'll go for the laptop. Together. Then we can settle up."

Sydney was locked in place by Zile's gaze. She knew exactly what "settling up" meant. Her only hope was to give Zile everything he wanted and pray that would keep him from killing her.

"I was hiding at the back of the closet when the Canadians came," Sydney said, shifting her eyes to the braided rug at her feet, the stain of Randy's blood still visible. "I might know where Randy hid the stuff and the money. Let Maude leave, and I'll go through all the hidden spots."

Zile wagged his head back and forth, appearing to contemplate the pros and cons. "Nope."

"Granddad?" Maude stood, looking meek and helpless. "I really need to pee."

Zile studied her with a skeptical squint. "Okay. Leave the door to the shed open. I want to hear you."

Maude trotted forward past Zile and Gonzo into the kitchen toward the shed lavatory with the mincing steps of someone desperate for relief. Sydney kept her eyes on Zile and Gonzo, wondering what the hell Maude was up to.

She heard the shed door creak and her peripheral vision registered that Maude took a big step sideways, away from the shed. Sydney closed her eyes, picturing Maude slipping out the kitchen door to the porch, willing it to be true.

For herself, a little bit of her heart held out hope for survival, but now she was primarily trying to figure out how to take Zile with her.

"Speak. Let's hear about the hiding places," Zile said. He waved the gun in her direction like he was shaking a wand.

Time to comply. "There's a hidden closet in back of the woodstove," Sydney said. "It's the only place big enough for the bags. There should be at least three. A bag of miscellaneous stuff, the bag from the Canadians, and a bag of Randy's money."

"Fine. You open it." Zile pointed with the gun. "No, stop." He waved to Gonzo. "She's full of tricks. There might be a gun in there. Better you open it."

Sydney stood and edged away from the couch. "You might want to leave all of it."

"And why the hell would I do that?"

She eyed the hidden closet. Gonzo was already maneuvering his enormous bulk in back of the glowing stove. Sweat ran down his cheeks and soaked his hair.

"There's a lot of fentanyl in one of those bags. Pure, I gather. Or pretty close. It's been sitting there, freezing and baking. If it gets out—even a tiny bit—we're all dead."

Zile squinted, and she saw his eyes slide from her back to Gonzo. "Be careful taking that stuff out," he said, and raised the gun to point past Gonzo toward the stove.

"How do I open this?" Gonzo asked.

"Press the bottom right corner," Sydney answered. Seeing Zile's attention waver, she backed herself around the living room, closer to the dining room.

As Gonzo bent over, his jacket brushed the stove. Within seconds it started to smoke. Zile didn't appear to notice. Sydney held her breath, waiting to seize an opportunity.

"It's in here," Gonzo said, his voice full of glee. "I can see a backpack."

Holding the backpack in his left hand, he fished inside and tossed out one bag onto the living room floor, followed by a second. As he turned with the third bag, the lower part of his jacket caught fire. He squealed and backed away from the stove, tripping over his own feet and landing on the bag he was carrying.

Sydney wasn't sure which bag he had fallen on or if they were in any genuine danger from fentanyl poisoning, but she screamed, anyway. "Shit! We're dead!"

Gonzo was rolling on the floor to put out the flames and onto the other bags. Zile danced back away from the stove, and Sydney willed her feet to take off.

Before she could take a step, Maude appeared from the kitchen, carrying an oversized bottle of rut gut vodka. Sydney halted, shocked to a standstill to see her sister was still in the cabin.

Maude unscrewed the top and lifted the bottle overhead. She swung it down to her knees, forcing the release of a large splash directed straight at Gonzo, followed by another.

The vodka hit Gonzo's blazing jacket, and he screamed as the flames blazed higher. Maude shifted the bottle so that she held it by the neck and slammed it onto the hot stove. Sydney did not wait to appreciate the results. She was already headed for the French doors in the dining room.

She fumbled with the lock, cursing her fingers. She felt Zile pull the trigger before she heard the blast, and ducked as a bullet struck the wall above her head. She rose to her feet to kick the door with everything she had left. The lock broke with a crack, and she yanked the door open. Another shot sounded, and the bullet whizzed by into the open air as she stumbled out onto the deck.

Sydney rounded the corner of the cabin in time to catch Maude leaving by the kitchen door.

"Run, run, run! Up the trail to your truck. Snow's too deep to get to my car. He'd catch us," Sydney said. Maude grabbed her elbow and yanked her through the snow. They had a long climb to safety.

40

Hypothermia

Sydney hoped they had chosen the best path up the hill. Following the unplowed lane to the lake road required a steep climb with several feet of snow underfoot. To add to her misery, she had abandoned her jacket, hat, and gloves in the cabin. She was breathing hard, running on adrenaline and fear.

The route back to her car was flatter but much longer. *Too late for that option.* Sydney pressed on, hoping to catch a second wind. Maude, also coatless, was running like a locomotive through the snow. Sydney shifted her path to follow in Maude's steps.

She risked a glance over her right shoulder. Zile burst from the side door from the living room. He was followed by Gonzo, now minus his jacket. The light was too dim to see clearly, but if Gonzo was suffering from his burns, he wasn't showing it, based on the way he was powering up the hill.

At their current pace, the two large men would soon cut off Sydney and Maude as they came up from the farther side of the cabin.

"Into the woods, Maude," Sydney said, in between gasps for breath. "They'll catch us if we don't hide."

Maude darted off the path to her left and into the trees.

The last vestiges of daylight were nearly gone. Sydney could see her way, but details were dimming, and she needed to move with caution. She hoped that applied to Zile and Gonzo as well.

Once upon a time she had known these woods. Softened by passing years and heavy snow, nothing looked familiar. She scanned left and right as they zigzagged up the steep slope. At least the snow was not quite as deep under the cedar and pine trees, which also provided a bit of cover.

To her right, she caught sight of a familiar landmark—a rocky outcropping. If they could reach it, they would be hidden from Gonzo and Zile on the edge of the woods.

"Right. Turn right. But watch out. There's a deep crevasse. Keep to the left of the rocks," Sydney said, trying to keep her voice low.

"Got it." Maude picked her way over hidden rocks, holding on to tree branches.

Sydney cast a quick glance at the base of the outcropping. She recalled vividly that there was a steep, rocky drop of six to eight feet deep, now hidden by a great deal of snow. To the unsuspecting, the snow made it appear that the land sloped gently away.

The two sisters paused on the left side of the outcropping, panting and listening. Sydney cocked her head. She could hear Gonzo's heavy breathing and slow self-talk as he moved up the edge of the woods to their right. Where the hell was Zile?

A grunt and muttered curse came from behind. Zile was following them through the woods.

Sydney motioned with her fingers and leaned in close to Maude. "Circle around these rocks and wait at the edge for Gonzo to come into the woods. Once he does, get back in the lane. You'll make faster time. Head for your truck."

"What about you?"

"I'll be right behind you, but do not wait for me. Got it?"

Maude started moving.

Walking backward, Sydney followed Maude, keeping an eye out for Zile. She could hear Gonzo's voice, now much closer. She figured he must have entered the woods.

"I'm not feeling so good, Zile. My back and arms are really burning. Maybe I inhaled some of that stuff like she said."

Sydney placed him about twenty feet to the right of the rocks. "Keep going."

That was Zile's voice, only about thirty feet in back of them.

Sydney scrambled up the uphill side of the outcropping, trying to stay low. The cold had penetrated every limb. Her movements were clumsy.

Voices. Were there really voices or was she imagining it? Sydney risked standing up to look. In the failing light, she saw dark shapes, making their way down the lane.

Gonzo appeared like a specter on the edge of the woods, grasping at Maude. Maude rocked back and forth, elbows flailing, making herself hard to hold on to. She screeched and kicked and tumbled free. Sydney saw that Maude had left the woods and was moving uphill to meet the two figures coming down the lane.

Women's voices rang out. "Maude!" said one. Sydney recognized Cassandra's cry.

"I'm coming to you," cried out another. *Lilith!*

A pulse of light pulled Sydney's attention back toward the cabin. Through the trees, she could see the cabin windows flickered with flames, and smoke poured from the door.

Sydney turned to look for Gonzo. Where the hell had he gone? That was when she saw Zile less than twenty feet away on the opposite side of the buried crevasse.

He was pointing the gun straight at her.

She felt the heat on her back from Gonzo's body before she heard him. He reached the crest of the outcropping and rose to pull her into a deadly bear hug. She lifted one foot to run and slipped, falling hard onto the buried rocks as a gunshot echoed.

Gonzo grunted and landed on top of her with a thud. She gasped for breath as she kicked and shoved until he rolled away—over the side of the outcropping and into the deep snow below.

Sydney wiped away a warm trickle on the back of her neck. In the dark, it was black and slippery. Blood. Not hers. A gun—

a revolver—lay close to her left hand. She reached for it and tucked it into the back of her pants.

Sydney rose to her feet and tried to follow Maude, but her feet failed her. She seemed to hit every stone and boulder on her way down from the outcropping. Writhing from the pain in her right knee and left hip, she knew hypothermia was closing in fast. She stumbled to the edge of the woods and fell again. She felt the gun slip out and into the snow.

A firm hand grasped her arm and pulled her to her feet. Wiping snow from her face, she made out Cassandra pulling Maude uphill. Lilith let go of Sydney's arm and bent to pick up Gonzo's gun.

Flames were licking the side of the cabin, highlighting the scene in ghoulish red.

"Kill her!" screamed Zile. He left the woods and stood about twenty-odd feet away. He still held the Luger. "She killed Randy. She killed our family."

Sydney looked straight into Lilith's eyes. Lilith raised the gun. *How could she miss at three or four feet?*

"You killed Randy," Lilith said. She was staring at Sydney, but her left hand rose to point Gonzo's gun at Zile. "*Rotkonseraken:.* He is the devil. The bad thing I let into my life. *Rariwaksen.*"

Lilith turned to face Zile and shifted the gun to her right hand. "You killed him. All those years. Doing your business. A disgrace to my people."

Zile stopped and hunched down. "She is stealing Maude. Our last hope."

"Our last hope for what?"

Sydney saw Zile draw a bead on her, and she dove for the nearest tree. Two shots rang out close together. Wood splinters showered down on her back.

She waited for another shot—the one that would rip through her body. When none came, she risked a peek around the tree and saw Zile crumple into the snow as Lilith marched toward him. The older woman bent forward and whispered something at Zile's motionless figure.

Sydney looked over at Gonzo, lying about fifteen feet away. A dark stain was spreading through the snow under his body. His face was turned toward her. Highlighted by the growing flames from the cabin, she could see his eyes were open and not blinking.

Using the tree as a brace, Sydney pulled herself upright. She limped over to stand next to Lilith, staring down at Zile. His eyes were open, too. She knelt and felt his neck for a pulse. *Zippo.*

Now the tears spilled so easily. Sydney hurt all over, but the snow was sweet and cold. She was ready to sit down and rest.

"No, you don't," said Lilith's voice in her ear. An arm hooked under Sydney's armpit and swung her up to her feet.

When Sydney protested, Lilith gave her a shove. "Get going. Cops will be here soon." She turned and tossed her gun toward Gonzo's body.

"What if they're not really dead?" Sydney asked, turning back downhill.

"You really are hopeless. They're dead. Trust me." Lilith gave Sydney another shove.

41

Toxic Shock

By the time Sydney and Lilith caught up to Cassandra and Maude, Sydney was barely able to raise her feet. Cassandra took one look and removed her coat. "You're in shock, and it's freezing. Put this on." She yanked off her woolen hat and jammed it down over Sydney's hair. Lilith took off her jacket and handed it to Maude.

It wasn't much, but enough for Sydney to feel the difference. The wind no longer cut her like a knife. With Lilith's firm hand on her back, she inched uphill as Cassandra and Maude forged ahead.

"Just remember," Lilith said every few steps, "Zile shot Gonzo because he was going to shoot Maude. Gonzo's a big guy. He didn't keel over right away. He shot Zile."

After hearing the litany about five times, Sydney summoned the energy to say, "We could also tell the truth. Zile shot Gonzo by mistake. Then he was going to kill me and maybe you, too. Everyone knows Zile would be capable of that. You saved my life."

Lilith's face was unreadable in the gloom. She pushed Sydney forward a bit more gently. "I like my version better," she said after a few more steps.

Maude and Cassandra were already in Cassandra's car with the heater running full blast when Lilith and Sydney reached the road. Cassandra jumped out and stuffed Sydney into the driver's seat and handed her a water bottle as Lilith climbed into the backseat.

"You and Maude need to be in front. Soak up that heat. And drink some water," Cassandra said, squeezing in with Lilith in back.

"This thing is blowing cold air," Maude said. Her voice sounded faint and exhausted.

"Give it a few minutes. I'm going to set up a couple of flares so the cops can find us more easily. They should be here any moment."

Sydney pointed her chin to the column of smoke rising over the woods, visible even in the dark. The glow of the fire reached the top of the trees, and sparks flew in the breeze. "I think we've got the signal fire thing covered."

She reached over and grabbed Maude's hand. "I'm twice saved. Make that three. You saved me, and Lilith saved me. In a sick way, Zile saved me from Gonzo."

Maude squeezed Sydney's hand and tilted her head back, eyes closed. "It's a Jaquith tradition."

The car heater was kicking out a bit of warmth when three law enforcement vehicles pulled up, two from the Hartwell Police Department and one from the Oriska County Sheriff's Department. Lilith leaned forward from the backseat. "Remember our story."

Sydney watched through half-closed eyes as Cassandra got out to greet the officers. Based on arm waving and head nodding, she appeared to be giving the high-level overview. The problem was, Cassandra didn't know about all the fentanyl and other nasty stuff going up in smoke.

Sydney left the car and tottered over to the little group. In the glow of the headlights, she recognized Chief Carver, Detective Payne, and Officer Ellyn Ranz from Hartwell, and Deputy Cox from the Sheriff's Department.

"Don't go down there without protection," she said through

chattering teeth. "There were a lot of nasty drugs in that cabin. It's possible Gonzo got an accidental exposure."

Chief Carver walked to the top of the path down to the cabin, hands on hips as he peered downhill. "We can't accept your assessment that those men are dead. We need to verify it ourselves. How far away from the cabin are they?"

Sydney made a guestimate. "Sixty to one hundred yards? Uphill."

Carver gestured to Ranz and Cox. "Okay. You two go down with the usual protection for drug exposure. If you start feeling odd or if the smoke turns, you get out of there. I want you to verify if they're dead or not and radio what you find. By the time you reach them, the fire department and EMTs should be here, and they'll know what to bring down."

"Or not," Cox said.

"Or not." Carver swiveled around and checked the road. "Is there any other way to drive in there?" he asked Sydney.

"No, someone could snowshoe or ski in from the other side of the lake, but they'd have to be very motivated."

Carver grunted. "We'll close off this road. Good thing it doesn't get much traffic. I'll put another car on the Hartwell road near your house as a precaution—in case someone gets *motivated*."

He guided her to the passenger side of his car. "Hop in." Once he had settled with a pad of paper on the driver's side, he continued. "We need to get statements from each of you individually. You'll have to come to the station for a formal statement as well. No avoiding that. I'm hoping we won't have to detain you—any of you—but we need to err on the side of caution if there's been a homicide. Two homicides."

Sydney's jaw had stopped chattering, but her stomach muscles were still clenching in prolonged flutters. "Got it."

"Start. Why were you down there?"

KISS. Keep it simple, stupid. "I was looking for Maude. She was upset, and I know she's a junkie. Or at least a user. This was one place to check."

"But your car is parked down the road."

"I drove by and saw Zile's truck. He's been harassing Maude. I thought I'd better go in from a different direction. That was when I texted Cassandra."

"How did Maude's truck get here? Did she drive it?"

Sydney bit her lip. She didn't want to get her sister in trouble. "I don't know, Chief. Maybe they came to the house and Gonzo drove it."

"Yeah, right. Maybe it flew here. Don't kid a kidder, Sydney. Go on."

"Zile saw me outside the cabin." Sydney cleared her throat as she considered mentioning carrying her grandfather's shotgun. *KISS.* "He forced me to come inside. He was looking for Randy's stash because he said this was where Randy died," she said.

Carver's facial expression didn't change as he stared at his pad. "And?"

"I helped Zile find what he was looking for. I knew where all Randy's hiding spots were in that place. But Maude got to leave first."

Sydney noticed Carver's pen stopped writing. He was watching her.

"I pointed out the best candidate. Behind the stove. Gonzo screwed up, and his coat caught on fire; the bags looked like they were bursting and I knew some of that was fentanyl. When I saw Zile was distracted with Gonzo, I cleared out." Another quick decision—Sydney decided not to mention Maude's intervention. If Maude decided to say something, Sydney could "conveniently" remember later.

"And they chased you."

"Yup."

"And Zile shot Gonzo."

"By mistake. Gonzo was coming up behind me. It was getting dark. I fell down right at the split second Zile fired, and Gonzo reached me."

"And who shot Zile?"

Sydney stumbled over Lilith's version of the truth. The words wouldn't come out. "He looked like he was going to shoot at me again. Lilith picked up Gonzo's gun and told him to stop. I dove behind a tree, and I heard two shots. I suppose it's possible he shot himself?"

Carver let out a bark. "Yeah, right. Why did Ms. Elway say Gonzo shot him?"

"She wasn't really there. She had already started uphill with Maude." Sydney rotated in her seat to look Carver in the eye. "That's what Lilith told her, and it's the story Lilith wants."

"Why would she do that? Yes, it will be a bit of trouble, but she should have no problem claiming self-defense."

"She was married to Zile for over forty years. She's been living a lie for decades."

Carver tapped his pen on the pad several times. He scribbled something and opened his door. "Go back to Cassandra's car and keep warm. I need to coordinate with the fire department," the chief said, gesturing toward the vehicles pulling into their midst.

"There's one more thing," Sydney said.

Carver stopped, one foot still in the car. "Make it quick."

"I was here the night your father died. He trapped me in that cabin and said he was going to kill me, exactly like he killed Caleb." Sydney watched the blood drain from Carver's face. "Wait. Don't go. Listen. I got away when Zile showed up and surprised your father. I heard two shots as I was running home. Zile is carrying a 9mm pistol. You'll find it down there. Isn't that the same caliber gun that killed your father? Same as killed those guys with Randy? He told me down there that he had killed your father in the woods and taken him to Schwarzer's quarry. We know Zile does have a habit of moving bodies."

Sydney held her breath. She was well aware Carver could arrest her right then and there, but at least she had told her version of the truth—with a few shortcuts.

Carver straightened up. "I've got other priorities at the moment. We'll see what that gun tells us. Go wait in Cassandra's car." He slammed the door.

* * *

Maude and Lilith chose to stay warm in Lilith's truck. Sydney dozed in Cassandra's car, alternately bored and fascinated, watching the responders do their jobs.

The Oriska fire department consisted of volunteers, augmented by the professional fire team from Hartwell and a hazmat group from Ithaca and several EMT vehicles. Cassandra moved around outside, poking her nose into every detail.

"That all looks very cordial," Sydney said when Cassandra came to the car for a warmup.

"Ha! Barely," Cassandra said. "The fire department sent down a couple of EMTs to make sure Zile and Gonzo were really dead and then they got the hell out of there."

"I hope the answer was yes. Much as I hated those two, I wouldn't have left them if they were alive."

"Oh, they were definitely dead, and not of hypothermia, although I guess it will take some time for the official report. They'll leave the bodies there for now because it's a crime scene."

"What about the fire?"

"Hopeless. No way they could get a truck down there in time, and with all that fentanyl, it's not a happy scene. They're going to let it burn."

"I wonder how Maude will feel about that," Sydney said. She turned to stare out the window at Lilith's truck.

"You did say she started the fire to save you. I'm guessing she'll be reconciled to it."

"I think she did it to save me, but I doubt she thought any further than that."

After about two hours, Chief Carver waved all the women to meet at the top of the road to the cabin. "Maude, Sydney, Cassandra. You are free to go, but you need to come to the station tomorrow and make formal statements. Lilith, you need to come with us until we can verify how things played out."

Cassandra jumped forward. "Give us a break, Carver. Shame on you." She turned to Lilith. "I'm calling Steve as soon as I get cell phone coverage."

Lilith's eyes glittered, and she glared at Sydney before she turned to address Cassandra. "Forget Steve. I'll be fine. You need to go rescue Buster. He'll need feeding and some water. He can be a bit defensive, but he's a good dog. If you take a couple of biscuits and rub behind his ears, he'll settle down."

"Don't count on that," Sydney said to Cassandra as Lilith climbed into the back of Carver's car.

Cassandra slapped Sydney's back. "You've always been fearful around dogs, Sydney. They sense it from you. Remember, I'm the go-to person when it comes to handling animals. Lilith knows that."

42

Accounting

Sydney barely remembered the short drive home or the quick trip to bed. The last thing she said was, "I hope that dog doesn't eat Cassandra alive."

The next morning, her aching body woke her up before dawn. Every limb hurt in a unique way, but at least her mind had returned—with a small, niggling, warm sense of release.

As the sky brightened, she looked over the fields and woods to the west and watched a faint curl of smoke rising from Hangnail Pond. She figured the old wooden cabin burned like a match and would be ashes now. She also wondered if drugs like fentanyl were destroyed by heat, or if the woods and pond would now be contaminated, or if a toxic cloud hovered overhead.

Over oatmeal, Sydney tried to engage Maude.

"How are you feeling?" she asked.

"Like shit." Maude stabbed the oatmeal with her spoon. "How am I supposed to feel?"

"Sad? Mad? Furious? Relieved?"

Maude tossed her spoon into the bowl with a loud clatter and stalked out of the dining room. She came back and slapped down a plastic bag—filled with cash.

Sydney jumped up, sending her chair flying. "What is that? Is that money from the cabin?"

Maude offered a smug, condescending smile. "It's almost twenty-five thousand dollars."

"I don't care if it's a million. How did that get here?"

Maude resumed her seat and tucked into her oatmeal. "When I dashed into the living room with the vodka—saving you by the way—I scooped it up as Gonzo was flailing around, and stuffed it under my sweater."

Sydney remained as far away as she could from the package. "It's contaminated."

Maude tapped the bag with her spoon and scooped up more oatmeal. "Maybe it was. Maybe not. But not to worry. I scrubbed it outside in the snow while the cops were dashing around."

"Fentanyl absorbs through the skin, you know."

"I was all covered up. When we got home, I washed the bag thoroughly and threw it out. Then I put the money into the laundry in a pillowcase. And I washed my clothes and everything."

"Where is the pillowcase?"

"In the trash," Maude said, and leaned back in her chair. "Jeez, Sydney. You think I would let anyone rest their head on that, even after cleaning?"

Sydney righted her chair and sat down at the table. "It's all yours," she said. "You'll probably need it to pay for cleaning up whatever is left of the cabin."

They both rotated to look out the back windows and studied the dwindling column of smoke.

"It's all over the news already. They mention my grandparents and Gonzo, but not us," Maude said. "I don't have to accept that inheritance, you know."

Sydney pushed her oatmeal away. "Maude, so much of all this mess is about our dark side. Greed for money, mostly, but also power and control. Control over people. Your grandmother, our mother. Me. As far as I'm concerned, I'm not touching that money."

Maude picked up her spoon and mimed eating the money.

"That property on the lake is probably worth a lot more than what is in the bag," Sydney said. "If you invested this to clean up the site, made a genuine driveway down the hill, and put in a septic system, you might double your money or more."

"Hello, Sydney. There's no building."

"Hello, Maude. Who would have wanted that cabin? Not exactly a selling point."

Maude stopped talking, and her eyes took on a faraway glaze.

"What about your grandfather? And Gonzo? Does that make you sad?" Sydney asked.

Maude didn't hesitate. "Gonzo was creepy. He wanted to marry me." She wiped her face and stuck out her tongue. "My grandfather was different. Keep in mind I thought he was my father for a long time. Sometimes he looked at me in a way that really made my skin crawl. Like he wanted something else." She looked up at Sydney. "Not recently. Recently he was too pissed off for that."

Sydney's mouth felt dry. She swigged her coffee.

"Did your grandmother know?"

"She said I was overly imaginative, but I could see she worried. She tried to keep us apart."

Sydney picked up the dishes. "Yeah, God forbid she should actually do anything about it."

"Hey." Maude grabbed Sydney's arm. "She did kill the son of a bitch."

"And not a moment too soon."

After breakfast, Sydney plugged in Randy's computer. It hummed a bit, but the screen stayed black. She plugged it into the monitor in her mother's office in case it was merely having display issues. No luck.

"I'm so glad we didn't have to depend on that working yesterday. We'd be stone-cold dead," Maude said.

"Yeah, *I* would be for sure. We're lucky your grandfather was a bird-in-the-hand type like he said."

"Is that it?"

"We'll give this to your grandmother. She should take it to a PC repair place and have them remove the disk drive and try to read it," Sydney answered.

"Can't you do that?"

"Even if I had all the equipment, I'm suffering from a lack of motivation."

"She did save your life. And I'd get half of whatever is in that bank account. I'd be rich."

"It's not going to be enough money to retire on at the age of nineteen, kiddo. Your grandmother should go to the same bank Mom used and work it that way. She's the legal executrix. If the authorities don't demand all of it, she may owe taxes. She'd be smart to give you any money in tiny increments."

"Sydney, I gotta say that you take all the fun out of being rich. Just saying."

With a lot of prodding, Sydney managed to get Maude into the car by 10:30.

"When you talk to the police, keep your statement nice and simple. I came to rescue you. Zile let you go. You started up the hill. You were going to drive to the house and call the cops. The next thing you knew, I was running away from the house," Sydney said.

"I'm not supposed to say I rescued you?"

Sydney stayed quiet as she negotiated a curve in the road. "Up to you. I didn't mention it. Don't say more than you need to, but don't lie." *Good advice coming from an incurable liar.*

"Should I say I saw Lilith shoot Zile?"

"Did you?"

"Nah, I was tucked under Cassandra's arm and running for my life in the other direction."

"Tell them that."

Sydney sat in a stiff plastic chair, checking her cell phone for email while she waited for Maude to finish her statement. She looked up and saw Lilith strut out from the back of the police station.

Maude's grandmother stopped in front of Sydney. "I'm leaving. Free. No thanks to you."

Sydney looked up from her phone. "It's time to tell the truth, Lilith. I knew you'd be in the clear."

"Zile's name will be trampled."

Sydney put down her phone to stare at Lilith. "Zile stalked

Maude over the years. I know you tried to hide that—to *manage* that. Like you tried to manage Randy. And you never did anything to help me." She paused to swallow. "I do have something to tell you."

"Go on. I'm tired and I want to go home."

"There's a tree in Randy's woods. A maple tree. Just uphill from the Blanchards' sugar bush. It has a mask carved in it. Well, partly carved. Kind of the outlines." Sydney circled her fingers around her face to indicate features.

"You mean like a Halloween mask?" Lilith was squinting at a point in the middle of Sydney's forehead.

"No, I mean like an Onondaga mask." Sydney's voice sank to a squeak. She glanced up. Lilith's face had turned to stone.

"And how did it get there?"

"Randy was supposed to take care of it, but he never did," Sydney said. She figured Lilith could draw her own conclusions as to the culprit.

Lilith busied herself with her coat and gloves. "You really are a piece of work, Sydney. Is there anything else you'd like to *share* with me?"

"I love Maude and Maude seems to love you. When it really counted, you came through. And you saved my life. Thank you."

Lilith grunted and left.

Sydney put her head down and pretended to read email. She had planned to tell Lilith about Randy's laptop, but she couldn't choke out the words. She'd let Maude handle that bit of news. Sydney was grateful, but the less she saw of Lilith the better, and she knew the feeling was mutual.

Sydney took her own advice and kept her statement as straightforward as possible. As Detective Payne finished his questions, Chief Carver stepped into the room and motioned with a jerk of his head for Payne to leave.

He leaned against the door and fixed Sydney with a stare.

"The gun Zile was carrying matches the gun that killed my father. And matches the gun that killed Randy's friends. Gonzo too."

Sydney remained quiet.

Carver continued. "Also, as you said, there does seem to be this habit of moving bodies, which points to Zile. Based on our conversation last night, I could bring charges that you impeded the investigation of my father's death. Or even for being an accessory."

Sydney knew she should feel alarmed, but a calm peace settled around her. Maybe she should tell the truth more often.

"If that happens, I'll get Steve on top of this," she said. "I assume the prosecution would have to explain motivation, and I'd be thrilled to describe what your father wanted me to do to him and for him, and how he planned to kill me when I declined. Not only that, he confessed to killing Caleb Elway. Caleb's down in Schwarzer's quarry. He deserves some justice. I'd like nothing more than to get him some and be very public about it."

The two stared at each other. Carver cleared his throat and looked at the floor.

"You're a good cop, from what I hear," Sydney said. "Steve says you're an excellent leader. No scandal. Which is quite remarkable in my book." She paused to study the palms of her hands, collecting her thoughts. "Your father was a son of a bitch, but he's long dead. I didn't kill him, and I wasn't there when he died. I was on my way to California. But I will call out what he did if I need to. Don't let an asshole like me ruin all the good work you've done."

"What did you say to Chief Carver?" Maude asked as they climbed into their mother's car. "I could have sworn he was crying."

"I simply told him how much his father meant to me," Sydney said, and put the car in gear. "Time to go see Grandpa and give him the news."

"Something tells me he'll be all over this already, but I'm sure he'll love hearing the details."

43

Farewells

When Sydney and Maude arrived at the Presbyterian Church Fellowship Hall to set up their mother's memorial service, cars were already parked outside, and the hall was bustling with volunteers. Some were setting up chairs, others were arranging flowers, and a large crew was laying out food, supervised by Rob.

Sydney felt her eyes swell and her nose tingle with emotions that threatened to turn into real tears. She feared there would be mass confusion with the last-minute switch from the funeral home, but Martinson's had made the right call. Francine reached out to her "coven," and Rob must have called in some favors as well. Bruce Martinson put signs on the funeral home door and in his parking lot. Clusters of white balloons graced the church parking lot, and a small sign announcing upcoming events showed Leslie's memorial at the top.

Feeling standoffish was not allowed. Francine made sure Sydney was introduced to everyone. She remembered some from her childhood, but most were new to her. Maude appeared to know everyone and spent most of her time moving from one guest to another, dispensing hugs and tissues.

"Naturally if you waited until summer, the crowd would be much larger," Francine said. "All those snowbirds would be back, along with the summer folks. But you'll have to come back to put her ashes in the cemetery when the ground thaws, right?"

Sydney was spared having to answer by the arrival of her grandfather and Patricia Atwood from Valley View. Only a few days ago, she would have sworn on a mountain of bibles that she would never return once she pried herself free of this place.

Maude guided David and Patricia to a table with pictures, some of Leslie's paintings, and other mementos—her first swimming badge, a spelling prize, her high school diploma . . . Leslie's hoarding habit had provided a treasure trove of worthless but emotionally charged items.

Sydney made a beeline for Cassandra. "How'd things go with Buster? Are you going to keep him?"

"Absolutely. Lilith doesn't want him. He was Zile's dog. He deserves a fresh start. He loves hanging out with my other dogs."

"It is a far, far better thing you're doing than that mutt deserves, Cassandra."

"He's not a mutt, and he's actually a sweetheart."

"You won't prove it by me."

"When you get to California, you guys should get a dog. It's great for the nerves."

"Not a chance. Meanwhile, I'm so glad you're here. There are so many people."

"That's a bad thing?"

"Wonderful. A bit overwhelming is all."

Cassandra waved to Steve, who entered with his mother.

"Mrs. Lee looks happy," Sydney said. "I don't think I've ever seen her smile before."

"That's because every time she saw *you,* it meant trouble. She's happy because Steve and I are getting married this summer."

After the hugging was over, Sydney checked out Mrs. Lee. She did seem very content. "Glad she's on board."

"She and my mother were chummy. Mostly I think she's thrilled at getting Steve married off and maybe adding some grandchildren." Cassandra paused to give Sydney a punch in the arm. "I expect you to come back for this event, girl. Besides, you need to set up your mother's headstone and spread some ashes. And your grandfather needs regular attention."

"Hmm."

"What do you mean, 'hmm'? Your mother was born and spent most of her life here. You know this is where she would want to be."

"Let me get out of here first, please. I need to stabilize my life in California, including Maude. One trauma at a time."

"This place has reset its claws into you, Sydney. You'll be back."

The service was short, followed by more milling around. Sydney spoke about how much she appreciated the community that had accepted and loved her mother—a more genuinely heartfelt sentiment on that day than when she wrote it the week before.

Maude spoke about the joy of finding her mother and a family, including Sydney and their grandfather, as well as her love of this place, the place of her people. Sydney noticed that Lilith slipped in as the speaking started and left before the socializing began.

David's speech started by saying his thank-yous.

"As I look around this room, I see people I grew up with, many people I worked with, others I taught in high school, and close friends I've made over the years. I am happy and proud of many things in my life, but one of my finest achievements was my daughter, Leslie, although arguably I didn't have much to do with that."

He let a bit of chuckling rise from the crowd. "She was a passionate, talented being. Smart and fearless. I think she got those qualities from her mother. While I am devastated to lose my daughter prematurely, I am so proud of my two granddaughters, Sydney and Maude. It thrills me to see such intelligent and strong young women of great courage and heart."

He went on to add some more observations, but Sydney was sobbing into her hankie and missed the rest.

44

Taillights

Sydney stuffed the last box into the back of the rental trailer hooked up to Maude's truck. In their typical odd couple fashion, she and Maude fought bitterly over how much stuff to take from their mother's house.

Sydney would have been happy to leave almost everything behind. Maude wanted to hire a moving company and *take* everything. Sure enough, Maude appeared carrying a small table with two boxes on top.

"That won't fit, Maude. We don't even have enough space in California for this much."

"So we'll buy a new house with money when we sell this house."

"A house like this goes for over two or three million where I live. Higher in fancy towns like Palo Alto. Besides, we could be waiting a long time for this place to move. We'll be using that money to visit Grandpa." She thought of her grandfather's cache of secret pills and the future visit when he might need them.

"Don't worry so much. It will all work out."

"Did you say goodbye to your grandmother?" Sydney asked.

"I went around to her place yesterday," Maude answered. "Perfect timing. She had some cousins and brothers visiting. Going to do some work in the woods, they said. It was nice to be able to see them before the trip."

Sydney turned to gaze across the back fields to the trees ring-ing Hangnail Pond. Her attention hovered for a moment and returned to the task at hand. She closed the back of the trailer and locked it, then checked the items they had stored in the back of Maude's truck.

"I gave her Randy's laptop. And I told her it was from you. With your thanks for saving your life, of course."

"Of course."

"She said, '*Iahothenon Khieaterea:ah:.*'"

"Meaning?"

"'It is nothing, my granddaughter.'"

Sydney chuckled. "That is the nicest thing she ever said to me."

Maude waved her arms in the air. "Sydney, this is *huge*. She called you her granddaughter. You're like . . . family."

After all these years . . .

"Tell her goodbye for now. How do I say that?"

"*Ó:nen ki wáhi.*"

"Time to go. I'm going to take one last look around inside," Sydney said. "Maude, have you gone to the bathroom?"

Maude's glare said *yes*.

The house already seemed much emptier. The life she had known had evaporated—not entirely a bad thing.

Sydney paused in each room, making sure she committed ev-ery detail to memory. She reminded herself that she had already left this house for good years before.

In the living room, the squeak of a floorboard raised the hackles on her neck. Randy used to sneak up like that.

"I'm keeping my promise like you asked," she said. "I'm tak-ing her with me. We're a family now."

She swung around but found she was alone with the remain-ders of her mother's life.

Finished with her mental inventory, Sydney left the house via the mudroom into the barn.

Outside, Cassandra and Steve were waiting, with Buster in tow.

"Buster said he wanted to say goodbye," Cassandra said after she gave Sydney a hug.

"Be a good dog, Buster," Sydney said, and patted him with a light brushing stroke on the head. Buster ducked his head with ears back and growled.

"Don't worry about him. You can see him when you come to visit your grandfather. And don't worry about your mother's car. I'll make sure Francine takes good care of it."

"The least of my worries," Sydney said. "Francine's cars last forever."

"So, which route are you going to take?" Steve asked. "Head to Route 81, see your grandfather, and then north or south?"

"I think we should drive through Canada to Alaska," Maude answered. "We could check out what real winter is like."

"We're going south to see the Grand Canyon and Death Valley," Sydney said. She tucked two final items behind the front seat: a cardboard box holding the cremains of Leslie and another with mementos from Randy's life, plus their promise rings in a special maple box their grandfather had made decades ago. They were leaving about half of her mother's ashes with Cassandra for burying and scattering in the summer when they returned for the wedding. "We can scatter some ashes and a few pieces from Randy's life every time we see something spectacular."

"Works for me," Maude said.

Sydney put her foot on the step up into the cab. A hand pulled her back down.

"I want to drive," Maude said. "You should let me drive. I'm a good driver, and the State of New York says my license has been restored." She held out her hand.

Sydney stepped back and studied her sister. Maude's eyes were bright. She looked happy and ready to take on the challenges ahead, blissfully unaware of how difficult those would be. It was going to be a very long trip.

"Okay. What the heck."

Sydney tossed Maude the keys.

*   *   *

As they drove toward Valley View, Sydney felt an unfamiliar tingle in her lower belly. She grew alarmed as the tingle grew warmer and spread up her torso, to her chest, neck, and jaw.

She realized her fear was melting away. The terrible mass of pain and terror she had been carrying inside for over twenty years was dissolving like rock salt in warm water. She had tried to kill it with drugs and alcohol, nearly killing herself in the process. Being clean meant learning to live with it without those crutches. Now the terrible ache was slipping away, into the ether, all on its own.

She leaned over and glanced into the right-side mirror. No, she still looked the same. She stole a quick peek over at Maude in the driver's seat. She was tempted to ask Maude if she could see a difference.

Maude was bobbing her head in time to the music from her headset connected to her phone, filling her senses as she focused on the road ahead.

Maude was right—she was a good driver. She turned to look at Sydney and grinned—the smile that was perfect parts Randy and Leslie—her own little sister.

Sydney decided to wait and let this feeling expand before she tried to name it or pin it down. The rolling hills covered in deep snow sparkled in the winter light. She would be home in California soon enough. Her feet were pointed west. For now, she could enjoy this world.

She smiled into the western sun.

Acknowledgments

A shout-out to my editor, Michaela Hamilton, and the Kensington team, as well as my agent, Anne Hawkins, of John Hawkins and Associates, for their wonderful guidance in shaping this book.

A special thank-you to Doug George-Kanentiio and the People of the Longhouse, the *Haudenosaunee*. The Iroquois contributed so much to the founding principles of this country, to my early life, and continue to enrich our society into the future.

Longtime friends Cassandra Harris-Lockwood and Steve Lee Lockwood were an endless well of information, contacts, and guidance on everything about life in Central New York these days.

More notes of appreciation to Lieutenant Saul Jaeger of the Mountain View, California Police Department and Captain Erik Roth of the Mountain View Fire Department for first-hand insights on the challenges faced by first responders.

Along with recognition to all those who lent me their names, there is a special place in heaven for those who support writers through their agonies, like the Martinez-Graham clan: Susanne Martinez and Nancy Sitton with centering advice, Jenny Martinez with her insights, David Graham's good-natured agreement to play any role I had in mind, and especially to Cassie for all the nonjudgmental affection. Kristin Bailey provided invaluable support for so many book-related activities.

As always, the Clydes writers group rules. I couldn't have shaped this tale without them. Sisters in Crime, the Guppies, and Mystery Writers of America have helped me to continue to grow and extend my writing community.

Connect with Us

Visit us online at
KensingtonBooks.com
to read more from your favorite authors, see books
by series, view reading group guides, and more.

 Join us on social media

for sneak peeks, chances to win books and prize packs,
and to share your thoughts with other readers.

facebook.com/kensingtonpublishing
twitter.com/kensingtonbooks

Tell us what you think!

To share your thoughts, submit a review,
or sign up for our eNewsletters, please visit:
KensingtonBooks.com/TellUs.